A BLANCO COUNTY MYSTERY

This one is for my good friend John Strauss.

ACKNOWLEDGMENTS

YET AGAIN, heaps of appreciation to Tommy Blackwell, Jim Lindeman, Becky Rehder, Helen Haught Fanick, Mary Summerall, Marsha Moyer, Karen Bennett, Linda Biel, Leo Bricker, Kathy Carrasco, Don Gray, Phil Hughes, John Strauss, and Pam Headrick. A tip of the hat to Allison Byers for the sausage ball recipe. All errors are my own.

1

LESTER HIGGS HAD never had sex in a bathtub before, but now that he was seeing Kelly Rundell on a regular basis, he was enjoying all kinds of new and exciting experiences.

Sex in a vehicle, for instance. Not parked—moving.

Sex in the dressing room of a Walmart.

Sex on a picnic table at the state park in broad daylight.

Sex in the back row of a movie theater in Mason, Texas.

Sex in a mind-boggling variety of locations—some risky, some merely creative or unconventional. Frankly, it went against Lester's rather conservative upbringing in Sweetwater, Texas. Fornication. A sin.

Worth every damn minute, Lester thought as Kelly positioned herself on top of him, sloshing a small amount of water over the edge of the tub. Her long red hair, still dry, cascaded over her shoulders. She was a vision. Gorgeous.

The only real drawback with Kelly was her marital status, in that she *was* married—to Claude Rundell, the president of First County Bank in Blanco. Adultery. Another sin. Well, shit. Why not? One good sin deserved another, didn't it? Claude was roughly twenty years Kelly's senior, as was Lester, which led him to believe that Kelly had a thing for older men. Fine by Lester.

He was happy to be with a woman of any age at the moment, because his personal life had been drier than a popcorn fart for a good, long while. His job as foreman at the Hawley ranch kept him busy—and isolated. Hard to find a woman to date when you spend your day tending cattle, mending fences, and relocating deer blinds. At the end of the day, you're too exhausted to go into town. On the rare occasion when you do work up the energy—maybe visit a dance hall on a Saturday night— what do you find? Young ladies who spend the evening shooting selfies and checking their phones. Who needs it?

Lester had about given up on meeting anyone when he'd spotted Kelly at the Sonic Drive-In, the two of them parked side by side, making eyes at each other. Lester finally worked up the nerve to holler something about the way she was eating that corn dog, and she laughed, and things sort of progressed from there. Quickly. As in having sex that very night. That had been two months ago, and he'd learned a lot about her—and Claude—since then.

According to Kelly, she and Claude hadn't had sex in more than three years, because Claude had lost his drive completely. Not that it had ever amounted to much, and besides, if he'd ever truly loved Kelly, he'd never done much to show it. Bought her all kinds of cars and jewelry, but that wasn't love, was it? He didn't want to spend time with her. They had nothing to talk about.

Kelly began to work her hips up and down and Lester plumb forgot about Claude and cows and deer blinds for the moment. Kelly's breasts bobbed gently in rhythm with her movement, and the water in the tub began to roll in gentle waves.

"That feel good?" Kelly asked.

"Mmbbhhhaaaa," Lester replied, his mouth just above the water line.

She grinned. "I thought so. Should I stop?"

"Nnnuuumuhhh."

He was just happy to prove that men his age weren't all like Claude. In fact, Lester figured he was just as virile as he'd been in his twenties. There were times, fooling around with Kelly, when he had to dial his excitement level back a little or risk finishing up earlier than he'd like.

Like now.

Good Lord, this felt amazing. Lester couldn't remember a woman ever making him feel this much pleasure. And if Kelly felt any shame or guilt about what they were doing, she sure didn't show it. She seemed to live by her own rules.

Lester heard a dog barking outside. That would be Cooter, his Australian shepherd. More of a barker than Jake, the Lab mix. Lester had to confine them to a couple of acres around the house during deer season, but now, in the off-season, they had the run of the ranch. Odd that they were up near the house this time of day, instead of chasing rabbits.

The dogs were a handy distraction, because Lester was already reaching the point where his vision was beginning to narrow and he knew he wasn't going to last much longer. And Kelly was well on her way, too, judging by the depth of her breathing and the way her neck was flushing a deep red.

More barking. Lester figured Jake had found something to play with, like a deer antler or a chew toy or just a particularly exciting stick, and Cooter was jealous. That's how it usually went.

Kelly grabbed Lester's hands and placed them on her breasts, and her hip action was increasing, sending more water sloshing out of the tub.

Another bark. Closer now. Cooter and Jake had entered through the doggie door. Lester should've blocked it off before he and Kelly had gotten into the tub. The dogs were probably in the kitchen, wondering where Lester was.

Kelly was moaning now. Totally focused. Eyes closed.

Lester heard toenails clicking on the hardwood floors in the hallway. That was Jake, searching the house. Cooter had a much quieter gait.

"Yes," Kelly said. "Yes."

In his peripheral vision—with his concentration understandably fragmented—Lester was aware that Jake had just nudged the door open and entered the bathroom. Tail wagging. His usual joyful self. Happy to please. Carrying something in his mouth.

"Yes!" Kelly said, unaware of Jake's presence. "Yes!"

Lester was doing his best to hang on—to last just a minute longer—

And then Jake trotted to the rim of the tub, playful, wanting to share his find with Lester—to be praised for finding it. *I brought you a prize!*

It was only then—with the object mere inches from Lester's face—that he realized it was no chew toy. It wasn't any kind of toy at all, or even a piece of rope or a deflated ball.

It was a human foot.

Jake wagged his tail and dropped the foot into the water.

And Kelly began to scream.

2

RED O'BRIEN WAS stuffing a wad of Work Horse chewing tobacco into his cheek and ruminating about the potential lawsuit against him when he spotted Dickie Loftin in the parking lot of the Lowe's Market in Johnson City. Of course, Red's legal woes flew right out of his mind at that point, because Dickie Loftin was one of his personal heroes. A goddamn legend. A voice for the common man. And funnier than hell, too.

But was it really Dickie Loftin? Hard to tell, because it was late in the evening and the parking lot wasn't lit all that well. Red popped the glove box of his ancient Ford truck and retrieved a pair of binoculars, which he always kept on hand, because you never knew when you might see something interesting, like a good buck on the side of some county road.

The man in question was standing beside an immaculate black Hummer, parked where it had lots of room to itself. No other vehicle was within twenty yards.

Red zoomed in.

The man was smoking a cigar, and Red knew for a fact that Dickie Loftin smoked cigars. Hell, yeah, he did—right on stage, during his act. Drank whiskey, too, poured straight from a bottle he opened in front of the audience, so they'd know it wasn't iced tea or some bullshit like that.

Dickie was just smoking and leaning against the passenger side of the Hummer, waiting on somebody inside the store. Cool as hell.

Fucking Dickie Loftin. Amazing—if it was really him.

The man was wearing a baseball cap, which cast shadows across his face, but if it wasn't Dickie, it was his twin brother, if he had one. Looked like this guy had the same wrinkles around his eyes and mouth. Gray hair poking out. Not some Hollywood pretty boy.

Red grabbed his cheap Korean cell phone and dialed Billy Don.

"You get one already?" Billy Don said, because he knew what Red was doing tonight.

"Guess who I'm lookin' at right now," Red said.

"Tom Landry."

"He's dead, genius."

"That's why it would be so impressive."

"It's Dickie Loftin," Red said.

"Bullshit."

"Ain't lyin'."

"Where?"

"In the parking lot at Super S."

"Lowe's Market."

"Whatever, but yeah, and I'm pretty sure it's him."

"Oh, here we go. 'Pretty sure.'"

"No, man, it's him."

"You've been needing glasses for a long time now. Just saying."

Billy Don had been using that expression—"just saying"—a lot lately. Something he'd picked up on Facebook. It was annoying as hell.

Red said, "He's like 40 yards away, and I'm looking at him through binoculars. That good enough?"

"What would he be doing in Johnson City on a Friday night?"

"Got no idea. But he's gotta be somewhere, right? Might as well be here."

"That makes a lot of sense."

"Be a smartass, but you're gonna be jealous when I walk over and meet him in a minute."

"Send me a picture of you and him."

"I will."

"Then do it."

"You can count on it."

"I'll be waiting."

"It'll be a pleasure to shut your fat mouth," Red said.

Billy Don started to reply, but Red hung up. Then he took another look through the binoculars.

Shit, yeah. That was Dickie Loftin. Red had no doubt at all now. Wouldn't hurt to say hello, would it? Maybe get a picture together? He opened his truck door and—

Forty yards away, Dickie Loftin flipped his cigar butt into the night and climbed back into the front passenger seat of the Hummer.

Well, shit.

Red decided to walk over there anyway, because Dickie was a man of the people, and he wouldn't mind opening the door for a fan, would he? Hell, no. He'd be downright grateful. That's just the way he was. Always happy to sign an autograph or say hello, unlike some of those snobby West Coast elitists. Okay, to be honest, Red had heard about a couple of incidents where Dickie had gotten a little hotheaded, but so what? It would only be a quick hello. Why would he be bothered by that?

So Red strutted over and stopped beside the passenger door of the Hummer. Red hadn't realized Hummers were so damn high off the ground, especially when they were jacked up even farther, like this one was. Red was looking up at the window, but the glass was tinted—dark enough that Red couldn't see inside the vehicle. But he knew Loftin could see him.

Red gave a wave. "Hey, there, Dickie," he said, feeling kind of funny about it, almost like he was talking to himself.

He waited, but there was no response. The window didn't go down. The door didn't open.

"I'm sure you get this all the time," Red said, "but you're looking at the biggest piece of white trash in Texas. Seriously. Ain't nobody more white trash than me."

Still no reply.

Red said, "I'm so white trash, I had tater tot casserole at my wedding reception." Red grinned at his own joke. "I wrote that'n myself. You can use it if you want. No charge."

Maybe Dickie was making a phone call or something. Maybe that's why he wasn't responding.

Red couldn't resist offering another zinger. He said, "I'm so white trash, some of my mail still goes to the county jail."

Nothing. Not the slightest hint that anybody was even inside the Hummer.

Okay, just one more. "I'm so white trash that my mother used to—"

"Hey!"

Red looked toward the grocery store and saw a big guy coming this way, carrying a 12-pack of Lone Star in one hand and a plastic gas can in the other.

Red waited.

When the man got closer, he said, "The hell're you doing? Step back from the vehicle."

He appeared to be in his thirties. Dressed in jeans, Red Wing boots, and a tight black T-shirt. Not as large as Billy Don, but not far behind.

Well over six feet and mostly muscle, from the looks of him. Probably weighed 250. Close-cropped black hair. Thick stubble on his face. On the outside of his left forearm was a green tattoo of a skull wearing a sailor's cap. Didn't look like a professional tattoo.

Red shrugged and moved away from the window. "Just saying hi to Dickie."

"Dickie who?" the man growled.

"Dickie, uh, Loftin," Red said.

"The fuck're you talking about?"

Red was starting to get nervous, and then he realized what was going on. This guy must be a bodyguard. He had the build and attitude for it. Part of his job, obviously, was to stop Dickie Loftin from being swarmed by fans. That was understandable. Even a great guy like Dickie needed some alone time now and again.

"Okay, I gotcha," Red said, smiling. "Dickie wants some privacy."

"You brain dead or something?" the man snapped, edging closer.

"No, it's cool," Red said, taking another step backward. "I ain't gonna bother him."

"Ain't nobody to bother," the man said.

"Got it," Red said. "Understood. Dickie ain't in there. But tell him I said hi."

The man shook his head like he thought Red was an idiot, then he walked around the front of the Hummer and climbed into the driver's seat.

"Just wanted a picture is all," Red muttered, regaining some of his nerve. "No need to get all bent out of shape."

As the big guy cranked the engine, Red took a few steps to his right, and now he could see through the front windshield. It would be interesting to see how Dickie was reacting to all this. If he was anything like he seemed on stage, he wouldn't be happy with the situation, and he'd be upset with his bodyguard. He made fun of celebrities all the time for acting like jerks.

But the passenger seat was empty. Dickie must've moved to the rear seats, just so he wouldn't have to deal with Red. Maybe he wasn't such a great guy after all.

The big man glared at Red a little more through the windshield and then pulled away. Red watched and saw the Hummer pull up to one of the gas pumps near the highway, and he was tempted to drive over there for another go at it, but he knew where he wasn't wanted. Most of the time.

9

The next morning, Red was seated in his recliner when he heard a vehicle slowly navigating up the rough caliche driveway to his trailer. Billy Don's Ranchero. Red recognized the sound of the engine.

The engine died, and then a car door closed, and then the entire trailer shook as Billy Don climbed the steps to the porch. The door swung open and Red's 300-pound friend, poaching partner, and trailermate stepped inside with a box of doughnuts.

"You're home early," Red said.

"Never went to sleep. Where's Dickie?"

Billy Don was razzing him.

"Funny."

"So he ain't here? I figured y'all was best buds by now. I even stopped at the Lowe's Market and got some Krispy Kremes, just in case your bullshit turned out to be true. But I guess it was a waste of time."

Krispy Kreme Doughnuts was one of the many brands Dickie Loftin endorsed, along with Odor Eaters, Natural Light, and a stool softener that had been pulled from the market after causing several cases of intestinal bleeding. Allegedly.

"It *was* him," Red insisted.

"Uh-huh."

Billy Don offered Red a doughnut, so Red took two, glazed.

"I ain't lying," Red said, and he told Billy Don everything that had happened. By the time he was done, Billy Don was working on his fourth cinnamon twist and had stopped paying attention to anything Red was saying. Par for the course. So Red turned his attention back to the fishing show.

"Hey, I got some good news for you," Billy Don said. "Maybe."

"What?"

"When I stopped for the doughnuts, I ran into Liz—that gal that runs the produce section?—and she said Dub Kimble went missing last night."

Red turned the TV volume down.

"Went missing how?"

"Went pig hunting and never come back."

"Who's saying this?"

"His girlfriend called the sheriff first thing this morning."

"Mandy?"

"Is that her name? The one with big hooters."

"Where was he hunting?"

"On his place," Billy Don said.

"And he just never came back?"

"That's what Liz says."

"Liz likes to gossip about all kinds of crazy shit that don't even make sense."

"Yeah, but then Jacob came along and said he heard the same thing."

Red pondered that for a moment.

Interesting. Very interesting. But was it actually good news? The first thing Red thought of—being the cynic he was—was that if Dub Kimble had truly gone missing, the cops would come straight to Red to see if he had anything to do with it. That totally sucked, because he'd been in that situation before—a suspect in a crime—and it was a major hassle. Problem was, if anything *had* happened to Dub, Red had a motive. A big one.

Well, he'd cross that alligator pit when he came to it.

Red got out of his recliner to grab a third doughnut.

"You know he lives near Stephenville, right?" he said.

"Dub does?" Billy Don said.

"No, Dickie Loftin."

"So what?"

"Point is, it ain't that far away, so it wouldn't be that weird to see Dickie in Johnson City."

"And it wouldn't be that weird for you to *think* you saw him," Billy Don said, now going to work on a doughnut covered with green sprinkles. Red hated that kind.

"It was him," Red insisted.

Billy Don didn't reply. Just kept stuffing his face. It wouldn't surprise Red if Billy Don polished off more than a dozen doughnuts, crullers, fritters, and whatever else he had in the box. Red had once seen Billy Don eat a box of Twinkies and a pound of cashews in one sitting. It was impressive and disgusting at the same time. Chased it down with Big Red.

"By the way, what were you doing in the produce section?" Red asked. "Get lost?"

3

BLANCO COUNTY GAME WARDEN John Marlin remembered the time a young hunter in south Texas decided to hop into his hunting rig—complete with camo paint job and elevated shooter's seat—and cross the Rio Grande into Mexico for a visit to a small-town brothel. There, he went on a three-day bender, drinking heavily and spending all his money on the ladies—until he exited his cheap motel room one morning and discovered that his rig had been stolen. It was obvious the party was over, so the young man did what anybody would do in that situation—he paid a taxi to take him back to the United States. Only then did he learn he'd been the subject of an intense search-and-rescue mission. *Oh, hey, were you looking for me? Sorry about that. I had no idea.*

That episode happened before the age of cell phones, when it was much easier to "lose" someone for an extended period. Marlin himself had dealt directly with dozens, or perhaps hundreds, of missing-hunter cases. Most were resolved in a matter of hours, or by day's end. Usually it turned out that there had been some sort of miscommunication, or plans had changed, or an excursion had been extended, or the hunter had simply moved on to a different site without telling his friends or family where he'd gone. That sounded exactly like something Dub Kimble would do, based on Marlin's previous encounters with him.

Less frequently, however, someone had genuinely gotten lost or injured. That's why, in these situations, a game warden had to assume the hunter in question was truly in need of immediate assistance. You had to assess the situation quickly, then decide, sometimes on a hunch and with very sparse information, whether a full-scale search was warranted—knowing it could turn out to be a tremendous waste of manpower and resources.

"What time did he leave?" Marlin asked Mandy Hammerschmitt, Dub Kimble's live-in girlfriend.

Mandy was in her early thirties and pretty in a late-night beer joint sort of way. She had a full figure and hair the color of blanched almonds. Her eyes—her best feature—were an electric blue. She appeared to be drinking tomato juice over ice in a clear plastic tumbler, but Marlin suspected it contained a generous splash of vodka. It was 10:13 in the morning. Apparently, she'd begun painting her toenails shortly before Marlin arrived. The smell of the polish was overwhelming in the closed trailer.

"Huh?" Mandy said.

"What time did Dub leave the house last night?"

They were seated on a plaid sofa so faded and tattered that most charities would turn it down. Unfortunately, it was one of the nicest pieces of furniture in the single-wide trailer. The carpet felt sticky under Marlin's boots and the place smelled like a Dumpster behind a fast-food restaurant.

"About nine thirty, maybe ten," Mandy said. She grabbed a small bottle of bright red nail polish off the coffee table and raised her bare left foot onto the couch. Still on the table were several emery boards and one of those little gizmos with a coarse spinning cylinder—basically a sander—for removing dead skin. "I'm sure it's nothin', but I figured I'd better tell someone, seeing as how I can't find his sorry ass." She sounded more irritated than concerned—like it wasn't the first time Dub had caused her grief.

"Was anyone with him?" Marlin asked.

"Nope." She was carefully—painstakingly—applying the polish to the nail on her big toe. She apparently goofed up, because she grabbed a tissue, wiped some of the polish away, and began again. Ironic that she was so meticulous about her feet when the house itself was downright sloppy and neglected.

"And he wasn't planning to go anywhere else?"

"Nope."

"When did you realize he was missing?"

"Huh?"

Totally focused on her feet.

"When did you realize he was missing?"

"This morning when I woke up."

"Okay, so walk me through it. You got out of bed and…"

"Well, he wasn't in there with me, but that wasn't weird or nothing, because he usually crashes on the couch when he comes in late. So I took a shower, and then when I come out here, I seen that he wasn't here and plus his truck wasn't out front."

She stopped with the nail polish and took a big swallow of tomato juice.

"What did you do next?" Marlin asked.

"I went outside and looked around, and sure enough, I found his truck on the north fence line."

"Locked or unlocked?"

"Unlocked. And I couldn't find him nowhere. I looked all around and hollered."

"Did he have a phone with him?"

"Huh?"

"Does he have a cell phone?" Marlin asked.

She began on another nail.

"Oh, sure. He's always got that damn thing with him. Pays more attention to it than he does to me. Texting his buddies all the time like a bunch of schoolgirls. Except I seen that his phone was in his truck. And his wallet."

Leaving behind valuables was not a good sign. After a few more questions, Marlin would ask Mandy to give him directions to the truck. It couldn't be more than 500 yards away. He recalled that the north side of the small ranch bordered on a county road. Easy access. Just hop the fence.

"Any chance one of his buddies picked him up out on the road?" Marlin asked.

"That's exactly the kind of thing he'd do—just disappear without telling me—except I called most of 'em already and they ain't seen him."

Which didn't necessarily mean they were telling her the truth. Maybe Dub had gone drinking and wasn't ready to face Mandy yet. Maybe he was still sleeping it off. Or maybe he'd gone off with some friend Mandy didn't know about. A special friend.

"I'll need a list of names and numbers," Marlin said. "All of his friends and anybody else he might be with."

"All that shit will be on his phone," Mandy said. She hadn't made eye contact since she'd sat down. Too busy with her nail polish.

"Do you know if it's protected by a password?"

"Oh, yeah, it is. I forgot."

"You know the password?"

"Nope."

"Then I'll need a written list instead."

"Yeah, all right."

Marlin's gut told him Dub might come stumbling through the front door at any moment, hung over—but then again, Dub wasn't the predictable type. An example: The small ranch had been in his family for more than 120 years, and there had once been a nice little cabin on the place. But Dub had neglected it to the point that it had become uninhabitable and even dangerous. So, the previous spring, Dub had thrown a bonfire party and burned the place to the ground. "Easier than tearing the sumbitch down." That's what he'd told the small army of volunteer firefighters who'd responded to reports of massive flames licking the evening sky. Dub hadn't bothered to inform them of his plans. Now the only thing left of the historic structure was a pile of charred rubble.

"How tall is Dub?" Marlin asked.

"About five-ten."

Two toenails left to paint.

"What does he weigh, roughly?"

"Maybe two twenty. Ain't no Playgirl centerfold."

"What color are his eyes?"

"Usually red," Mandy said with a laugh. "But brown, mostly. His hair, too."

"What was he wearing when he left last night?" Marlin asked.

"Jeans and a blue T-shirt."

"Okay, and on his feet?"

"Tennis shoes. He don't like clomping around in boots."

"What brand?"

"Nike, I think. He buys 'em at Goodwill."

"What color?"

"Blue, I think."

"Was he wearing a hat?"

She had paused to drink some more tomato juice, so Marlin had to wait.

"Yeah, a red one. It's his favorite."

"Like a baseball cap?"

"Yeah."

"Anything printed on it?"

"It says something stupid about him being a bikini inspector."

Marlin was running out of questions. "Does he have any medical conditions—other than his bad back?"

"Nope. He's overweight, drinks too much, and eats pure crap, but he'll probably outlive us all."

Marlin nodded. He couldn't resist pressing further on the bad back. "Does he take pain pills for his back?"

Mandy kept a poker face. "Now and then, but not too often."

"Know if he took any last night?"

"Don't think so."

"And his back doesn't stop him from hunting? He can lift a dead pig?"

"If he shoots one, he calls one of his friends and they butcher it for him. He don't do no lifting himself."

Marlin nodded and let it go. "Okay, why don't you point me toward Dub's truck?"

9

Dub's phone and wallet were in the truck, just as Mandy had said. His rifle, too—resting against the passenger seat with the muzzle touching the floorboard, where eight empty beer cans were scattered. A twelve-pack carton, with four beers still in it, occupied the passenger seat, indicating that nobody had been with him. Keys were in the ignition.

Marlin used his phone to shoot multiple photos of the interior of the truck. Then he shot some video, too, just for good measure.

Then he tugged on some latex gloves and grabbed the phone from the console under the dashboard. Unfortunately, Mandy was right about it being password-protected. Marlin put it back where he'd found it.

Next he checked the wallet and found several credit cards and $43 in cash. Fairly solid indication that nobody had robbed him—not that Marlin had expected a robbery out here in the middle of nowhere, but you never knew. He found a driver's license and a frequent-customer card from a pizza joint in Blanco. He put the wallet back.

Then he grabbed the stock of the rifle—a Remington .270—with his left hand and worked the bolt with his right, ejecting a live round from the chamber. So the rifle probably had not been fired.

Marlin exited the truck and looked around. He'd noted earlier that the caliche road leading from the house to the truck was packed too hard to hold any prints—from tires or feet—but now Marlin began to check the surrounding area. Might find footprints. Might find an article of clothing or a beer can or something else to lead him in a particular direction. Might find a body.

But he didn't. After slowly searching the area for 20 minutes, he'd found nothing except deer tracks. Meanwhile, the clock was ticking. If Dub needed medical help, time was of the essence.

Marlin, back near the truck again, stood quietly and looked around. He looked to the north. Just past a row of cedar trees was the county road. Marlin knew the road well, as he knew every road in Blanco County. This particular road saw very little traffic, maybe fewer than a dozen vehicles a day. Not a single vehicle had passed in the time Marlin had been on the scene.

He walked over to the barbed-wire fence, eased himself over—

which wasn't too difficult, considering that he was six-four—and crossed the right-of-way to the pavement.

Two lanes. Faded yellow center lines. Pavement that would be in need of some attention in the next few years.

Marlin walked east along the side of the road. Didn't see much worth noting. Continued for about 50 yards, then crossed the road and came back to the west.

He passed his original starting point, and after walking thirty more yards, he spotted a scattering of glass in the road. He checked it out. Not glass from a beer bottle or a pickle jar or anything like that. Glass from a shattered headlight. Probably not important. Somebody hit a deer or something. Happened all the time. He pulled his phone out again, took more photos, and continued walking west.

Ten yards farther, he found a piece of molded automotive plastic in the high weeds along the shoulder. Probably part of a shattered fender or valance. The piece measured roughly ten inches by five inches. He photographed it, then bent down and studied it more closely. He was hoping to see a part number or any other stamped codes that might help him identify the make and model of the vehicle it came from, but he saw nothing. He continued walking.

He stopped again, abruptly, still on the edge of the shoulder. Eight or tens yards ahead, in the bottom of a small dip in the road, was a large pool of dark liquid. Marlin walked closer.

Blood. Had to be. Fairly fresh, too. Deep maroon, but not yet brown or black. From late the previous night or early that morning. Marlin had seen enough blood during his career to make accurate assessments based on color and coagulation.

The pool was large enough that Marlin felt confident whatever had done the bleeding, animal or human, it had died in that spot. There should be a carcass or corpse, either in the road or somewhere nearby. But where was it? No way predators had dragged it off, not without leaving trails of blood. Marlin took a knee right at the edge of the pool, hoping to see telltale pig or deer hair, but he didn't see any hair at all. Also didn't see any tire skid marks on either side of the pool. The driver had never applied the brakes. Drunk? Asleep? Simply not paying attention?

Time to bring in the sheriff's office.

4

THAT AFTERNOON, Billy Don came rumbling down the hallway into the living room, where Red was trying to take a nap in his recliner, and said, "Okay, I asked him."

"Asked who what?"

Red wasn't in a good mood. This thing with Dub Kimble was starting to worry him.

"Dickie Loftin," Billy Don said. "I posted on his Facebook page asking if he was in Johnson City last night."

He held up his iPhone. He'd bought it not long ago, after they'd come into some serious money from a pig-hunting contest, which they had then parlayed into a much larger amount at a blackjack table in Vegas. To be honest, Billy Don had done the parlaying while Red had watched and rooted him on. Who would've guessed that Billy Don—who once claimed that a "burner phone" was one you were supposed to set on fire when you were done with it—would've been a skilled blackjack player?

Red was still making do with his cheap Korean cell phone that didn't always work properly, but he had to admit he was leaning toward buying an iPhone himself. No doubt Billy Don would razz him about stepping into the modern world, but it would probably be worth it.

"You can do that?" Red said. "Send a message to a famous person like that?"

He had also been harboring a secret urge to join Facebook himself. He was almost disgusted with himself. What kind of self-respecting country boy joins Facebook? As far as Red could tell, half of the stuff on there was pictures of food and pets, and the rest was arguments about politics and other bullshit. On the other hand, Billy Don seemed to have fun with it.

"Yeah," Billy Don said, "if it's an official page, but that don't mean they'll answer it. Sometimes they do and sometimes they don't. Or they got somebody running their page for them. Some of 'em are more likely to answer a tweet."

Red had heard the word "tweet" a lot, but he still wasn't sure exactly what it was. Hell if he was going to ask Billy Don.

"Well, you just let me know when he says I was right," Red said.

Billy Don sat down in his usual place on the couch, which was so sunken in from his weight that his butt was no more than a few inches above the floor. "His feed don't say nothing about him being here. Last post was three days ago, from Abilene when he was up there for a show. Oh, hey—somebody just left a comment under my post saying they think they saw him here, too."

"See?" Red said. "I was right."

"Maybe. Or it was just a guy who looks a lot like him."

"Wanna put your money where your blowhole is?" Red asked.

Billy Don looked at him. "What you got in mind?"

"Thousand bucks says it was him."

"Not a chance," Billy Don said.

"That's what I thought," Red said.

Red went back to his nap attempt and Billy Don continued messing around with his phone. That was one good thing about the phone—it kept Billy Don distracted. Kept him from babbling all the time.

Just as Red could feel his eyes getting heavy, Billy Don said, "Well, shit. My post is gone."

Red waited.

"I think they deleted it," Billy Don said.

"They can do that?" Red asked. He was honestly curious. He didn't know how Facebook worked.

"Yeah, it's their page." Another minute passed with Billy Don on his phone. "I still see posts from other people, but mine is gone."

Red didn't really care either way.

"Wasn't like I said anything ugly," Billy Don said. "Why would they get rid of it?"

Red had to admit that was a pretty good question, but he had a question of his own. "Any news on there about Dub?"

9

"Did something happen to Dub? Is that what this is about?"

Marlin was having his second conversation with Mandy Hammerschmitt, this time across a table in an interview room at the sheriff's office. Bobby Garza, the Blanco County sheriff for many years now, was seated to Marlin's right.

"The truth is, at this point, we just don't know," Marlin said. "But we need to ask you some more questions, so please bear with me if this gets repetitive."

While they were talking, Henry Jameson, the forensics technician, was processing the county road and Dub's truck, with permission from Mandy granted earlier. No warrant needed. She'd also given the investigative team the go-ahead to search the house if they deemed it necessary, and to provide them with Dub's toothbrush and other personal items, so they could compare his DNA to that of the blood on the county road.

At the same time, deputies were using tracking dogs to search a wider area on Dub's ranch and surrounding properties, and a local helicopter pilot had agreed to fly the area to see if he could spot anything.

There was a slim possibility that Dub had been struck by a vehicle and then taken to a hospital in Austin or San Antonio. Marlin wasn't placing much hope in that. Wouldn't that person call 911? Generally, yes, unless the person happened to be intoxicated or in violation of some other law.

Back to Mandy. Garza would lead this interview, which was being video-recorded. Marlin would chime in as necessary.

"Walk us through your evening," Garza said. "What were y'all doing before Dub went out hunting? Were you together? Did he receive any calls?"

"Is Dub dead?" Mandy asked. "Is that what's going on?"

"Not as far as we know," Garza said. "But we're searching for him and hope to know more soon. The best thing you can do to help him is provide as much detail as possible."

Garza had always been a warm and comforting interviewer—or a tough interrogator, when needed. Right now, he was still in interview mode. Marlin had told him earlier that Mandy had shown no signs of deception when he'd questioned her at the trailer.

"Fire away," Mandy said. She had her arms tightly crossed. It appeared she had touched up her makeup since Marlin had first seen her at the trailer.

"Tell us about last night, before Dub went out to hunt," Garza said.

He was a few years younger than Marlin. Good-looking guy. Dark hair and a square jaw. Always had a confident demeanor about him.

"I started getting supper ready at around nine, and while I did that, he was watching TV and messing around on his phone, like usual."

"Do you know the password to his phone?" Garza asked, even

though Marlin had already told him that Mandy had said she didn't have it. Didn't hurt to see if her response was consistent.

She let out a snort. "Yeah, right."

"He never shared it with you?" Garza asked.

"Hell, no."

"So it never came up, or you asked and he refused?"

"That's just the way Dub is. He don't like me messing with his stuff."

"Just his phone?"

"His rifles, his tools, whatever. Heaven forbid I don't put a screwdriver back in the right place. But I don't really like him messing around with my shit, either, including my phone. Listen, I really think Dub just ran off with one of his friends. Don't you? Have you called 'em all? They mighta lied to me, but they'd be honest with you."

She appeared genuinely hopeful, but concerned. They hadn't told her about the pool of blood yet.

"We've called everyone on the list you gave me," Marlin said. "Nobody has seen him. If you can think of anybody else to add…"

She was already shaking her head.

"Or anyplace else he might be…" Marlin added.

Still no.

Garza proceeded to ask her a variety of questions for fifteen minutes, and while she answered freely and appeared completely forthcoming, she gave them nothing useful. As far as she was concerned, Dub had simply gone hunting and hadn't come back. End of story.

"You and Dub been getting along all right lately?" Garza asked, shifting gears.

"Yeah, I guess," Mandy said, frowning just enough to indicate she'd sensed the change in questioning.

"No big fight last night or anything like that?" Garza asked.

"Just the same old stuff."

"Which was what?"

"Well, you know, we're always snapping at each other."

"About what?"

The frustration was apparent on Mandy's face. "Well, last night, he was bitching that dinner was late. He's just such a…"

She didn't finish.

"Such a what?" Garza asked, not letting up.

"Okay, we got our problems, you know? Just like anyone else. But there wasn't nothin' going on last night any different than any other night."

Garza and Marlin both waited patiently. She had something to say, but she couldn't say it just yet. She was working up to it.

Finally Garza quietly said, "What are the problems you're talking about?"

She shook her head and a tear ran down her left cheek.

"He seeing someone else?" Garza asked. "Something like that?"

She let out a sigh. "Don't they all?"

Marlin and Garza remained quiet.

"Can I smoke in here?" Mandy asked.

"I'm afraid not," Garza said, "but we'll take a break soon. Why don't you tell us about the person Dub was seeing?"

"Well, that's the thing—I don't know for sure who it was. Or how many. All I know is he'd sometimes come home smelling like perfume, or he'd go into the other room to take phone calls. That kind of stuff. I think one of them mighta been Kelly Rundell."

Kelly Rundell's behavior—or rumors about her behavior, true or not—created gossip by the truckload in Blanco County. She was a beautiful young woman married to the president of First County Bank, who was twenty years older than she was. If the rumors were accurate, Kelly had had affairs with at least half a dozen men—apparently her way of getting back at her husband for neglecting her and denying her the children she wanted. Or maybe the two of them simply didn't love each other. Either way, Marlin thought it was a sad situation. Why live like that?

"Why do you suspect that he was seeing Kelly?" Garza asked.

"I heard about it from friends," Mandy said, "and then Dub and Lester Higgs had words at the café a few weeks ago. Hell, you probably know that, since somebody called the law."

"That's true," Garza said, "but at the time, neither of them would tell us what the problem was."

"Well, Lester is seeing Kelly now," Mandy said, "so you can probably piece it together."

"Did you ever confront Dub about your suspicions?" Garza asked.

"Yeah, but he always denied it."

"Did y'all talk about that last night?"

"No, not that. We were just bitching at each other. Something stupid. I can't even remember what it was. Oh, I remember. He made some wise-ass comment about the biscuits, so I told him to go to hell, and it didn't get any better after that."

Garza nodded and waited. She still had something else to say. Marlin could sense it.

She took a deep breath. "Okay, I might as well go ahead and tell ya, because you're gonna find out anyway. I've seen on TV how these investigations go. I got fed up with Dub screwing around behind my back, so I did a little stepping out myself. I went out and got me a boyfriend. And you know what? I don't regret it for a minute. Not a single minute."

5

"THIS AIN'T GOOD, Dickie," Creed Loftin said. "Ain't good at all."

"I know."

"We don't need word getting out. This isn't the kind of PR we were looking for."

"Think I don't know that?"

Dickie Loftin was stunned. No other word for it. Amazing how quickly his charmed life had gone off the rails. One bad decision was all it had taken. Followed by an even worse one. How many more was he going to add to it? What choice did he have now?

"We gotta do something about those guys in Johnson City," Creed said.

"What the hell *can* we do? Just keep denying it was me. Say it was someone who looks like me."

"That might not be enough. What if someone took a picture? That guy at the grocery store? He had time to do it before I came out."

"Doesn't matter. Still deny it."

"What if he took a picture of the Hummer?"

Dickie had been through rough waters before. Back when he'd hit the big time, critics had called him a plagiarist. A shameless ripoff. A comedy thief. The lowest of the low, within the world of entertainment. Others had said he was merely a snappy writer and clever marketer who knew how to appeal to mass audiences and capitalize on trends. His routine—as anybody alive in the past few years could tell you—was *I'm So White Trash...*

I'm so white trash, I drive a tractor to church on Sunday.

I'm so white trash, I've got more tires stacked in my yard than on my truck.

And so on.

Didn't take a genius to see the similarities between that and the classic "redneck" spiel perfected by Jeff Foxworthy many years earlier.

But Dickie had gotten past the harsh criticism. And he'd get past this.

"Dickie?" Creed said.

"Let me think."

"You been thinking since last night."

They were holed up in Dickie's house on the south side of Stephenville, Texas, which was about 65 miles southwest of Fort Worth. A straight shot up Highway 281 from Blanco County. Easy two-hour drive on a Saturday. Normally Dickie would've napped on the way home, but not this time. Now they were seated in two overstuffed easy chairs in front of the 85-inch LED TV in the recreation room. A gift from the nice folks at Samsung—one of the brands Dickie endorsed. Just like Harrah's Casino had sent him a poker table, and Brunswick had sent him a pool table. Dickie's wife Lola was in New York City with some of her girlfriends, thank God.

The TV was tuned to the old Steve McQueen movie *Bullitt*, but the sound was low and neither of them was paying any attention to it.

"Can't just let it lie," Creed said.

Dickie didn't reply.

"You know that, right?"

"No, I don't know that," Dickie said. "Just calm your ass down."

The taxi in the movie had a bobble-head dog visible through the rear windshield. That's how Dickie felt right now—his head going in different directions, out of control.

Creed said, "You never shoulda gotten out of the—"

"I know, goddammit, but what's done is done," Dickie snapped. "I don't need you harping about it. Jesus Christ, all you've done is talk all day. I can't think straight. Just let me think, okay? Please?"

They sat in silence for a long moment. Old habits die hard—that's what Dickie was thinking. Lola hated when he smoked cigars in any of their vehicles, and he'd hear about it for weeks if he lit up. So he'd gotten out of the Hummer in Johnson City. Stupid mistake.

"Just trying to keep all of us out of trouble," Creed said.

Creed stood and walked over to a rack of dumbbells against one wall. Grabbed the 75-pounder and began to curl it with his left arm as if it were a plastic movie prop. That's what Creed did when he was stressed out. Lift. He also did it when he was excited, bored, confused, depressed, angry, or sad. He'd always been that way, even back when he and Dickie were just kids. Got his first weight set when he was about eleven years old. Ever see an eleven-year-old walking around with sculpted biceps and six-pack abs? It just looked weird. But that was Creed back then. Now he was a walking wall of concrete.

"Let's think this through," Dickie said. "If I say, yeah, I was in Johnson City, so what? Who cares?"

"That ain't the way to play it," Creed said, not even breathing heavily. He'd moved the weight to his right hand.

"Why not?"

Creed finished his reps, then walked back to his chair. "Why admit it? What do you gain from it? Why do the cops' jobs for them?"

Creed had experience with law enforcement, whereas Dickie had never even been arrested, despite the image he projected on stage. Hell, it had been eight years since he'd even received a traffic ticket. Did that mean he should listen to Creed? Creed was Dickie's bodyguard, driver, general assistant, social media manager, and brother—but legal advisor?

"What happens if they figure out where it happened?" Dickie asked. "They'll start talking to everyone who lives around there, including Skeet, and it won't be long until they figure out who was at his place last night."

"Maybe so, and that's unavoidable, but we don't want them to know we were in Johnson City." Creed said. "Don't say we were there, but don't say we *weren't* there, either. Just keep our mouths shut—that's my advice. You have the right to remain silent. They have to prove we drove that particular stretch of road."

"Then we just sit tight? That's what you're saying now?"

"Except for the people who said they saw you in town."

"What about 'em?"

"We've gotta do something about that."

"Like what? What're we supposed to do?"

"We just need to make sure they keep quiet, that's all."

"How?"

"I'm not sure yet. But let me take care of it, okay? You can't get bogged down in all this shit. I'll figure something out. And it's better if you aren't involved, you know what I mean?"

Dickie looked at him long and hard. Creed didn't always make the best decisions—an understatement—but he was offering Dickie a chance to wash his hands of everything. To stop worrying. To let someone else clean up the mess.

"Just don't do anything stupid," Dickie said.

"I just heard something good," Billy Don said, stepping into the living room with a mixing bowl cradled in the crook of his arm, stirring the contents with a wooden spoon.

"What the hell are you making now?" Red was in his recliner again, this time watching that old classic, *Bullitt*. Best car chase ever filmed, despite the same green VW Beetle appearing over and over, and more lost hubcaps than you could count.

"Sausage balls," Billy Don said.

That was something else that had changed about Billy Don since he'd gotten the iPhone. He would get recipes off the Internet and cook or bake stuff. Some of the items had turned out pretty good, so Red had stopped making fun of him—calling him "Betty Crocker" and such.

"That ain't like Rocky Mountain oysters, is it?" Red asked, grimacing at the thought of eating bull testicles. Who would do that? It would be just like Billy Don to trick him into eating something that disgusting.

"Nope," Billy Don said. "Just deer sausage and Bisquick and a couple other things."

Red grunted.

"Cream cheese."

"Yeah."

"Cheddar cheese," Billy Don said.

"Hmm."

"You mix it all together and bake—"

"More than I need to know," Red said.

Billy Don turned to go back into the kitchen, then remembered why he'd come into the living room in the first place.

"What I heard is, it sounds like Dub Kimble mighta got hit by a car."

Red turned the volume down. "So they found him?"

"I don't think so. But they figured out he got hit by a car."

"Who figured it out? Where'd you hear that?"

"Facebook."

"But who said it?"

"I don't know. Just somebody on Facebook."

"Somebody you don't even know?"

"Yeah, but they said they heard it from somebody who heard it from somebody that works at the sheriff's office."

By now, Red figured it was a crock of shit. Just a rumor. "Was it his cousin's uncle's brother?"

"You don't believe it?"

"Sounds like fake news to me," Red said.

"I'm just passing along an interesting bit of information, that's all."

"Passing along bullshit."

"Why're you being such a dickhead?"

"Just good at it, I guess."

"You got that right."

"When did this supposably happen?" Red asked.

"Don't know. Nobody knows."

"What I figured."

Billy Don went back into the kitchen, then came right back out again. "Oh, I figured out why you got a stick up your butt. If they don't find Dub pretty quick, ain't the cops gonna come talk to you about it?"

"It took you 'til now to puzzle that out?"

"Just for that smart-ass remark, you ain't getting any sausage balls."

Billy Don went into the kitchen and didn't come back this time.

Red sat there thinking about the situation. Was it true that Dub had been hit by a car? If the person said "car," did that include trucks? Problem was, Red's truck was so old and beat up, it would be hard for the cops to tell whether or not he'd hit anything recently. Which would make it easy for them to pin it on him.

Well, shit. How had everything gone to hell so quickly?

6

MANDY'S SECRET BOYFRIEND was a handsome young man named Tino Herrera. According to his Facebook profile, he was born in Ecuador but had moved here "to persue the American dream" and was now the assistant manager at the Dairy Queen in Fredericksburg, Texas, thirty miles west of Johnson City, in Gillespie County. Herrera seemed to be tagged in lots of photos with attractive young women, either individually or in groups.

Marlin was riding shotgun as Garza's county car cruised at 80 on Highway 290. A quick background check revealed that Tino Herrera had been busted twice for possession of marijuana, but the last time had been nearly three years earlier.

Normally they wouldn't rush to interview Herrera until they were better prepared, but in this case, they wanted to inspect his vehicle for damage as soon as possible, and they wanted to question him before Mandy warned him they were coming. She had promised she wouldn't contact him before they met with him, but Marlin figured it was 50/50 on her sticking to it.

"He moved here seven years ago," Marlin said. "Twenty-three years old."

"How old is Mandy?" Garza asked.

"Thirty-two," Marlin said.

Garza made an expression, like *That's interesting.*

Once Mandy revealed the relationship with Tino, she hadn't held anything back. She'd been seeing him for about four months. Just a fling, at first. Couldn't help herself. He was such a hunk. Like a movie star. And a gentleman, too. When she'd first met him, instead of calling her up to the counter when her order was ready, he'd delivered it to her table, with a smile that made her heart thump in her chest. And extra French fries! Later, as he watched her from the soft-serve machine, she couldn't resist eating her corn dog in a suggestive manner. That sealed the deal.

Was Dub aware of the affair? Not as far as Mandy knew. And she figured he probably wouldn't have cared, anyway. He didn't seem to care about her one way or the other. She was crying when she said that. She was upset, but did she have anything to do with Dub's disappearance? Marlin would've guessed the answer was no.

As they passed through Stonewall, Garza said, "Any brilliant deductions?"

"Not really, but whatever happened, it almost certainly had to be an accident."

"Followed by a cover-up," Garza said.

"I think that's the most plausible scenario," Marlin said. "Somebody hit Dub in the dark, panicked, and decided to dump the body somewhere. Maybe the driver was drunk, or just scared."

"Makes sense," Garza said, "because if it was intentional, how do you arrange something like that? You'd have to lure him into the road somehow. I guess you could work something out—some kind of trap—but it doesn't seem likely."

"And if you're going to get rid of the body afterward, why not just shoot him or stab him, instead of running him down with a vehicle? Much easier that way, and you don't screw up your vehicle."

"Good point," Garza said.

They rode in silence for a moment.

"We need to compile a list of everyone who lives on that road and drives it regularly," Garza said.

"Agreed."

"That also means Tino is probably a dead end. Lester Higgs, too. And Claude Rundell. Their motives are meaningless if it was an accident."

"Probably," Marlin said. "And Red O'Brien."

Garza nodded. They hadn't discussed O'Brien yet, but they were both familiar with his motive—the lawsuit Dub Kimble had been threatening to file against him.

O'Brien was one of the most colorful—and irritating—residents in Blanco County. An inveterate poacher, along with his partner in crime, Billy Don Craddock. Both of them were talented tradesmen, but they avoided work whenever possible. They also made life choices that would leave most people scratching their heads. The two of them had won a pig-hunting contest some time back, and then, from what Marlin had heard, they'd gone to Las Vegas and turned their original $50,000 winnings into something like $140,000 each.

What had O'Brien decided to do with his share? At first, he'd tried to go into business with an old man who'd created a deer-attractant spray. Marlin had seen firsthand that the spray worked amazingly well, but the old man wound up dead, and for a short while, O'Brien had been a suspect. They'd ruled him out, just as they would need to rule him out in this investigation.

Next, from what Marlin had heard, O'Brien had decided to build a massive tree house resembling the Alamo on this property. Not a tree house like the kind kids play in, but an actual house in the trees, complete with plumbing, electricity, HVAC, and all the other modern comforts and conveniences. What kind of person decides that's the best use of that much money? Regardless, it wasn't to be, because on the first day of construction, Dub Kimble had fallen fifteen feet and injured his back. Allegedly.

"It would be nice if Henry could nail down that piece of molded plastic," Garza said as they entered the Fredericksburg city limits.

Henry Jameson was a fine forensic technician, but his availability was frequently limited. Blanco County's relatively low crime rate couldn't justify the salary of a forensic technician and associated expenses, so several years earlier, Garza had worked a deal with four other counties, pooling resources, giving them all access to Jameson's services, as needed. All five counties together kept Jameson busy, which meant the occasional wait to have items processed.

"Crossing my fingers that piece came from the vehicle that hit Dub," Marlin said, "rather than being some random piece of debris."

"Speaking of which, I bet that's Tino's Honda right over there," Garza said, pointing, as they approached the Dairy Queen.

Records showed that Herrera owned an eight-year-old Civic. It was blue, but Marlin could already tell that the Civic's light blue didn't match the darker blue from the fragment he'd found at the crime scene. Garza circled the Honda and they saw no damage to it anywhere. Then he pulled into a parking spot.

"Well, if we accomplish nothing else, at least we can grab a Dilly Bar for the ride home," Marlin said.

9

They spotted Tino Herrera hovering near a booth occupied by three young ladies who appeared to be high-school age. Tino was, by any standard, a good-looking young kid. Dark hair, dark eyes, high cheekbones. Eyelashes so long, it looked like he was wearing mascara. Tino had just said something that made the trio of girls giggle. Two other tables were occupied, one by a solo male diner and another by an elderly couple.

Marlin grabbed a booth in a back corner while Garza went to the counter and ordered a cup of coffee from one of the other employees. While Marlin waited, he sent a text to Blanco County Chief Deputy Lauren Gilchrist, who was leading the search for Dub Kimble.

Anything?

No immediate response, so he set his phone on the tabletop.

Tino was still chatting up the ladies. The kid was a player. That was Marlin's immediate assessment. Tino probably hit on every woman that came into the place. Marlin watched him. The kid was completely at ease—laughing, joking, chatting. Marlin couldn't hear the words, but the girls in the booth seemed to be eating it up.

A text came from Lauren: *Found a red baseball cap w blood on it.*

Not good. Marlin sent a reply: *Anything written on it?*

Garza came to the table and sat down with his coffee. They'd agreed they weren't going to push Tino hard. Don't spook him, just in case. Don't march in and demand to talk to him. Play it from a different angle.

Lauren replied: *Licensed bikini inspector.*

Marlin was disappointed, although not surprised, to see that. Now it was all but certain that Dub Kimble had been hit by a vehicle, then moved, possibly still alive, but much more likely dead. Marlin told Garza about the text.

"That's a shame," the sheriff said, his voice low, even though the nearest customer was several tables away.

Marlin noticed that Tino was eyeballing him and Garza, so Marlin held up one finger, meaning *Come talk to us.*

Tino said one more thing to the girls and then made his way across the room.

"Good afternoon, gentlemen. I hope Eddie at the counter remembered to give you our law-enforcement discount."

If he was nervous, he didn't show it. He had more of an accent than Marlin was expecting.

"Tino, right?" Garza said.

"Yes, sir."

Garza and Marlin introduced themselves, and Garza said, "Mind if we ask you a couple of questions?"

"I'm working right now, but—"

"Probably take five minutes," Garza said. "And you're the boss, right? Not like you'll get in trouble."

Tino appeared puzzled or possibly curious, but still not nervous. "Okay, yes, sir. What's going on?"

"When was the last time you were in Blanco County?" Garza asked.

The question was designed to lock Tino into a story right away.

"May I ask what this is about?" he said.

Mandy had revealed that she'd called Tino last night, after Dub stormed out, but she said she hadn't talked to Tino since then. Theoretically, he wouldn't know anything about the situation yet.

"We'll get to that in just a sec," Garza said. "You been to Blanco County recently?"

"Uh, three days ago, I think. But I wasn't hunting or fishing."

He was making some assumptions based on the presence of a game warden. Or pretending he didn't know what this was about.

"What were you doing in Blanco County?" Garza asked.

"Visiting a friend."

Now Tino was finally starting to look a little anxious.

"The friend being Mandy, right?" Garza said. "Yeah, she told us. You went over to her place. And you haven't been back to Blanco County since then?"

"No, that was the last time."

"So that was Wednesday night?"

"I think so. Or Tuesday night."

"But you weren't in Blanco County last night?" Garza asked.

The three girls were exiting the restaurant, casting furtive glances at Tino as they left.

"No, sir," Tino said. "Not last night."

"Where were you?" Garza asked.

"Last night?"

"Right."

"I worked from two until nine. It was probably more like nine-fifteen or nine-thirty before I got out of here."

"And then what?"

"I went over to a friend's house and drank some beer."

"What's your friend's name?"

"Conrad."

Garza pulled a napkin from the dispenser and a pen from his breast pocket. "We'll need his phone number, please."

Tino took out his phone to check the number, then scribbled it on the napkin. "Did something happen to Mandy?" His voice was quivering.

"No, she's fine. It's Dub. You know Dub, right?"

"I've, uh, never actually met him."

"He went missing last night," Garza said.

Tino blinked twice. "Missing how?"

"In the sense that he is gone and nobody knows where he is."

The glass door to the restaurant swung open and two customers walked in and went to the counter.

"Is he okay?"

"We don't know. But I'm sure you can understand, given your relationship with Mandy, why we're asking."

"Absolutely. Yes, sir. But I had nothing to do with it. I promise."

"We're just ruling people out," Garza said. "So the more you can help us out, the quicker we can get out of your hair."

"I'll help however I can."

"That's your blue Honda out front?" Marlin asked.

"Yes, sir."

"Do you own any other cars or trucks?"

"No, sir."

"Do you routinely borrow or drive any other cars or trucks?"

"No, just my Honda."

"What kind of vehicle does Conrad own?"

"A truck. A Chevy truck."

"What color?"

"Green."

Marlin was seeing no signs of guilt from Tino. No hemming and hawing. No body language that indicated deception.

"Can you think of anyone who might want to harm Dub?" Marlin asked.

Now, for the first time, Tino seemed to hesitate.

"Just Mandy," he finally said, appearing rueful. "But she wouldn't actually do anything."

"Why might Mandy harm him?" Marlin asked.

"She wouldn't, like I said, but she might want to because of the way he treats her," Tino said.

"Tell us about that," Marlin said.

"Okay, well, she never, uh, got together with me until Dub had cheated on her many times. I mean a lot. For years. So she got tired of it."

"Understandable," Marlin said.

"Anyway, one night Dub accused her of fooling around, and she denied it, and then he started yelling at her, and pretty soon he called her a two-bit whore."

Tino paused there, and it was obvious he was looking for a reaction.

"That's pretty ugly," Marlin said.

"Exactly. What kind of man says something like that? Mandy lost her temper, and then she went into the bedroom and came back with a pistol she keeps in the nightstand. Dub ran out the door, and by the time she made it onto the porch, he was forty or fifty yards away. Still—"

"What happened?" Garza said.

"She fired a shot," Tino said. "Not to hit him, please understand. Just to scare him."

Garza said, "I bet it worked, too, huh?"

7

CREED'S FORMER CELLMATE was named Alan Bricker. Funny. Name like that, it sounded like he should be selling insurance or designing websites. Wearing black-framed hipster eyeglasses. Eating kale.

In reality, Bricker was a lifelong recidivist who'd earned his most recent stint in Huntsville—the one where he and Creed had met—by breaking a glass tip jar in a college student's face. The victim's transgression? He'd gawked a little too long at Bricker's date inside a nightclub in Austin's Warehouse District. Stupid kid ended up with a broken nose, a concussion, and a line of stitches running from his forehead to his upper lip.

Bricker seemed to have no conscience, and as far as Creed was concerned, for his purposes, that was a plus, not a minus. Bricker also had no impulse control—hence the tip jar incident—and that was more of a concern. Creed would have to keep a close eye on him. Make sure he didn't say or do anything stupid.

Creed wanted Bricker along merely for the intimidation factor, just in case the men in Johnson City didn't cooperate. Bricker had a way of looking at people and making them uneasy. Amazing that a man one hundred pounds lighter and ten inches shorter than Creed could be twice as scary, but it was true, and Creed was smart enough to acknowledge it.

"Hey, bud. Long time, no see," Bricker said when Creed picked him up on Saturday evening at the corner of Burnet Road and Rutland in north Austin. He was wearing oil-stained blue jeans and a black T-shirt for a metal band called Accept. He had a lock-blade knife in a sheath belted on his hip.

"Jesus friggin' Christ," Creed said, clasping Bricker's hand. "Been a long damn time. Staying out of trouble?"

"Sheeyit," Bricker said. "Not hardly. It follers me around."

Damn, that funky accent. Creed had forgotten how silly it sounded. Sort of a mix between the Texas flatlands and the hollers of Appalachia.

"I hear you on that," Creed said, and he pulled away from the curb, going south on Burnet.

"Where we headed?" Bricker asked. He had a pinch of Copenhagen behind his lip, as usual.

"Grab some supper?"

"Screw that. Let's get a drink. There's a great little joint about a couple miles down the road."

Creed nodded.

"This is a goddamn nice ride," Bricker said, scoping out the interior of Creed's black BMW coupe.

"Thanks."

"This leather?"

"Damn straight."

"So what's the problem you mentioned on the phone?" Bricker asked.

Creed laughed. "You get right to it, huh?"

"That's why we're here, ain't it? Or are you wanting to go get our nails done?"

Creed kept his speed slow and steady. After all, they were both on parole.

"I need some help with a… situation," he said. "*Might* need some help. I'll pay you real good either way."

"What's the deal?"

On the drive down to meet Bricker earlier, Creed had debated how much to tell him and how much to keep to himself. It would be better to keep Dickie out of it completely—but that simply wouldn't be possible. Besides, if Bricker had all of the details, he might come up with some good ideas of his own. He was a clever little son of a bitch, at least when it came to this sort of stuff.

So Creed told him the full story, start to finish, with all the gory details.

Bricker never even batted an eye. Then he said, "Ain't nothin' a couple of smart guys like us can't fix."

Creed was relieved to hear that.

"Right here," Bricker said, pointing to a place called Ginny's Little Longhorn Saloon. "I need a cold beer quick."

9

Red was in the middle of his third beer when Willard Fisk walked into TapZ32 in Johnson City.

"There's Willard," Billy Don said from the stool next to Red's.

"I see him. Don't—"

"Willard!" Billy Don called, waving to catch Willard's eye.

Too late.

"You did that on purpose," Red muttered.

Willard Fisk was a Blanco County homebuilder and occasional client. Used to be a friend, too, until Red decided to build an Alamo tree house in his backyard a few months earlier. Willard had offered to pitch in with the planning part of it, which was damn nice of him—or so Red had thought. Wasn't long before Willard started saying that a lot of the great stories about the Alamo were myths, including the one about William Travis drawing a line in the sand and asking patriots—those who were willing to die for the cause—to step across it. Willard said the whole thing probably didn't happen. Said nobody even mentioned that alleged incident until forty years later. What kind of authentic Texan would say such a thing? Even if it didn't happen—and Red figured it probably did—it *sounded* like something that would've happened, and wasn't that good enough?

"Hey, guys," Willard said, taking a stool on the other side of Billy Don.

"Hey, Willard," Billy Don said.

Red grunted.

"What's going on?" Willard asked.

"Same old bullshit," Billy Don said.

Red sniffed.

"Guess y'all heard about Dub," Willard said.

"Yep," Billy Don said.

Red said nothing.

"Figure that's real convenient for you, isn't it, Red?" Willard asked.

Red spun in his direction. "The hell's that supposed to mean?"

Willard's eyes bulged in surprise. "Take it easy. I didn't mean nothing by it."

Red glared at him. "You're kind of a know-it-all, huh?"

"Jeez, where is this coming from?" Willard said.

"Dang, Red, settle down," Billy Don said.

"I was just kidding around," Willard said. "Not that it isn't true."

"What isn't true?" Red asked.

"I didn't say it isn't true. I said, 'Not that it isn't true.'"

"Whatever you're saying, I disagree with it," Red said.

Willard looked like he was stifling a laugh. "All I meant was, now that Dub is missing, maybe your legal troubles will disappear, too. If that's even the way it works. I'm no legal genius."

"Or any kind of genius," Red said.

"Fair enough," Willard laughed. "Let me buy y'all a beer. Peace offering."

"Now we're getting somewhere," Billy Don said.

Red didn't say anything, because he wasn't the kind to object to a free beer. But he still didn't appreciate Willard bringing up the potential lawsuit. It was a painful reminder that Red's cash—now standing at somewhere around $121,000—was at risk, all because of Dub being a clumsy idiot. On the very first damn day of building the tree house with a crew of volunteers, Dub managed to fall and injure his back. Least that's what Dub claimed. Red wasn't sure he bought it.

In hindsight, Red realized that every last man on that building crew knew that he was rich, and it wasn't a big stretch to think one of them might've been tempted to pull a scam. Red had talked to a lawyer about it, and he'd said Red was definitely looking at some liability. Medical bills. Loss of income. That sort of thing. The lawyer pointed out it wasn't real smart of Red to supply beer to all of the volunteers and then ask them to climb ladders.

"Red?" Willard said. "Beer?"

Red shrugged. "Do what you want."

Willard signaled the bartender and said, "Same thing for them and a Pecan Street for me."

The bartender went to the taps and came back a minute later with the beers. Willard paid and gave him a tip.

After the bartender had moved away, Willard said in a quiet voice, "You want my opinion, they oughta be taking a real good look at Lester Higgs."

"Why Lester?" Billy Don said.

"Well, I heard he's been seeing Kelly Rundell, and she used to have a thing going with Dub, if you didn't know."

Red hadn't known that, so he said, "Everybody knows that."

Willard said, "Apparently, Dub and Lester almost got into it at the Kountry Kitchen a few weeks ago. Couple of waiters had to step in and keep 'em apart. Somebody even called the law."

"My money woulda been on Lester for sure," Billy Don said.

Red was interested, but skeptical.

"Who'd you hear all this from?" he asked.

"I'm not at liberty to say," Willard replied.

"I won't tell nobody," Red said.

"Sorry, Red."

"Was it Homer?" Red asked.

Willard's cousin Homer Griggs was a reserve deputy.

"I can neither confirm or deny that assumption," Willard said.

"Then I'm gonna figure it was Homer," Red said.

"I can't stop you from that," Willard said.

"And that's your way of saying it was him, right?" Red said. He might believe the rumor if it came straight from a deputy, even though deputies sometimes made Red's life a living hell.

"Maybe so, maybe not," Willard said.

Red wanted to punch him.

9

After the discussion with Tino, Marlin went to his office within the sheriff's department and spent several hours writing affidavits, hoping to secure search warrants for Dub's, Mandy's, and Tino's cell phone records and location data. He'd present the affidavits to Judge Hilton in the morning.

When he was done, he texted Lauren Gilchrist again.

Update?

The sun was setting and the searchers would soon knock off until the morning. At this point, there was little chance that Dub would be found alive. Homer Griggs, one of the reserve deputies, had called all area hospitals earlier, inquiring about any unknown male fitting Dub's description. No luck.

Nothing new, Lauren replied.

She was an outstanding chief deputy, earning respect immediately from everyone who worked with her. She also happened to have been Marlin's girlfriend back in his college days. Sure, it had been awkward at first, but they'd gotten past that, and Marlin had even grown comfortable with the fact that Lauren was now dating his best friend, Phil Colby. In fact, she and Colby had gone out a few times years ago, after Marlin and Lauren had broken up—something Marlin had not known until recently. That had taken him a little longer to digest, but everything was fine now. His wife Nicole wasn't the jealous type, so she'd had no problem with Lauren's presence from the start. Nicole and Lauren had even seemed to hit it off, which wasn't surprising, because Lauren was every bit as strong-willed and sharp-witted as Nicole.

Marlin simply sat at his desk for a moment, thinking.

Earlier, Bobby Garza had spoken to Tino's friend Conrad, who had confirmed that Tino had come over to his house at about 10:00 or 10:30 on Friday night to drink beer, and that he had stayed until nearly four in the morning. That provided Tino with a fairly solid alibi.

After sharing that information, Garza had gone home to have a late dinner with his family. Now the building was fairly quiet. Marlin could hear Darrell, the dispatcher on duty, talking in another part of the building, but he couldn't make out any of the words.

What happened to Dub Kimble? If it was a hit-and-run—an accident followed by felony fleeing—the driver was probably drunk, on drugs, unlicensed, or had some other motivating factor for running. And he had to have moved the body in an effort to conceal the accident. But where had he—assuming it was a male—taken it? Was the driver alone, or were there passengers? What time had it happened?

Marlin turned toward his computer and opened a map centering on the location where he'd found the pool of blood on the county road.

On the south side of the road was Dub's small ranch. His neighbors to the east and west on the same side of the road owned properties of similar size. Marlin knew all of them—nearly a dozen landowners in total—and he made a mental note to check what kinds of vehicles they owned.

To the north of Dub's place, on the other side of the county road, was a much larger property—two thousand acres. A working cattle ranch owned by a car dealer out of San Antonio. Skeet Carrasco—a flamboyant guy with annoying ads on the radio and TV. A corny slogan, too. *Come see Skeet and get back on the street!*

Marlin had met Skeet Carrasco a couple of times, and if his cheesy, good-ol'-boy TV persona was an act, he kept it up full time. He closed each commercial with a full-toothed grin and a wink, and Marlin almost expected him to do that in person.

Skeet Carrasco regularly invited some of his largest clients and best salespeople to his ranch to hunt. And drink. Marlin had heard about some wild parties on the Big Ram Ranch. In fact, one Saturday night about a year earlier, Marlin had stopped a slow-moving vehicle, thinking it might be poachers, only to find five young attractive women inside, all dressed in skirts and high heels. Escorts? Why did he get that feeling? It didn't help that a couple of them made flirtatious remarks, including a suggestive comment about his handcuffs, while the rest of them laughed. They said they were lost, looking for Skeet Carrasco's place, and Marlin gave them directions.

The entrance to Carrasco's ranch was about a half mile west of the spot where Marlin had found the pool of blood.

Interesting.

8

"WHAT WERE THEIR NAMES again?" Bricker asked on Sunday morning, with some Copenhagen in his mouth.

They'd crashed at Bricker's apartment the night before, getting in late after barhopping, and now they were in Creed's BMW, heading west on Highway 290 toward Blanco County. Crossing a bridge over Yeager Creek at the moment. Pretty country through here. Very little development. Just cedars and oaks and hills covered with caliche. Gorgeous day. Seventy degrees at the moment. Not a cloud in the sky.

"One is Billy Don Craddock and the other is Danny Ray Watts."

Creed had taken screen shots of the comments on Dickie's Facebook fan page before he'd deleted them. Now he had the names memorized and their Facebook profiles bookmarked.

Billy Don Craddock's Facebook profile photo was an old Ford Ranchero. There were no photos of him anywhere else, but Creed figured Craddock had to be that pushy little son of a bitch from the Lowe's Market parking lot. His comment on Facebook had simply said: *Think Dickie might of been in Johnson City, Tex last nite. Was that you?*

Danny Ray Watts was the man Creed and Dickie had encountered at a stoplight right after they'd left the Lowe's Market. The booze and cigar together had made Dickie queasy, so he'd rolled down the window, just in case, and right then Watts had pulled up beside them.

Watts yelled, "Hey, Dickie!" and Dickie had responded by rolling his window up and giving the guy the rod in the process. Stupid. Later, Watts's comment on Dickie's Facebook page said: *Think i saw Dickie in Johnson City. If so, he is a real a-hole, what a disapointment.*

"Know where we can find them?" Bricker asked as he spit into a beer bottle.

"Shouldn't be real hard to find out."

"You decide how you want to approach this yet?"

Good question. Last night, he and Bricker had sat in the beer joint until closing, drinking and brainstorming, and both of them had come up with some pretty wild options.

At one point, Bricker had lowered his voice and said, "If you just wanna take 'em off the board, I'm okay with that."

That took Creed by surprise, for sure. So he laughed, like Bricker was joking, and said, "Yeah, right."

Bricker said, "That's the easiest and quickest way. I could do it myself, if you want. Keep your hands clean."

Creed figured it was the alcohol talking. Macho BS on Bricker's part. No way he really meant it. Now Creed decided it would be best to pretend they'd never had that discussion.

"Still thinking," he said.

Bricker didn't have much expression on his face. Just kept watching the miles roll past. "I ain't never been in these parts. They got a lot of deer?"

"Oh, yeah. Crawling with 'em."

"Pigs?"

"Yep. Some exotics running around, too. They get out from the high-fenced places."

Bricker nodded, pleased with the information, as if he were some aristocrat planning to buy a ranch and build a custom home on it. His type was much more likely to drag a mobile home onto an acre and let the weeds grow to shoulder height around it.

Take 'em off the board.

Creed couldn't help contemplating that, as insane as it was. Not seriously considering it, of course, but just running it through his mind, brainstorming on the logistics of it, the way a man might ponder the best way to rob a bank, even when he knew he'd never do it in a million years. More of a mental challenge than anything else.

Take 'em off the board.

How would something like that even work? How exactly would Bricker go about it if Creed gave him the go-ahead? Creed pushed that whole idiotic idea out of his head. Sounded like something a crackhead would do. Stupid. Rash. Impulsive.

They crossed Middle Creek, then Miller Creek, and a short while later, they followed a sweeping right-hand curve onto Highway 281. Johnson City, seven miles ahead.

9

"How the heck're you doing?" Skeet Carrasco said as he came out the front door to meet Marlin in the circular drive in front of his home. Big grin on his face, walking with all the confidence in the world—the same demeanor that had no doubt served him so well when selling cars, hands on, back in the early days.

Carrasco looked more like a wealthy patriarch in a soap opera than a car magnate. Handsome, with short, graying hair that was expertly cut. Square jaw. Light blue eyes. Perfect teeth. Capped, for sure, and as white as the inside of a coconut, all the more pronounced because of his tanned face. Tall, too. Almost as tall as Marlin.

Marlin shook his extended hand. "Good to see you, Mr. Carrasco."

"Aw, call me Skeet. You picked a gorgeous day to come out. Wanna see the ranch?"

"I—"

"I love to show the place off, I'll admit it. If I recall, I've never given you the tour."

They'd met twice, yet Carrasco was acting as if they were longtime buddies.

"You haven't. I'd like that," Marlin said. Good chance to talk.

Earlier, on the phone, Marlin hadn't told Carrasco the reason for the visit, but most landowners weren't surprised when the game warden wanted to stop by and say hello, especially on large hunting ranches. Some of them did what Carrasco was doing—giving Marlin a big welcome, as if to show they had nothing to hide. No sir, no poaching going on here. Everything is by the book.

"Let's take my truck," Skeet said, and he began walking toward a black Ram dual-cab truck on the far side of the circular drive. That was his brand—Dodge, and the offshoot Ram Truck line. He owned half a dozen dealerships around Texas.

After they were both seated inside the cab, Carrasco dropped it into drive and said, "How about we start at the creek? It's running real good right now."

9

Red was behind his mobile home—staring upward at the horizontal support beams attached to a large oak tree—when he heard a vehicle coming up the drive. Early for visitors. He walked around the side of the house and saw an SUV parking out front. It looked just like the SUVs Blanco County deputies drove, except it didn't have the distinctive paint job and logo on the door, because the person driving it didn't routinely go on patrol.

Crap.

Not unexpected, but still, crap.

Out stepped Bobby Garza. Not just some deputy, but the sheriff himself. Coming to talk about Dub Kimble.

Crap.

Red had an overwhelming urge to sneak away quietly before Garza spotted him. But the difference this time—and it was a big difference—was that Red hadn't done anything wrong. How often was that the case?

Garza climbed out of his SUV, and Red was just about to call out, but the sheriff walked over to Red's truck and began to study the front of it. Even got down on one knee and inspected the undercarriage, obviously looking for damage. Maybe the rumor about Dub getting hit by a vehicle was right. After a moment, Garza stood up and turned around.

"Hey, Sheriff," Red called, walking closer.

"Red."

"Admiring my truck?" Red asked.

"It's a nice one, no doubt," Garza said, playing along.

"Them little dents and dings is just character," Red said.

"That's what I've been saying about myself lately."

Red laughed, maybe a little too loudly.

"You got any idea why I stopped by?" Garza asked.

"To give me another one of them fancy citizenship awards?"

Garza chuckled. "Not this time, sorry. No, I need to—"

The front door to the trailer swung open and Billy Don poked his head out. "Oh. Hey, Sheriff."

"Billy Don."

Billy Don grinned. What a jerk. "You here to ask Red about Dub Kimble?"

"I'm afraid that's between me and Red," Garza said.

"Fair enough, but there ain't no way Red would do nothing to Dub, even though he's got a motive bigger than Dodge."

"Jesus, Billy Don!" Red said.

"Well, everybody knows it, Red," Billy Don said. "Might as well deal with it head on. In fact, probably ain't nobody with a bigger motive than you, except maybe Lester Higgs, or maybe Claude Rundell, and since you was all alone on Friday night—"

"Billy Don!"

Garza said, "Red, why don't you hop in my vehicle and we'll go back to my office for a chat?"

Crap.

9

"The great thing about this truck," Carrasco said, "is you got all the modern conveniences and comforts. Heated bucket seats. Premium leather. Touchscreen navigation. Hell, it's more than navigation, it's a command center. Look at the size of that screen. You got your satellite radio, Wi-Fi hotspot, Bluetooth, voice commands…" He was shaking his head in amazement. "Remember when we were kids? Lucky if we had an AM radio. What was your first car?"

"Sixty-nine Ford truck," Marlin said. "Big blue thing."

"Felt like driving a damn tank, I bet."

"Pretty much."

"Nowadays we're driving around with more technology at our fingertips than you'd find on a goddamn spacecraft back then." He chuckled. "Hell, look at me—back in sales mode. Sorry about that. Not that I couldn't make the wildlife department a hell of a deal on an all-new fleet—first class all the way—but that's a topic for another time."

He was easing the truck slowly down a rough caliche road to a valley with Middle Creek running through it like a shiny silver ribbon.

"Beautiful place," Marlin said.

He'd stopped at Judge Hilton's house earlier to have his affidavits signed, but he'd suffered a setback. The judge had granted warrants for Mandy's and Dub's phone records, but not for Tino's. Said Marlin hadn't established probable cause, and even though Marlin was disappointed, he could understand the ruling. However, with luck, he was hoping the cell phone companies would provide Mandy's and Dub's call logs and location data in a day or two.

"Thank you, sir," Carrasco said. "I love it here, and the truth is, I worked my ass off for this place. Earned every acre. Eighty-hour weeks, back when I was younger. Now I've cut that back to sixty, and the crazy thing is, the recession almost killed me anyway. I didn't see it coming, and I had to lay some people off, and that just about broke my heart. Made me wonder if all those hard years were worth it."

"Come to any conclusions?" Marlin asked.

"Well, yeah, it's worth it—but you've gotta do what's best for the business itself, not for any particular person. That's just the harsh reality of the world."

"Guess it helps to have a place like this where you can blow off steam," Marlin said.

Carrasco grinned as the truck bounced and swayed. "Sounds like you mighta heard some stories about my parties."

"A few."

"You'll have to come out to the next one. You married?"

"I am."

"What's her name?"

"Nicole."

"Well, you and Nicole will have to come out. We definitely manage to have a good time out on the ranch. It's one of the ways I thank my employees and some of my top clients. Nothing too wild, though. Believe me, I've heard some of the rumors myself, and I'm afraid that's all they are."

Marlin was tempted to ask about the carload of young women who had needed directions to the ranch that night. Were those ladies for employees or clients? Probably not the right time for that.

"Did you happen to have some folks out this weekend?" Marlin asked.

Carrasco didn't react for a long moment. He appeared to be distracted—focusing on the road ahead—or buying time to decide how to answer. Maybe he'd figured out why Marlin was here, and it had taken him by surprise that a game warden would be involved in a hit-and-run investigation.

"Hang on a second," Carrasco said as he navigated over a particularly rough patch. When he reached the bottom of the hill, the road became smoother. He stopped in a flat, grassy area about twenty yards from the creek and looked at Marlin. "Is this about Friday night? Yesterday afternoon, some deputies asked if they could look around on my place, up near the county road, and I noticed a helicopter buzzing around. Of course I told 'em they could look wherever they wanted. They said they were searching for an injured person. Is that right?"

"We're not sure what happened yet," Marlin said. "Or when it happened."

"Was it a hunting accident or something?" Carrasco asked.

"We're looking into it," Marlin said. "At the moment, we need to figure out who was in the area, in case anybody saw anything that might be helpful. Did you have any guests Friday night?"

"As a matter of fact, I did. Had some people out to visit with a special friend of mine."

"Who was that?"

"Dickie Loftin."

"The comedian?"

"That's right. We were roommates at A&M. Been close ever since. He lives up near Stephenville, but he comes to see me once or twice a year. Did you know he was in one of my ad campaigns before he hit it big?"

"I think I remember that," Marlin said.

"I like to take credit for making him a star, but obviously Dickie's a talented guy and deserves all the success in the world."

"How many people were here for the party?" Marlin asked.

"I guess around twenty-five or thirty. Not a big group."

It was a larger group than Marlin would have liked, considering that each of them would have to be checked out.

"What time did the party start?" Marlin asked.

"It was more of an afternoon thing. Most everybody got here between two and three."

"How late did it go?" Marlin asked.

"Oh, maybe eight or nine. Hard to keep track when you're hosting. Some people left earlier. Dickie spent the night."

"Was he the only guest who did?"

"Yep. He enjoys having some time to decompress. Would be a long drive back to Stephenville after having a few cold beers."

"So he left yesterday morning?"

"That's right."

"What time?"

"I guess it was about ten or eleven."

"Did y'all hear anything unusual Friday afternoon or evening?"

It was a long shot, considering that Carrasco's house was roughly half a mile from the county road. Even a blaring horn might not be audible that far away.

"Not that I recall," Carrasco said, "but we're a loud group. Everybody talking and laughing at once."

"Was the party mostly indoors or outside?"

"On my back patio," Carrasco said. "It was a nice afternoon, so we gathered out there around the pool."

"Anyone swim?"

"I told everyone to bring swim trunks, but nobody took me up on it."

Marlin was running out of questions—for now.

"What I'm going to need," he said, "are the names and phone numbers of everybody who was here Friday night, including Dickie Loftin. We need to rule each one of them out, one by one."

Carrasco had an expression on his face now, like *Boy, you are putting me in a tough spot.*

"Dickie really values his privacy," Carrasco said. "He loves his fans, but if his phone number gets out..."

"I won't share it with anyone outside the sheriff's office," Marlin said. "I might not even need to call anyone else on your list. Right now, we're still piecing together what happened."

Carrasco nodded. "I can tell you that Dickie never even drove over there where y'all were mostly searching. It was east of here, right? Seemed like the helicopter stayed over in that direction."

"I can't say for sure."

"Well, Dickie would've come from the west and left the same way."

"I'll keep that in mind," Marlin said. "If you can remember roughly what time each person left the party, that would be helpful, too," Marlin said. "Maybe jot that down beside each name."

"I'll do my best, but that might be kind of spotty," Carrasco said. "Not like I was watching the clock."

"An estimate is fine."

Once Marlin got the list of names, he could find out what make and model of vehicle each person owned, including the color.

"So is the person okay?" Carrasco asked. "I'm assuming the search yesterday didn't turn anything up."

"They're still looking," Marlin said.

"Sure hope he's okay," Carrasco said. "Or she."

9

MARLIN—WHO HAD questioned Red O'Brien more often than any other law-enforcement officer in Blanco County—had cautioned Bobby Garza that O'Brien would be nervous, even if he had nothing to hide. It was just his nature, based on his previous experiences with law enforcement.

Marlin was right. O'Brien was fidgety, seated on the far side of the table. Not comfortable in an interview room, just as he hadn't been comfortable during the ride over. Kept asking questions, which Garza deflected until he could get everything recorded.

This interview, Garza felt certain, would amount to nothing more than a hurdle he had to cross to move on to other possibilities—like his renewed interest in Mandy. The fact that she had fired a shot at Dub one night after an argument was intriguing. For now, Garza and Marlin had decided to hold that information in their back pocket. See what else they could learn before interviewing her a third time.

"This won't take long," Garza said to Red O'Brien. "Want anything to drink?"

"Jack and Coke?"

Garza smiled and nodded. "Sure thing, but I'll have to leave the Jack out."

"In that case, I'll pass."

Garza sat down across from him.

Like most law enforcement officers in and around Blanco County, Garza had had plenty of his own experiences with O'Brien—mostly bad, but not all. And both Marlin and Garza agreed that deep down—way, way down, much further than most people would be willing to look—there was something redeemable about O'Brien. There was an incident several years back during which O'Brien and his partner in crime, Billy Don Craddock, had saved Marlin and a young boy from a taxidermist who had defrauded and then killed one of his customers. O'Brien had placed his own life in jeopardy and truly acted heroically in a stressful situation, and he and Craddock later received a citizenship award during a public ceremony. For a time, they'd had the respect of everyone in the county. It was a great opportunity for O'Brien to reexamine his life and focus on the positive, rather than reverting to bad habits—but it wasn't long before Marlin caught him poaching deer out of season. Disappointing.

"When was the last time you saw Dub Kimble?" Garza asked.

"So something did happen to Dub?" Red asked.

"We're not sure what happened," Garza said. "But we're—"

"I heard he's missing and mighta got hit by a car," O'Brien said.

"One step at a time," Garza said. "When did you last see him?"

"Couple of weeks," Red said. "I went over to his place after his so-called accident to see how he was doing."

"You don't think it was an accident?" Garza asked.

O'Brien obviously realized he had said something dumb. "Well, okay, maybe it was real, but who knows? I know he fell, because a lot of people saw it. Question is, did he *mean* to fall, and even if he didn't, did he really get hurt?"

"You think maybe he fell on purpose?" Garza said.

"That's the thing—I got no way of knowing. Neither does anybody else."

Garza nodded, like that was perfectly logical. "Tell me about the last time you saw him."

"Okay, well, I went over to his house—because I *was* feeling bad about what happened—and right off the bat, I could tell he was laying the groundwork to turn it into some kind of payday."

"How so?"

"He started saying his back was all screwed up, which meant he couldn't work, and maybe I oughta help him out."

"What did you say about that?"

"That he could kiss my sweet you-know-what. We're all grown-ups around here. *He* decided he wanted to help me out with the tree house, and *he* also decided to consume a few adult beverages, and then *he* had an accident, and why is that my fault? He wants me to pay? Maybe that's how they do things in Austin—keeping it weird and all that crap—but you and me both know that ain't the way we do it in Blanco County."

"Did y'all argue?"

"Not so much. More like me calling him a freeloader and then he asked me to leave."

"And you did?"

"Hell, yeah."

"And that was the last time you saw him?"

"Yep. But then I started hearing he was gonna sue me. I'm sure somebody's already told you that, and if not, you're gonna hear it sooner or later. And I realize that don't look so good for me. It's like when Harley Frizzell died and y'all thought I did it."

"We never thought that, but go on," Garza said.

"Well, I was a suspect."

"You weren't a suspect," Garza said, wondering why he was wasting his time. "I specifically called and told you that you weren't a suspect."

"But ain't that exactly what you'd tell a suspect?" O'Brien asked.

"Please," Garza said. "Finish what you were saying."

"About?"

"About Dub Kimble threatening to sue you."

"That's pretty much it."

"You heard he was going to sue you, and that's the end of it? You had no more contact with Dub after that?"

"No, sir, I didn't. And all I can say is, if something happened to him, I didn't have nothing to do with it. That's the God's honest truth."

Garza nodded slowly, but he remained quiet for a moment. Let O'Brien keep talking.

Red squirmed a little, but he stayed silent, too. Then his face brightened with something he suddenly remembered. "Lester Higgs is who you should be talking to," he said.

"Why's that?" Garza asked.

"I heard Dub used to see Kelly Rundell on the side, and now Lester's bang—uh, seeing her, and so Dub and Lester got into a little tiff about it a couple of weeks ago."

Garza nodded again. He had already talked to Lester Higgs, who had a rock-solid alibi for the night Dub Kimble disappeared. Higgs had been fishing in Port Aransas and had only come home this morning. He had a receipt from the motel and his three fishing buddies had vouched for him.

Likewise, Claude Rundell and his wife Kelly had spent Friday night at a hotel on the Riverwalk in San Antonio. Claude had spoken at some kind of banking convention that afternoon, and the convention organizers had offered him a room at the Menger Hotel. The Rundells and at least a dozen bankers and their spouses had gone to a pub called Durty Nelly's on Friday night, staying from ten until two in the morning. The Rundells had returned home on Sunday afternoon.

"We'll look into that, but tell me what you were doing Friday night," Garza said.

LAST LAUGH | 55

"This past Friday?" O'Brien asked.

"Yes, two nights ago," Garza said.

"Like, all night?"

For the first time, O'Brien seemed to be stalling.

"Yes, please," Garza said.

O'Brien let out a long breath and seemed to be thinking. "Not a whole lot, really. Just hung around the house. Watched TV."

"All night long?"

"Pretty much."

"You and Billy Don?"

"No, just me. Billy Don drove to Mason County to visit a buddy over there. Guy bought a place on the Llano River last year. Calls it the Fish Camp. He don't catch many fish, far as I can tell."

"What time did he leave?"

"The friend on the river?"

"No, Billy Don. What time did he leave your place on Friday to drive to Mason County?"

"About three o'clock. Three-thirty."

"What time did he get back?"

"Yesterday morning. He brought a bunch of doughnuts home."

"What did he drive?"

"His Ranchero."

"So you were by yourself from Friday afternoon until yesterday morning?" Garza asked.

"Just me and a friend."

"Who was that?"

"Jose Cuervo," O'Brien said, grinning.

"Clever," Garza said. "I've met him once or twice myself."

Neither man said anything for a moment.

"So...we about done?" O'Brien said.

"Almost," Garza said. "But I need to ask again, just to be sure. You didn't go anywhere on Friday night?"

"Nope."

"So you definitely won't change your mind later and say you did go somewhere after all?" Garza asked.

"No, sir. I stayed home. All night. Hell, I wish I'd gone somewhere, 'cause then I'd have an alibi. But I didn't, so I don't. Why would I lie about that?"

"So you're always honest with law-enforcement officers?" Garza asked, as if it were a little joke between the two of them.

"Well..." Red said, enjoying the joke.

"The reason I keep asking," Garza said, "is because I'm pretty sure

I saw your truck in town on Friday night."

It was a bluff.

O'Brien frowned. Then he smiled, looking embarrassed. "Oh, man. You're right. I did run into town at one point."

"What for?"

"Beer."

"Where'd you go?"

"Super S," O'Brien said. "I mean Lowe's Market. Still getting used to the new name, even though it's been a while now. Got beer and a bag of ice on account of my freezer being on the blink. Probably a Freon leak, but I ain't got around to fixing it yet. Don't have all the right tools."

Garza stared at him for a long moment, and it was plain that O'Brien was ill at ease, which was reflected in his rambling answer. He was hiding something—but what?

"Where else did you go?" Garza asked, wishing now that he hadn't specified where he'd seen O'Brien's truck. He'd said "in town," and it would have been wiser to leave that phrase out and make it more vague.

"To the store and back home," O'Brien said. "That's all."

"What time was it?"

"Man, that's a tough one. I'd say nine-thirty or nearly ten."

"What were you driving?"

"My truck," O'Brien said.

"Do you own any other vehicles I don't know about?"

"Nope, and none that I don't know about, either," O'Brien said.

"What about Billy Don?" Garza asked.

"If he owns any vehicles I don't know about, then I don't know about them."

O'Brien wasn't being a wise-ass. That was just his way of talking. And thinking. Scary.

Garza felt certain that O'Brien was a dead-end, but that didn't mean he could let it drop yet. He'd have to figure out why O'Brien was being evasive about his trip into town on Friday night. Meanwhile, there was no harm in letting him think he was in the clear.

"I appreciate your time," Garza said. "I'll have one of the deputies run you back home."

9

Creed and Bricker parked the BMW across the street from the auto shop in Blanco where Danny Ray Watts worked.

When Creed opened his door, Bricker said, "Whoa, hold up."

"What?"

"I don't wanna tell you how to do your business," Bricker said, "but I'm thinking maybe we should wait and catch him alone."

"That's fine. We ask him to step outside for a minute."

"That probably ain't a great idea."

First thought Creed had was: *Why?*

He closed his door. He waited a minute.

"Why?" he asked.

Bricker was dipping Copenhagen again, and occasionally spitting in a Coke can that was cradled between his thighs.

"What if he don't wanna cooperate?" Bricker said.

"Then we try something else."

"Yeah, but depending on how far you're willing to go down on the list, we might not want a bunch of people saying they saw us talking to him. Know what I mean?"

Witnesses. That's what he meant.

"I been thinking about that," Creed said. "Some of the things we talked about last night."

"Yeah?"

"And I think we might oughta rein it in a little. Dial it back."

Bricker took a moment to ponder that statement, then said, "Well, you're the boss. But I gotta figure maybe you're making a mistake."

"What I don't wanna do," Creed said, "is take a bad problem and make it worse."

"So what's the plan, then? You ever decide on one or not?"

Creed had forgotten just how *intense* Bricker was. The way he always seemed hungry for something extreme to happen. Back in Huntsville, he'd strut around like a damn rooster, his body language flat out daring bigger men, or even groups of men, to come at him. Most of them learned pretty quickly to leave him alone, because something about him wasn't quite right.

"Remember the angle about the TV show?" Creed said.

"That's the way you wanna go with it?"

"I think it's the best option."

Bricker made an expression like he thought Creed was making a big mistake. "So why do you even need me?" he asked.

"Watts is probably kind of pissed off," Creed said. "I'm gonna try to smooth things over, but I want you here just to, you know, shake him up a little."

"Shake him up how?"

"Make him realize it could go another way if he doesn't play along. Hell, Bricker, all you gotta do is be yourself. He'll get the message."

"You think?"

"I do. You on board for that?"

Bricker spit into the can, and Creed could see his small, yellow teeth. "Like I said, you're the boss."

10

IT QUICKLY BECAME clear to Marlin that the people on the list provided by Skeet Carrasco were not inclined to answer a call from an unknown number. He dialed seven straight with no answers and left the same voicemail every time.

"Hi, this is John Marlin, the game warden in Blanco County. I got your number from Skeet Carrasco. I need to ask you a couple of questions, so if you could call me back as soon as you get this message, I would appreciate it. Thanks."

Once again, he was in his office at the sheriff's department. He much preferred spending time in his truck, navigating the back roads of Blanco County, but when he was involved in a larger, more complicated investigation like this one, he had to make trade-offs.

He dialed the eighth number on the list—for a woman named Carlotta King, who had been the general manager for Carrasco's top-selling dealership for the past decade. She answered on the third ring.

"I was just talking to Skeet about you," she said. "He told me I should be as forthcoming as possible. Probably wouldn't normally expect that from a car dealer, huh?"

Her tone was friendly and self-deprecating. Marlin wasn't buying it, at least not yet.

"Depends on the dealer, I guess," Marlin said. "But I'm glad Skeet wants you to help."

Marlin had found a photo of Carlotta King on the website for her dealership in Bastrop. Nice-looking woman in her late forties or early fifties. Short dark hair with some gray sprinkled in. Eyes so noticeably violet, Marlin wondered if the photo had been photoshopped. King had a warm smile and appeared comfortable in front of a camera. Probably starred in some of the dealership's TV commercials.

"He said someone went missing near his ranch on Friday night," she said.

"Yes, ma'am, and we're talking to everyone who was in the area," he said.

"That's a shame. I'll help if I can."

"I appreciate that. What time did you arrive at Skeet's place?"

"I guess about two thirty," she said. "I know because I stopped for gas in Johnson City and my receipt has the time on it."

"Can you tell me who was already there when you arrived?"

She slowly reeled off thirteen of the twenty-seven names provided by Carrasco. She had a good memory, even for the people she had only just met that night. A skill she had honed as part of her job, Marlin suspected.

"Of course, the special guest for the afternoon couldn't be bothered to show up until five-thirty," she said.

"Dickie Loftin?" Marlin said.

"Interesting guy," she said, clearly using that adjective as code for something else. "You met him?"

"I have not," Marlin said. "What was your impression?"

"That he would've sooner been somewhere else," she said. "Like maybe he didn't want to let his buddy Skeet down, but it was kind of an imposition. It was obvious Skeet invited him down just to show him off, and I'm sure Dickie realized that, and so did everybody else. It was kind of awkward when he first arrived. Everybody was just sort of clustered around him, like we were waiting for him to entertain us."

Marlin appreciated that she was freely sharing, but he doubted any of this information would be useful. Before he could ask about some of the other guests, she continued in an amused tone.

"At one point, later in the afternoon, after we weren't all watching him like a trained monkey, Dickie and I were talking—just the two of us—and he noticed I wasn't wearing a wedding ring. So he asked about that, and I told him I got divorced a few years ago, and then, more or less out of the blue, he actually suggested that we should slip off to one of the bedrooms. Can you believe that?"

"Was he joking?"

"Not at all. I mean, did he honestly think that kind of approach was going to work? Or maybe it does sometimes, which is kind of sad. Up to that point, we were having a perfectly normal conversation, and suddenly he's propositioning me. Talk about white trash."

"How did you respond?"

"I pretended I didn't understand what he was asking, but I wish I hadn't. I should've thrown my drink in his face. Skeet would've been upset that I ruined the party, but who cares?"

Now Marlin was wondering about the other female guests present that night. Had Dickie Loftin put the moves on any more women? Had he been successful? If he had, what possible connection could that have to the Dub Kimble case? Probably none at all, but he had learned not to make assumptions, and that having an abundance of information—even extraneous information—was better than knowing too little.

"Did any of the other guests ever seem upset or agitated in any way?" he asked.

It was a long shot, and he got the answer he was expecting. "Not that I saw," she said. "Everybody was having a good time. Nothing unusual. May I ask who it was that went missing?"

"A resident who lives nearby," Marlin said.

"And…what does that have to do with the party at Skeet's place?"

"Probably nothing, unless someone happened to see something useful."

"Oh, you're looking for witnesses. I was starting to wonder if you thought someone from the party was somehow involved with some kind of crime."

"We don't know exactly what happened," Marlin said. "Just gathering information right now, and I sure appreciate your help. Can you tell me what time you left the party?"

"About eight-thirty."

"Had any of the other guests left by then?"

"Several, yes."

She named them, and added that she couldn't be certain it was a complete list. Others might have left without her being aware of it.

"I'm guessing you drove east from Skeet's place, going through Johnson City again," Marlin said.

"That's right."

"Did you happen to see any other vehicles on the county road on the way into town?"

"Not that I recall, now that you mention it. That's a very quiet road."

"You didn't notice anybody parked along the shoulder or anything like that?"

"Nope. Just a lot of deer, so I was driving very slowly."

Marlin was getting discouraged. Maybe Skeet Carrasco and Dickie Loftin and all of the partygoers had nothing to do with Dub Kimble's disappearance. Maybe Dub had been hit by someone else who lived along that county road, or a lost tourist, or some other random person just passing through. Maybe that person was in another state by now, with their damaged car already being repaired at a body shop.

Or if one of the guests *had* been involved, it was more likely they'd hit Dub on the way home, later in the evening. That would explain why the pool of blood hadn't been smeared by tires. Might also explain why the driver had fled the scene and taken the body, rather than reporting it. Too much to drink. They would've been charged with vehicular manslaughter, even if Dub had jumped right in front of their vehicle.

"So nothing unusual happened at the party that you can recall?" Marlin asked. "Nobody seemed nervous or upset?"

"No, it was actually a fun party and I met a lot interesting people. Oh, there was one thing that was a little...weird. Well, not weird, but it surprised me for a moment. When I went out to leave, there was a man standing between my car and the Hummer next to it. He was obviously relieving himself, so I waited a moment, and then I cleared my throat to let him know I was out there."

"Who was it?"

"Well, that's the thing. I didn't recognize him from the party. I don't think he ever came inside. But he spotted me and probably realized that I was a little spooked seeing him there in the dark, so he said hello and introduced himself. His name was Creed—Dickie Loftin's brother."

That got Marlin's attention. Creed Loftin was not on the guest list provided by Skeet Carrasco.

9

When Red came through the front door of the trailer, Billy Don was in his regular sunken spot on the couch, with his mouth full of something. He said, "Stho howb diggo?"

Some animated show was on the TV.

"What?" Red said. He noticed that Billy Don was holding a green bag of potato chips or something.

Billy Don made a gesture with one hand—*Hold on a minute*—while he finished chewing and swallowing whatever it was. Then he said, "Don't you hate it when pork rinds build up in the back of your throat and you start feeling like you're gonna choke?"

"Maybe if you wouldn't shovel 'em down your gullet a dozen at a time," Red said.

"They oughta have a warning label," Billy Don said. "Just saying."

"You can't eat a bag of pork rinds without instructions?" Red said.

Billy Don glared at him. "They get all clumped up. Why're you in such a foul mood?"

"Really? Weren't you standing out on the porch when the sheriff took me in? Didn't you in fact say some really stupid crap about me having a motive?"

"Yeah, but I told him you wouldn't have done it, *even though* you had a motive. Big difference."

All Red could do was shake his head in exasperation.

"So I guess it didn't go so good," Billy Don said.

"How'd you piece that together?"

"I'm about to get up off this couch and knock some manners into you," Billy Don said.

Red said, "Might as well go ahead, since you already stabbed me in the back."

He knew he was treading on dangerous ground, but he was pissed off—and his last remark seemed to get through.

"I was only tryin' to help," Billy Don said.

Red didn't care to discuss it, so he sat down in his recliner. Then he changed his mind and went into the kitchen for a Keystone Light tall boy. He brought one for Billy Don, too, because even though he was mad at him, what sort of monster fails to bring his trailermate a cold beer? Billy Don needed it, too, because he had stuffed his face again with more pork rinds.

When Red was comfortably seated in his recliner again, Billy Don said, "Okay, so what happened?"

"Sheriff is wondering if I had something to do with Dub's disappearance," Red said. "Just like I thought all along."

"Wadjoo tellim?" Billy Don said, his mouth full yet again.

"If you're under the impression I wanna see all that chewed-up crap in you mouth, you're sadly mistaken," Red said.

Billy Don eventually swallowed and said, "What'd you tell him?"

"He was asking about Friday night, and where I was, and I told him I was home all night, all by myself."

"But you—"

"I know," Red said. "And then he said he saw me in town. I think he was bluffing, but what could I do? Call him a liar? Try to pretend I wasn't? Anyway, I said yeah, that's right, now that you mention it, I *was* in town, but I only made a quick trip to the store for beer and went right back home."

"But you—"

"I know," Red said. "And he mighta thought I was lying."

"But you—"

"I know," Red said. "I *was* lying."

He took a long drink of his beer.

He just couldn't catch a damn break, could he? First, Dub Kimble went missing. Great news! But then here comes Bobby Garza, wondering if Red was involved. Horrible luck.

"You know, people get railroaded for shit like this all the time," Red said.

"Haven't we had this conversation before?" Billy Don asked.

"Maybe, but that don't mean they ain't gonna try to pin something on me."

"You mean something you *didn't* do?"

"Well, duh. They wouldn't really be pinning it on me if I did it, would they?"

Billy Don reached into the green bag again, but apparently there was nothing left but crumbs. He dropped the bag on the carpet beside the couch.

"So what're you gonna do?" he asked.

"Stick with my story and hope everything don't go to hell."

11

AT 12:38, according to the clock on Creed's dashboard, Danny Ray Watts came out of the auto shop, climbed into a white Ford F150, and drove away.

For reasons he didn't entirely understand, Creed found himself waiting for Bricker to say something. To tell him what to do. And he did.

"Give him a lead, but not so far that we lose him. And not so close that he figures out we're following."

Creed did as he was told.

Watts took Fulcher Street to a big, round water tank, where he hung a left on Kendalia Road and crossed the river. Creed followed.

"Friggin' beautiful," Bricker said as they crossed the bridge. There was a small dam to the right and the green river shimmered in the sunlight. "Think they got any bass in there?"

Creed didn't know how Bricker could be so calm. His heart was already racing.

They passed a row of long, humped greenhouses—some sort of nursery—with a sign out front: *Our business is blooming!*

Passed a gated property on the left. Nice limestone entryway. Some rich fucker's place.

Already out of town.

Passed some wide-open fields. All the cedars had been cleared, leaving oaks only.

No vehicles in front of Danny Ray's truck or behind Creed's BMW.

Passed another private road on the right, this one featuring a modest red gate with metal buzzard silhouettes on either side.

Creed's palms were getting sweaty and he didn't understand why. He was only intending to have a conversation with Watts.

Passed a narrow paved driveway on the left.

Long straightaway.

No cattle. No people. Nobody walking or bicycling.

Then some horses in a pasture, and a sign for stables on the right.

Still no people visible anywhere.

"Who owns all this land?" Bricker said. "Think it's passed down from one generation to the next or what?"

Talking like they were out for a Sunday drive. Creed didn't answer. Just kept driving. Forty yards from Danny Ray's rear bumper. Watts was poking along at thirty-five miles per hour.

Not unusual to have another vehicle following on a narrow two-lane road like this one. Watts wouldn't be suspicious in the least. Where was he going? Heading home for lunch? Done working for the day? Maybe he worked half days on Sundays.

More open fields. More gates and private roads. Very few houses to be seen.

When would Watts turn? Creed's mouth was dry.

They hit a long straightaway.

"You know what?" Bricker said suddenly. "This'd be a good place to talk to him. Pull up beside him."

"What? Here?"

"Pull up next to him. I'll wave him over."

"But we—"

"Hurry, before we miss the chance. Ain't nobody around. Do it, man!"

Creed stepped on the gas and began to gain on Watts's truck. Wasn't hard, at his slow speed.

Watts saw Creed coming and eased to the right. He was checking his side mirror. Probably wondering what kind of jerk would pass on this narrow road.

"That's it," Bricker said. "Keep going."

Creed would do his best to keep himself hidden behind Bricker. After all, Watts had seen him at the stoplight in Johnson City on Friday night. They'd had words.

Creed's front bumper was even with Watts's back bumper...

A little further.

And now the vehicles were side by side.

"Hey!" Bricker yelled.

Creed stared straight ahead, hiding behind his sunglasses, hoping he wouldn't be recognized.

"Pull over for a sec!" Bricker said.

"What's the problem?" Watts called back.

Both vehicles had slowed to twenty miles per hour.

"You got something hanging from your axle."

Damn. Bricker could lie with the best of them.

Creed glanced past Bricker's head and saw that Watts was slowly pulling over to the shoulder.

"Fall back and park behind him," Bricker said. Not asking. Telling.

Creed obeyed. Slowed down and came to a stop behind the Ford. All three men got out of their vehicles, and Watts was smiling, appreciative, so glad to be warned about the object hanging from his undercarriage—until he got a good look at Creed, and then his smile disappeared.

"What the—"

"I owe you an apology for the other night," Creed said, holding his palms up in a placating gesture. "My brother was a real asshole."

"He sure as hell was."

"Let me tell you why, if you've got a minute," Creed said, moving a little closer. "You're Danny Ray, right?"

"Were you following me?" Watts asked.

"The man's trying to apologize," Bricker said. His tone wasn't friendly. He had his hand resting on the sheathed knife on his hip.

Watts glared at him, then looked at Creed again. "I don't understand what's going on. How did you find me? How do you know who I am?"

Creed said, "Okay, yeah, let me explain. The other night, at the stoplight, you kind of caught us by surprise. See, here's the deal. Can I share a secret with you?"

By this point, Watts looked confused and suspicious. He was still standing in the wedge between his open door and his truck, ready to get back inside at a moment's notice.

"What?" he said.

"Between you and me," Creed said, "Dickie is thinking of filming a show down here in Blanco County."

Creed waited for a reaction—but he didn't get one. Or not the one he was expecting. Watts finally said, "So what?"

Bricker, standing ten feet to Creed's right, shifted his weight.

Creed said, "We came down to talk to a rancher about filming on his place, and he ended up turning us down, so Dickie was in a bad mood, and I'm afraid he took it out on you. Dickie felt bad later, so he told me to contact you and apologize. We saw that you commented on his Facebook page, so it was pretty easy to track you down. We could see where you worked."

"That's kind of creepy, if you wanna know the truth," Watts said.

Creed was baffled. Why wasn't this guy cooperating?

"You ain't never made a mistake?" Bricker asked. "The man's trying to say he's sorry."

"Dickie shot the rod at me," Watts said. "That's how he treats people?"

"And he feels bad about that, which is why we're here," Creed said. "And to make an offer. We need to keep it quiet about the show, because we're not even sure if it's gonna happen. So Dickie wants to give you five thousand bucks to keep it under your hat that you saw him in town."

Bricker was fidgety. Obviously losing his patience. If Watts was intimidated by Bricker, he sure didn't show it.

"Good Lord," Watts said, shaking his head. "So the apology is bullshit. You're just worried I might spread the word about your stupid show. That's what this is about."

"We're wasting our damn time, Creed," Bricker said.

"To be honest," Watts said, "I never liked Dickie."

"Oh, yeah?" Creed said. "Why's that?"

"He's a copycat. Stole all his best ideas."

"Well, fuck you," Bricker said.

"Whoa," Creed said. "Guys—"

"Fuck you right back, you little son of a bitch," Watts said, taking a step forward, not intimidated by Bricker in the least. The situation was falling apart. Creed thought he'd have to break up a fistfight—but what happened next was so much worse. He saw Watts's eyes suddenly widen with surprise, and then—

BOOM!

Watts stopped. Placed a hand on his chest. Creed could see a wet red stain spreading underneath Watt's palm.

Creed looked at Bricker and saw him lowering a small handgun—an automatic with a stainless steel slide. And he was grinning.

Holy shit. This can't be happening.

Watts began to cough. He placed his free hand on the side of his truck for support.

Creed took a few steps toward him, but what could he do? Watts dropped to his knees, then fell facedown on the ground. No movement at all. Not even a twitch.

"That's how you take care of bidness," Bricker said. "Hell of a shot from that distance with this little pea shooter."

Creed was gasping for air. His ears were ringing. He could feel a pressure in his chest. Was he going to faint?

"Man like that ain't nothin' but trouble," Bricker said. "I know his type. He wasn't gonna play along."

It felt like some sort of weird alternate reality. This couldn't be real, right? A bad dream.

"Leave him here or haul him off?" Bricker asked. He was looking around for something on the ground.

Creed couldn't think straight. "I said no."

"Said no to what?" Bricker stooped and picked up the spent shell from the gun.

"This. Everything."

"What are you talking about?"

"Oh, fuck," Creed said. "Can't believe you did that. I didn't know you had it." He bent and placed his palms on his knees. He thought he might throw up.

"Had what?"

"The gun."

"Take it easy, man," Bricker said. "Breathe. Ain't no big thing. But you gotta make a decision. Leave him or haul him off?"

12

DICKIE LOFTIN DIDN'T answer his phone, but Marlin hadn't expected him to. So he left a message—same as he had with the other party guests on the list. He really wanted to talk to Dickie about his brother.

Earlier, after talking to Carlotta King, Marlin had run a background check on Creed Loftin—and he was glad he did. Creed Loftin's record included one count of domestic violence eight years earlier, after an argument with a girlfriend, followed two years later by one charge for possession of cocaine. All of the charges had been filed in Erath County, where Stephenville was the county seat.

Marlin texted Lauren Gilchrist about the ongoing search—*Anything?*—knowing that if the answer were yes, he'd have heard by now.

Instead of texting back, she called.

"Nothing," she said. "I'm about to shut it down. You okay with that?"

She was deferring to him, because he had had more experience with searches.

"Seems like the right call," he said.

"You talk to Bobby?" she asked.

"Not in a couple hours."

"He's en route to a shooting on Kendalia Road. You know a guy named Danny Ray Watts?"

"I do, yeah."

Marlin had checked his hunting license a couple of times over the years, but he didn't know Watts well.

Lauren said, "One of his neighbors found him on the side of the road, shot in the chest. His truck was parked nearby, still running. STAR Flight is on the way."

"When did this happen?"

"Within the last twenty or thirty minutes."

"Any firearm on the scene?"

"Don't know."

"Is Watts conscious and talking?"

"Don't know that, either, but I sure hope so."

Marlin was sorry to hear about Watts's injury, but he was hoping it would prove to be a simple case—perhaps an accidental shooting—because anything more involved would mean that either Garza or Lauren would have to stop working on the Dub Kimble case. Limited manpower was always a concern when things got busy in Blanco County. That was one reason the sheriff, with his small staff, occasionally asked Marlin to take part in challenging investigations, especially those that originated as hunting- or fishing-related incidents.

"Okay, keep me posted, please," Marlin said. "Why don't we touch base this evening or first thing in the morning to see where we're gonna go next?"

Lauren agreed and they disconnected.

Over the next two hours, Marlin continued calling numbers on the list, and while several more of Skeet Carrasco's guests either answered or called him back, none provided any information that told him more than he already knew. Likewise, none appeared to be reluctant to speak or answer questions. Naturally, many of them were curious as to what had happened on Friday night. There had been talk among some of the partygoers, much of it speculation and inaccurate gossip.

As far as Marlin could tell, not one of them had met Creed Loftin or remembered seeing him. Odd, but maybe it was nothing. Maybe Creed Loftin simply wasn't the type to attend parties. Maybe he'd had a long day and preferred to wait outside while Dickie mingled with the guests. Maybe he was sleeping in the Hummer. Marlin had verified that Dickie Loftin did indeed own a black Hummer, complete with a hefty grill guard on the front.

Lauren sent a text: *Watts in surgery at Brack. Critical but stable for now.*

"Brack" was Brackenridge Hospital in Austin.

Marlin sent one back: *Details on shooting?*

Lauren: *No gun on scene, not an accident. Hoping Watts can talk when awake.*

Marlin: *Whose case?*

Lauren: *Looks like mine. More later.*

That meant Marlin and Garza would continue to work the Dub Kimble case together.

He placed his phone on his desk and sat quietly for a moment, pondering his next move.

He was tempted to call Henry Jameson for an update, but he knew from experience that Henry would call him or Garza as soon as he had any news about the piece of a fender or valance Marlin had found. He was hoping Henry could pinpoint the exact make and model of vehicle, along with a year of manufacture, but he knew that the same part might have been used over several production years, or for several vehicles from one manufacturer.

Marlin's phone vibrated with another text. Maybe Watts had already woken and revealed who had shot him.

But it was Nicole. *Coming home soon?*

They were both kept busy with their careers, but they made a point of having dinner together every Sunday evening, and Marlin wouldn't miss it.

You bet, he replied.

9

"Wanna hear the latest rumor?" Billy Don asked. He'd just emerged from his room at the far end of the trailer, where he'd been napping for the past two hours.

"About what?" Red asked.

"Hang on," Billy Don said, and he went into the kitchen. He came back with two tallboys, one of which he handed to Red. "About Dub Kimble," he said.

"What now?" Red popped the top on his beer.

"People are saying Mandy's been cheating on him with the manager at the Sonic Drive-In over in Fredericksburg. Or maybe it was the Dairy Queen. Anyway, she's been cheating."

"Oh, yeah?" Red asked.

This was interesting, considering what Willard had said about Dub cheating on Mandy with Kelly Rundell. Lots of cheating going on. Weird, because Red had a hard time finding even one woman willing to fool around with him. He also had a hard time understanding why Dub would cheat on Mandy, considering the size of her rack. All natural, too, as far as he knew. Those were hard to come by.

"But it gets better," Billy Don said. "They're saying the manager is a woman."

"No shit?"

"Yep. Gal's name is Tina. That's what everybody's saying."

"Who is everybody?"

"Just, you know, all of them."

"But who did you hear it from?"

"Scott."

"Scott from the feed store or Scott from the hardware store?"

"From the hardware store."

Red was glad to hear that. Scott from the hardware store was a reasonably trustworthy individual, whereas Scott from the feed store had once told Red he'd seen Elvis eating enchiladas at the Bowling Alley Café in Blanco, and he was dead serious about it.

Red thought about this new development for a moment. "Think the sheriff knows?" he asked.

"I would imagine so."

"Because that right there's a motive," Red said.

"Huh?"

"If Mandy has a girlfriend, maybe that girlfriend wanted Dub out of the way."

Billy Don did not appear convinced.

"And let's face it," Red said. "Some of those women are pretty rough."

"Which women?" Billy Don asked.

"You know. Women that like other women," Red said.

"You mean lesbians?"

"Yeah, those."

Billy Don made a clucking sound and began shaking his head.

"What?" Red said.

"Do you even hear what comes out of your mouth?"

"What?" Red repeated.

"You some kinda expert on lesbians?"

"I didn't say that, but Tina might've done it so she could be with Mandy, or Mandy might've done it so she could be with Tina, or maybe they did it together."

"Because lesbians are kind of rough?"

"All I'm saying is you see that kind of thing all the time—somebody killing their husband or wife or boyfriend or whatever 'cause they got someone on the side and wanna start a new life with that person. Even a woman and another woman."

"Even them," Billy Don said. "The lesbians."

"I'm not judging or anything," Red said. "Hell, I don't really care what happened or who did it or why. I'm just saying that this Tina and Mandy situation is good news for me, because they got a lot bigger motive than I do."

"Or maybe they had nothing to do with it at all," Billy Don said.

Red wasn't going to let his good mood be fouled by that possibility.

"Know what I'm wondering now?" he asked.

"Not really."

"If Dub had any insurance or not."

"His truck was only a couple years old, so I figure he must've," Billy Don said.

"Not truck insurance," Red said. "*Life* insurance."

Red was starting to think about all sorts of plans and possibilities, any one of which would clear him of any involvement in the disappearance of Dub Kimble. Imagine, for instance, if Mandy wanted to be with Tina, and she also had a chance to gain a lot of money in the bargain? Red figured that was a pretty big possibility, but he didn't mention it to Billy Don, because the big man was obviously in a mood to argue.

"What's that look on your face?" Billy Don said. "Got gas?"

"Even better," Red said. "I got a plan."

Billy Don lowered his beer can. "Oh, good Lord, no," he said.

13

"THESE BISCUITS TASTE like the underside of a toilet lid," Dub had said on that Friday evening before he went hog hunting.

Mandy slowly placed her fork on the table and glared at him.

"You forget an ingredient or something?" he asked.

She knew he wasn't serious. She made some damn tasty biscuits. He was just picking away, trying to start something, like he always did.

"Maybe I should just stop cooking altogether," she said. "You can fend for yourself. How about that?"

"Might live longer," he said.

"You are such an asshole," she said.

"Maybe if you'd learn to cook, we wouldn't have these little disagreements," he said.

"Well, maybe if you wouldn't screw everything that ain't nailed down," she said, and then realized she wasn't sure how to finish that sentence. She didn't have to.

"Maybe what's good for the goose is good for the gander," he said, rising from his chair.

"Maybe the gander was out there chasing tail long before the goose gave up on him," she said.

"Maybe if the goose actually liked to fool around now and then, the gander wouldn't be out chasing anything."

"Maybe if you knew what the hell you were doing in the bedroom, I'd be a little more interested," she said, knowing they were both sinking to a depth they'd never reached before.

"Oh, yeah?" he said, his face flushing bright red. "That's funny, 'cause Kelly says I'm the best she ever had."

She grabbed a biscuit and launched it like a Nolan Ryan fastball. She was pleased to see it hit him square in the forehead.

He let out a mean-spirited laugh. "That right there was assault with a deadly weapon."

She threw another biscuit, but he ducked under it and scurried out of the kitchen.

"Maybe you should go live with Kelly!" she yelled.

"Maybe I will!" he yelled back.

She could hear him out there rummaging around—gathering his stuff to go hunting.

Stay in here, she thought to herself. *Let it go. Don't say anything else.*

But she couldn't resist, because she was furious.

She went into the living room, where he was seated on the couch, but only so he could pull his ratty sneakers on.

"Kelly's gonna give you the clap," she said. "You wait and see."

"No problem," he said. "I wear a rubber."

"They make one small enough?" she asked.

"I'm done," he said as he stood. "It's not worth it."

"I was done a long time ago," she said.

"I could tell," he said, heading for the front door.

"If you go, don't come back," she said.

"Wasn't planning on it," he said.

And out the door he went, slamming it behind him.

Mandy stood there for a long moment, seething.

Then she marched into the bedroom and opened the top drawer of her nightstand. Inside was the .38 Dub had given her as a birthday gift a few months earlier. She hurried back to the living room and out the front door, onto the porch. Dub was still standing beside his truck in the semi-darkness, taking a leak.

Mandy raised the .38 and aimed at his head.

He wasn't looking in this direction. He'd never know what hit him. Could she make the shot? She hadn't practiced with the gun at all. Was it accurate? No telling, since Dub had bought it for $50 at a pawnshop. That's the kind of guy he was—bragging that he'd bought her a cheap, used gun as a gift.

If she did shoot, then what? Her life would be ruined, just because of this idiot. She was starting to cool down and come to her senses.

She raised the barrel a few inches and sighted into the space directly above his head. Then she pulled the trigger.

14

"YOU MADE THE right call," Bricker said. "I cain't always think things through myself, which is why I got busted so many times, but you made the right call. Spur of the moment like that, it ain't always easy."

They'd left the body. Of course they'd left the goddamn body. And the truck. What else could they do? Haul it somewhere and try to hide it? How often could you get away with that?

They were at a bar called TapZ32 in Johnson City. Late in the afternoon. They'd been sitting here drinking for several hours now, and Bricker—well, he was acting like it was just another day for him. Like none of that stuff had happened on Kendalia Road.

"Ever feel like you're destined for something big?" Bricker asked. "Something that'll make people remember you?"

Creed had a difficult time following Bricker's train of thought, and he figured it was probably because Bricker's brain was wired like a Chinese blender.

"That's how I feel sometimes," Bricker said. "Like the world is watching me, waiting for me to make my mark. Could be something good. Or maybe not. I don't know if everybody gets that feeling, but I sure do."

What the hell was he babbling about?

"Got that little Colt off a friend of mine for a hundred bucks," Bricker said, perfectly able to carry on a conversation by himself. "Great little pistol—fits right in my pocket—but, shit, with a barrel that short, he'll never believe I made that shot. What was that—thirty feet?"

Creed was thinking, *Are you insane? You can't tell anyone what happened.* He raised his beer to his lips and his hand trembled noticeably. Fortunately, Bricker was looking the other way, trying to catch the bartender's eye. Was he carrying the pistol right now in a bar? That in itself was a felony.

Jesus.

What a disaster. There was no way this would end well.

The bartender came around and Bricker ordered two shots of tequila.

The little fucker wasn't nervous, and he hadn't shown the slightest bit of remorse. In fact, he seemed downright thrilled about what had happened. He *wanted* it to happen. Creed realized that now. Bricker *wanted* to shoot Watts. That had been his intent all along. He'd just needed an excuse, and Watts had given it to him. Creed suspected that even if Watts had cooperated, Bricker would've found a reason to shoot him anyway.

The bartender dropped off the shots, along with two lime wedges and some salt on a small plate.

"Dude, you gotta chill," Bricker said, grinning at him. "You look like you found a roach in your oatmeal. It's all good, man. Over and done with. No worries."

Creed did his best to appear at ease. Unconcerned. Rolling with it.

Bricker raised his tequila shot in Creed's direction, and waited. Creed raised his own shot.

"Mission accomplished," Bricker said, and he downed his shot. Then he grabbed a lime and bit into it.

Creed did the same. The tequila hit his stomach like hot acid.

"Part one, anyway," Bricker said.

"Huh?" Creed said, fighting his gag reflex.

"Still got that other guy," Bricker said.

"What're you talking about?" Creed said.

But Bricker was signaling the bartender again.

9

Dickie Loftin was seated on the couch in his game room, trying to write some new "white trash" lines for the show in Houston, but he was getting nowhere. Total writer's block, because he was still too freaked out by the incident.

The Incident.

That's how he really thought of it. It had a formal name. It always would, no matter where things went from here.

And where *would* things go?

He'd been texting Creed throughout the day, but Creed had answered only once. *Will call later.*

Dickie had replied immediately—*All good?*—but Creed hadn't answered yet. That was three hours ago and Dickie was getting restless.

And then he'd gotten that voicemail from a game warden in Blanco County. Weird. Dickie had fully expected to hear from someone in law enforcement sooner or later, but a game warden?

He couldn't call or text Skeet, because they'd agreed that was a bad idea, for the time being. It seemed obvious that the cops, including that game warden, had figured out that Dickie was at Skeet's place on Friday night. Not a big deal. Completely expected.

Dickie tried to focus on the notepad in his lap. Lots of lines, but none of them good. Well, one was good.

I'm so white trash, I had tater tot casserole at my wedding reception.

Dickie had gotten pretty jazzed about that gem, until he realized it was one of the lines the redneck in the grocery store parking lot had told him. Couldn't very well use that one, could he?

Everything else he'd written was crap. Too distracted.

After he'd listened to the voicemail from the game warden, Dickie had thought, *How would I react if I had nothing to do with the disappearance of Dub Kimble whatsoever?*

The answer was, he'd have Creed return the call and tell the game warden they had no information to share, because they didn't know anything about it. Sorry. And that's what Creed would do, eventually. No reason to rush. Cops would expect a celebrity like Dickie to be difficult to reach. They'd expect to go through at least one person to get to him. They'd expect Dickie to take his time calling back, or to not return the call at all. Not because he had anything to hide, but because he was Dickie Loftin. A bona fide celebrity. Maybe not a superstar, but on the A list nonetheless. For the moment.

I'm so white trash, my favorite Walmart gave me a reserved parking spot.

Yowser. That was pure crap.

I'm so white trash, my daddy and I occasionally argue about who has the better mullet.

Better, but still not good enough for the stage.

I'm so white trash, I've got more ex-wives than teeth.

Okay, not bad.

Maybe he could get back on track and put The Incident behind him.

They stopped at the Sonic Drive-In on the east side of Fredericksburg, next to the Pizza Inn.

Billy Don had offered to drive his Ranchero, and Red had taken him up on it. After Billy Don had gone without a vehicle for so many years, now it was time for him to cover the cost of gas and oil for a while. Plus,

Red enjoyed being able to drink a beer or three without worrying about getting busted for DWI.

"What you want?" Billy Don said, scoping the menu to the left of his door.

"We ain't here to eat," Red said.

"Gotta get something or they'll run us off."

Red watched a young female carhop as she exited the building and carried a tray to a yellow truck parked on the other side of the breezeway in front of the building. Was that Tina? She was cute—red-haired and slender—but she couldn't be any older than her early twenties. Could you become an assistant manager at that age? Would Mandy be seeing a gal that young? Plus, the redhead didn't look like the type to keep company with another woman, but Red figured if he said anything about that, Billy Don would make fun of him. So he kept that observation to himself.

"Gonna get an order of tater tots," Billy Don said.

"Whatever," Red said. There were no more than eight or ten vehicles scattered on both sides of the building.

"So you want some tots?" Billy Don asked.

"I don't want nothing," Red said, starting to lose his patience. "If you want something, get it. But stop asking me."

Billy Don didn't reply.

Another young lady came out of the building, and then another. Any of them could be Tina. Would an assistant manager actually deliver orders? Well, sure. That's how you become an assistant manager—by rolling up your sleeves and getting the job done, even when it involves carrying a greasy sack of corn dogs to some redneck who'll try to look down your shirt or ask what time you get off work later, and then give you a twelve-cent tip if you don't give him a big smile.

"Gotta admit a chili cheese coney would hit the spot," Billy Don said.

"Just order," Red said. "Before I lose my mind."

Billy Don punched the red button and a moment later a cheerful male voice answered. Not Tina. Billy Don asked for a chili cheese coney and large tots, and then turned to Red and said, "You sure you don't want nothin'?"

Red glared at him.

"Okay, jeez. Just asking."

A few minutes later, the red-haired carhop came out to the Ranchero with a paper sack on a tray. Now Red could tell that she wasn't any older than twenty or maybe twenty-two.

"How are y'all today?" she asked, like it was the highlight of her day to bring them the order.

"Better every minute," Billy Don said, no doubt thinking he was slick.

Red didn't waste any time. "Is Tina here today?" he asked, leaning over to catch the redhead's eye through the driver's-side window.

"Tina?" the redhead said as she passed the sack to Billy Don.

"Yeah."

"There isn't a Tina who works here."

"The assistant manager?" Red said.

The gal frowned, puzzled, and then she said, "Wait, do you mean Tino?"

Red looked at Billy Don, who shrugged. He'd already stuffed five or six tater tots into his mouth.

"Possibly," Red said to the carhop.

"Okay, well, Tino is the assistant manager at the Dairy Queen," the redhead said. "That's probably who you're looking for. I've lived here all my life and I don't know anyone named Tina. Just Tino."

"We sure appreciate it," Billy Don said. He handed her several bills to cover his meal.

She made change and Billy Don tipped her forty-seven cents.

"If you talk to Tino, will you do me a favor?" the redhead asked.

"Sure thing," Red said. "What?"

"Tell that foot fucker to kiss my bare ass."

15

CREED SAT ON THE TOILET, the door closed, just for the opportunity to think, without Bricker yammering on.

They'd gotten a motel room in Johnson City. Nothing fancy. Two queen beds at the Best Western.

Creed was buying time by playing along with Bricker's craziness, because he had no idea what else to do. Trying to think of a way out of this mess, but nothing was coming easy. Should he call the attorney who'd helped him out last time? Cut a deal, in exchange for being a witness against Bricker? Too early for that. They might still get away with it. Besides, did he want to make an enemy out of Bricker? Hell fucking no. Not in a million years.

Okay, what other options did Creed have?

None. Not a damn one, except for waiting to see what would happen next.

"Which bed you want?" Bricker asked through the door. "Left or right?"

Creed didn't answer, because right now he was trying to compose a text to Dickie. The less Dickie knew the better.

"You fuckin' fall in?" Bricker said. "Which bed?"

"Don't matter to me," Creed said.

What kind of psychopath shoots an innocent man on the side of a county road, then concerns himself with social courtesies in a cheap motel room?

"I'll take the one on the right," Bricker said, "because I always gotta piss in the middle of the night."

"Good," Creed said. "Fine."

"Always drink too damn much beer," Bricker said, laughing. "That's the problem. Then it runs through me after I fall asleep."

Creed typed: *no problems. will call tmw. you focus on the show in houston. i'll take care of this.*

That was the best way to go about it. Keep Dickie out of it as much as possible. Creed sent the text, took a deep breath, and exited the bathroom.

Bricker was stretched out on his chosen bed, back against the headboard, checking his phone. "Found this guy Billy Don on Facebook," he said. "Doesn't say where he works. But we'll track him down, don't you worry."

Creed didn't doubt that Bricker would do exactly that, one way or another. What would Creed do then?

9

"Sounds like Tino gets around," Billy Don said.

Now they were seated at a booth inside the Dairy Queen, just two blocks down from the Sonic. Billy Don was eating a Chocolate Chip Cookie Dough Blizzard he'd gotten from the girl at the counter a few minutes earlier.

"And he's a little weird," Red said.

Billy Don shrugged as he dug into his Blizzard.

After the red-haired carhop had made the "foot fucker" remark, Red had asked what that meant, and she'd revealed that this guy Tino had a thing for feet. He loved fondling feet. Kissing feet. Licking feet. And especially rubbing his private parts on feet. It was the one thing that really seemed to excite him, according to the carhop, who obviously disliked Tino enough that she was willing to share embarrassing private details. And what had created the hard feelings? Turned out Tino had asked her to the prom a few years back, then ditched her at the last minute. According to Lydia—the carhop—Tino was the male slut of Gillespie County. That was the phrase she'd used. "Male slut."

Red was facing the counter, wondering where Tino was. The only employees he could see at the moment were three or four young gals, just like at the Sonic. Maybe Tino wasn't working today, despite Lydia saying she'd noticed his car parked there earlier. Maybe he was out somewhere fucking feet.

"Can't believe you thought it was someone named Tina," Red muttered.

"Can't believe you think you know so much about lesbians," Billy Don replied.

"Shhhh," Red said.

"What?"

"Don't say that word so loud."

"What, lesbians?" Billy Don said even louder, totally on purpose.

There weren't many customers inside the restaurant, but an older couple seated two booths away glanced in their direction. Red considered himself fairly open-minded about the idea of women getting together in the bedroom and such, and he'd even watched a few videos along those lines, but he knew some small-town folks could get a little uptight about that kind of arrangement.

"Focus on finding Tino," Red said, just to shut Billy Don up.

Red's plan—the one he'd described to Billy Don at the trailer—was simple. Figure out who ran Dub Kimble down, so Red wouldn't get pinned with it. Do some investigating on his own and prove he was innocent. Basically, it was the same plan he'd devised when Harley Frizzell had been killed and Red was a suspect, even though the sheriff said he wasn't. Cops were tricky that way—playing mind games to fool you into making a mistake. You couldn't trust them. In fact, they were legally allowed to lie right to your face. Crazy.

Earlier, at the trailer, Red had started his investigation by making a list of the people most likely to have harmed Dub, and it had ended up like this:

Tina

Mandy

Lester Higgs

Claude Rundell

Kelly Rundell

As Red was wondering if he was missing anyone, a young dark-haired dude emerged from the kitchen area. Average height. Average build. In his early twenties, or thereabouts. Red had no idea if the guy was good-looking or not, because Red was straight as an arrow and didn't ponder such things.

Was this Tino, the foot-fucking male slut? Probably. Red wished he'd asked Lydia for a better description. She'd simply said he was a cute guy who thought he was hot stuff, and she wished he'd get his ass kicked by a jealous husband or something. Might teach him how to treat people better. Funny thing, she didn't even mention that he was Mexican, even though his name indicated that he was.

"Think that's Tino?" Red said quietly to Billy Don, who was scraping the bottom of his paper cup with a red spoon.

"Nope," Billy Don said.

"Why not?"

"I just heard one of them gals call him Carlos. Maybe you should pay better attention if you're gonna be a detective. Hey, you know what you really are?"

"Huh?"

"A defective. Not a detective."

"Clever."

"Just thought of that right now. Almost the same word."

Red didn't have a witty comeback, so he said, "You were making too damn much noise with that ice cream. Stop smacking your lips."

Truth was, all the gunshots over the years had left Red with some hearing loss.

Carlos went back into the kitchen area, out of sight, but less than a minute later, another young dark-haired guy emerged, and Red made an audible sound of surprise, which caused Billy Don to look his way. Then Red turned to look out the window, toward the parking lot, to avoid eye contact with this new guy. He raised one hand to the side of his face to shield himself.

"What?" Billy Don said, placing his empty cup on the table.

"It's Tino," Red muttered, just barely audible. He pulled his feed store cap low, to hide his face.

"Huh?"

"It's him. That guy is Tino."

"How do you know?"

"Because I saw him on Friday night," Red said.

"Where?"

"About a quarter-mile from Dub's house. We need to get out of here before he spots me."

9

At seven o'clock, Bricker said, "Our boy Billy Don posted a picture earlier and said, 'Where am I?'"

They were still in the motel room, but Creed was getting cabin fever. They'd need to get out soon—maybe get something to eat, even though Creed didn't have much of an appetite. Too tense. Bricker, on the other hand, was relaxed enough that he had fallen asleep for about thirty minutes earlier. Kill a man, then take a nap later. Amazing.

"The picture shows a Dairy Queen sign against a limestone wall, with an archway entrance underneath it," Bricker said. "You can't really see anything else, but somehow a couple of his idiot friends knew it was in Fredericksburg. Would you be able to recognize a goddamn Dairy Queen from nothing but the entryway? Speaking of which, you hungry?"

"Yeah."

"I was thinking we should drive over to this Dairy Queen," Bricker said. "Maybe we can catch our boy before he leaves town."

Crap. Creed had walked into that one. What if they spotted Billy Don Craddock?

"He'll be long gone before we get there," Creed said.

"Maybe, but he might post another picture from somewhere else. Besides, what else are we gonna do? Sit around here all night? Might as well be out looking for him."

"Yeah, okay," Creed said. He still had no idea what he should do. If he told Bricker he was abandoning the mission, what then? Sooner or later, Bricker would blab to someone about shooting Danny Ray Watts.

"Then let's hit the road," Bricker said.

16

MARLIN WALKED INTO the kitchen with two bags from Ronnie's Barbecue and Nicole, standing at the refrigerator with the freezer door open, looking for something to thaw or reheat, said, "Oh, thank you. No wonder I love you so much."

"Wow," Marlin said, because Nicole had already changed into her comfy clothes for the evening, which included a thin cotton T-shirt, and the cold air from the freezer had had a noticeable effect.

Nicole looked down, then looked at him again. "You are a dirty old man," she said, closing the freezer door.

Even from five feet away, he could smell her shampoo. She'd been working in the yard earlier, and her gorgeous auburn hair was still damp from the shower.

"Not that old," Marlin said. "Just be glad I can form full sentences at the moment, considering that shirt. Want some brisket and potato salad?"

Between bites, Marlin told her about his interview with Skeet Carrasco, and his subsequent phone call with Carlotta King. He was interested in hearing Nicole's input.

She was the victim services coordinator for Blanco County, but prior to that, she'd been a deputy for several years, both in Blanco County and in Guadalupe County, where she was from originally. She'd developed sharp investigative instincts over the years.

"How long before you get the records back on those cell phone warrants?" she asked.

Geist, their white pit bull, was sitting patiently beside the table, hoping for a scrap. She didn't whine, but she stared intently.

"Hoping tomorrow," he said. It would be interesting to learn whether Mandy and Dub had spoken or texted on Friday evening, after their argument, and whether either of them had contacted anyone else.

Frankly, though, Marlin was surprised Nicole's first question wasn't about another suspect.

"No interest in Creed Loftin?" he asked.

"Not so much," she said. "Doubtful that he and Dickie hit Dub Kimble on the way to the party and then parked the Hummer right there for everyone to see. They probably would've skipped the party altogether. And if they hit Dub *after* the party, that means Creed stayed outside for some other reason, and whatever that reason is, it's meaningless, since the accident hadn't happened yet."

Marlin stopped eating and blinked at her.

"You hadn't thought of that?" Nicole asked.

"Well..."

She laughed. "Good thing you have your looks to fall back on."

She knew as well as he did that there are times during an investigation when something obvious simply escapes your notice.

"Still seems a little weird that Skeet Carrasco didn't put him on the guest list," he said.

"Agreed, but since Creed didn't come inside, maybe he just forgot. Or maybe he never even knew Creed was out there."

"But Dickie spent the night," Marlin said.

"Maybe Creed went inside after Skeet had gone to bed. Or he slept in the Hummer."

Marlin wasn't convinced yet. "When I talk to Dickie Loftin—if he ever calls me back—it will be interesting to see if he mentions his brother being with him."

They both ate in silence for a few minutes, just thinking. Geist stood up, then sat back down again.

"What about Lester Higgs and Claude Rundell?" Nicole asked. "For that matter, what about Kelly Rundell?"

"All three of them have alibis," Marlin said. "Good ones. They weren't around."

Nicole nodded and dipped her spoon into a container of beans.

"I guess you'll need to rule out Red O'Brien, too," she said.

She knew the situation between Dub Kimble and O'Brien—the injury and the possibility of a lawsuit.

"Bobby interviewed him, and it turns out Red was alone on Friday night. At first he said he stayed home all night, and then he changed his story and said he ran into town for some beer. Bobby's getting location data for his phone."

"That should be interesting," Nicole said. She handed a small bit of brisket to Geist, who took it gently from Nicole's fingers.

9

"I hit a lot of my favorite routes," Red said, trying to tell the story with as much flair as possible, because everybody loved a good storyteller, and Red considered himself to be quite talented in that area. "Miller Creek Loop. Sandy Road. A. Robinson Road."

They had just pulled out of the Dairy Queen parking lot and were heading east on Highway 290 in the Ranchero.

"All the usuals," Billy Don said.

"Yeah, and then I decided to drive out to Dub's place. Well, not his place pacifically, but to drive the county road out past his house and then all the way around, because we ain't never hunted that area much."

"'Cause they got too many high fences along that road," Billy Don said.

"I know *why*," Red said. "But I figured it wouldn't hurt to look, and since I was all alone, without you to nag me, I was free to do whatever I wanted."

"Hmph," Billy Don said. "Get to the part about Tino."

"Hold your horses," Red said. "This is good. So I was heading west, not quite to Dub's place, when ten or twelve pigs ran in front of the truck."

"Which means more like three or four," Billy Don said.

"Honestly, I still don't know why they won't let us shoot 'em from the road, seeing as what a nuisance they are."

The population of wild pigs in Texas had reached 2.5 million, and the agricultural commissioner had even proposed bringing about a "hog apocalypse" by poisoning them with a blood thinner.

"They don't let people road-hunt because people like you come along and fling lead in just about every direction," Billy Don said.

"Maybe, but I'm careful about it."

"You drink and hunt."

"So do you."

"I know, but I never said I was careful."

"Well, I'm an extremely careful hunter, even if I'm drinking. In fact, the more I drink, the more careful I am. But why don't you hush for a second and let me finish my story?"

"I'm all for that. The sooner, the better."

Red waited a moment before he proceeded, just to show Billy Don who was in control of this conversation. Then he said, "The hogs took off before I could take a shot, but while I was sitting there on the side of the road, here came a vehicle, and when it passed, my headlights lit up the driver. Wanna guess who it was?"

"Jackie Gleason?"

"Nope. Tino. That dude from the Dairy Queen."

"How can you be sure?"

"Because I got a good look, and it was him. Wanna know what he was driving?"

"The Batmobile?"

"That little blue car that was in the parking lot."

Billy Don made another grunt. "Not that I'm believing any of this bullshit, but did he see you?"

"Why don't you believe me?"

"Because it was dark and you were probably half drunk by then, and you *want* to have seen him out there. Other than that, no reason."

"It was him."

"Let's say it was. Did he see you good enough to recognize you?"

"Don't know for sure. Maybe. Couldn't take chances just now."

"On the other hand, if he did see you, so what?"

"Huh?"

"What does it matter if he saw you, or if he knows you saw him?"

"Okay, foller along. If I go to the cops and say I saw Tino near Dub's place on Friday night, I'll have to admit I lied earlier, and that I was actually in that general area."

"This is getting way too complicated," Billy Don said.

Red ignored him. "The only thing that's throwing me is the fact that if you hit a live human being with a little Jap car like that, you're bound to cause some damage."

"It *did* cause some damage," Billy Don said. "It killed him."

"I mean to the car," Red said.

"Oh."

They were already out of town, and the Ranchero's headlights weren't doing much to puncture the darkness ahead. No moon out tonight.

"See the way the gals were fawning over him?" Billy Don asked.

"Yeah, what was the big deal?"

"He's a good-looking guy," Billy Don said. "Got eyelashes like a woman."

"I guess I can't judge that sort of thing as well as you can," Red said.

"Don't be a pinhead. You're telling me you can't look at George Clooney or someone like that and see that he's a handsome guy?"

"I guess you and me is wired a little bit different," Red said. "Besides, he's fishing off the company pier. Not real smart."

"Huh?"

"You never heard that phrase before?"

"Nope."

"Fooling around with gals you work with," Red said. "Never a good idea, believe me."

"You've done it?" Billy Don asked.

"Couple of times."

"For realz?" Billy Don said. Another one of his stupid Facebook expressions.

"Absolutely," Red said. "Lived to regret it."

"But it's so hard for them young gals to resist guys like you and Tino," Billy Don said, plainly giving Red a hard time.

"Yeah, whatever," Red said.

Another mile passed. He reached into the ice chest on the floorboard and grabbed a cold beer for each of them.

"Think he done it?" Billy Don asked.

"That's the question, ain't it?"

"Yep. Which is why I asked."

Red took a deep, dramatic breath. "I'd say it's a real good possibility."

"So how are you gonna go about proving it if you don't tell the cops what you saw?"

"Working on that, Billy Don. Working on that as we speak."

So far, he had nothing.

9

On the way to Fredericksburg, on a curve near the small community of Stonewall, the headlights of Creed's BMW briefly illuminated a passing vehicle—an old Ford Ranchero, just like the one in Billy Don Craddock's Facebook profile.

"What?" Bricker said.

Creed realized he'd opened his mouth involuntarily when he'd first seen the Ranchero—having the spontaneous urge to say something, and then realizing he shouldn't.

"Maybe we should stop at Luckenbach on the way back," Creed said, thinking fast.

The turn to that destination—made famous in the song by Willie and Waylon—was just up ahead.

"Maybe so," Bricker said. "But let's see how things go in Fredericksburg."

17

WHEN BOBBY GARZA got to his office early on Monday morning, he found an email waiting from the cell phone company that serviced Red O'Brien's phone. That was fast. He quickly scanned the attachments and shook his head in exasperation. A damn complication he didn't need at this point.

He'd been hoping the information would show that O'Brien had gone into town on Friday evening, stopped at Lowe's Market, and then gone back home—without going anywhere else. In other words, he was hoping Red O'Brien had told him the full truth about his comings and goings.

But O'Brien had lied.

Garza sent a text to Marlin: *O'Brien was all over the county on Fri night.*

Marlin was out on a poaching-related call at the moment. He was, after all, a game warden, and his first responsibility was enforcing hunting and fishing laws, but Garza knew that Marlin enjoyed taking part in broader investigations, and the sheriff was grateful for Marlin's contributions, when he had the time.

Garza went for a mug of coffee and by the time he got back, Marlin had replied: *Anywhere near Dub's place?*

Garza sent a detailed response: *Looks that way. Pinged off the nearest tower several times. Also pinged off towers in central and northern part of county.*

Marlin said: *Aggravating. Hoping to get records for Mandy and Dub today or tmw. Will touch base w you. Any progress on the Watts shooting?*

Garza knew that Marlin was hoping Lauren could get back on the Dub Kimble case as soon as possible.

Not yet. Hoping Watts wakes up soon. Lauren talked to the RC late yesterday, putting word out, asking for leads. Phones should be ringing soon.

"RC" was the *Blanco County Record*, the largest newspaper in the region.

Want me to take a run at Red when I'm done with this call? Marlin asked. Garza grinned. *Absolutely.*

9

"Don't lose your shit, but we got a problem," Bricker said the next morning when Creed woke at seven-fifteen.

Creed had slept for maybe three hours—tossing and turning like a fish on a pier, consumed by the feeling that his life was over for good.

Of course, they hadn't found Billy Don Craddock in Fredericksburg the night before, but they'd spent at least an hour looking around while Bricker waited to see if Craddock posted anything else on his Facebook page. He hadn't, fortunately. Then they'd eaten at Sonic, and then they'd swung through Luckenbach, which was dead. Then they'd come back to the motel and Bricker had fallen asleep almost immediately, which was a blessing in itself. Gave Creed time to think—but ultimately, he'd gotten nowhere.

"What?" Creed said, propping himself up on one elbow, wondering what kind of problem might have cropped up overnight.

Bricker was sitting at the end of his bed, fully dressed, looking at his phone. "Danny Ray Watts ain't dead."

There was only one way to describe the feeling that swept over Creed right then. It was like the moment in a horror movie when a woman suddenly realizes the psycho killer is calling from inside the house.

Creed's entire body began to tingle with panic.

His face went warm in an instant.

Holy hell. This changed everything.

"How do you know?" he asked. His voice sounded hollow and foreign.

"Newspaper website." Bricker shook his head, still reading. "He's in critical condition. Sure as hell looked dead to me."

This was a catastrophe. No other way to categorize it.

Creed hadn't been happy about being an accessory to murder, but at least he'd had a chance at getting away with that. Now, though, he was an accessory to *attempted* murder, which was a lesser charge, but he was more likely to get caught. Watts might be able to identify the people who'd done it.

"Why haven't we heard from the cops yet?" Creed asked, doing his best to sound calm.

"Relax," Bricker said.

"It's only a matter of time before—"

"*Relax*," Bricker said again, still looking at his phone. "Says anyone with information should contact the sheriff's office. That's good news. Means he probably can't talk. At least, not yet."

Creed didn't know how to respond, so he got out of bed and grabbed his clothes—same ones from yesterday, because they hadn't planned on staying the night—and went into the bathroom. Left the door open so he could hear.

Bricker said, "That's the only thing that makes sense. He can't talk yet. If he could, they woulda been knocking down our door last night. He might be brain-dead or something, for all we know."

Creed found some comfort in that. Maybe Watts would still die. Maybe he was in a coma and would never recover. Maybe he would wake up with no memory of what had happened. There was hope. Creed's nerves were starting to settle down a bit.

He got into the shower and let the lukewarm water pour over him. Gave himself time to ponder this new situation. And he surprised himself by coming up with an idea.

It was Creed and Bricker against Watts. Two against one. That gave them an advantage.

Hold on a second.

Couldn't Creed and Bricker claim that Watts had pointed a gun at them? Maybe some kind of road rage incident. Self defense? The cops would wonder why they hadn't found Watts's gun on the scene. Creed and Bricker could say they'd grabbed it off the ground and taken it with them. But why? Who knows? Panic, maybe. People do strange things under stress. Hire a lawyer to talk for them.

It was a tragedy, really. This young man—Danny Ray Watts—lost his temper and fired a shot at my clients. They had no choice but to defend themselves. We still have that right in Texas—to defend ourselves from an attacker. And, sad as it may be, this is a good example of why we need that right.

Damn, that wasn't bad. It could work.

"Hey, no jerking off in there," Bricker called out.

Red didn't get many phone calls, and despite what Billy Don sometimes said, it wasn't because Red didn't have all that many friends. He had just the right amount, thank you very much. No, it was because most people texted nowadays, or they communicated on Facebook or those other "social media" sites Red didn't fully understand. He had a vague idea how Twitter worked, but what the hell was Snapchat? And Instagram? And Tumblr? Red had gone this far in life without needing those things, so he figured he could continue without them just fine.

Point was, Red didn't get many calls, and the majority of those he did get, well, he'd just as soon he didn't. It was always salesmen or scammers with foreign accents or just some dude asking for "Tonya," who apparently used to have this number and liked to have a good time.

Or, every now and then, it would be a cop of some sort.

On this particular morning, it was the Blanco County game warden, John Marlin. Red had long ago programmed Marlin into his phone as "Possum Cop," because that's what a lot of people called game wardens.

Until that moment, Red had been doing some research by watching an old *Mannix* rerun, trying to pick up some pointers. After all, Mannix was a damn good detective. Solved every last case he worked on.

Red was tempted to ignore the call from Marlin, but he was also curious. So he answered.

"I need to ask you a couple of questions," Marlin said right off the bat. "You got a few minutes for me?"

"Uh, well, I—"

"You home right now? I'm about a mile away."

"Uh, yeah."

"I'll be there in a few minutes."

Why did cops always have to be so damn pushy?

18

SEVEN MINUTES AFTER CONCLUDING his text conversation with John Marlin, Bobby Garza received his second curveball of the morning. That's when Darrell, the dispatcher, buzzed his office and informed him that a man named Tino Herrera was saying he needed to speak to the sheriff right away. He was holding on line three.

Garza took the call and Herrera said, "Sheriff Garza, I've been thinking about our conversation on Saturday, and I need to clarify something I said."

"Oh, yeah?" Garza said with as much nonchalance as he could muster. "What's up?"

9

"I know we've had our differences over the years," Marlin said, "and most of those differences have revolved around various violations of hunting and fishing laws."

He and Red O'Brien were standing outside O'Brien's trailer, below the porch, in the flat caliche parking area. O'Brien had stepped outside as soon as Marlin had pulled up.

"Can it really be a violation if I don't happen to agree with a particular law?" O'Brien asked.

"Well, sure it can," Marlin said, while trying to remain as affable as possible. "Take the hunters I was just talking to. They were shooting dove over their own lease, but some of the birds were falling onto the neighboring ranch. So they were climbing the fence to get them."

"Makes sense," O'Brien said.

"But they didn't have permission to climb the fence. They were trespassing."

"So you wrote 'em up for that?" O'Brien said.

"Just a verbal warning," Marlin said. "These guys made an honest mistake, and once I informed them of the law, they were more than happy to comply. They know I was just doing my job. On the other hand—with you and me—I sometimes feel like you think of me as the enemy. I'm the bad guy that comes by to ruin the party. You get what I'm saying?"

Marlin was trying an unusual tactic, but he thought it might pay off.

O'Brien said, "Well, I don't know about that. I'd say it's more like we simply disagree about the interpretation of various statues."

"Statues?"

"Rules and reg'lations and whatnot," O'Brien said.

"Okay," Marlin said, "but I'm sure you understand that I have to enforce the law whether you disagree with it or not."

O'Brien said, "I guess."

"But just like with those dove hunters, I'm not here to cause trouble for you. In fact, I'm trying to help you out of a jam. See, the truth is, nobody thinks you had anything to do with the disappearance of Dub Kimble. That's because you didn't, right?"

"Of course not."

Marlin was trying hard to gain O'Brien's trust, if only for the next few minutes, but it wouldn't be easy. Marlin knew from past experiences and conversations that O'Brien cultivated a deep wariness of just about anyone in a position of authority—including cops, judges, lawyers, doctors, teachers, preachers, scientists, librarians, and the occasional restaurant hostess.

"Good," Marlin said. "What you need to understand is that anytime someone has a motive in a case like this, we need to rule that person out. Problem is, we haven't been able to do that with you. That's my goal right now—to rule you out, so you don't have to worry about any of this anymore. Sound good? I'm not here to get you to admit to anything else that might've happened that night—even if, say, maybe you took a shot at a deer or pig alongside the road."

"I didn't!" O'Brien insisted.

"Good," Marlin said. "But even if you did, I wouldn't care about that, just this one time. All I care about is what happened to Dub Kimble. I'm not trying to trick you."

It was a damned trick. Red was sure of it.

Even if Marlin was convinced Red didn't harm Dub, he was still trying to bust him for road-hunting on Friday night. That's just the way these game wardens operated. They never let anything go. Red had experienced it firsthand, and he'd seen it plenty of other times on the TV show called *Lone Star Law*, which featured Texas game wardens suckering decent, hardworking citizens into confessing to crimes almost too small to matter. The good news was, Red was pretty sure he'd learned enough over the years to outsmart just about any game warden.

Marlin said, "I talked to Bobby—Sheriff Garza—and he said you weren't totally up front with him about where you went on Friday night."

"Not on purpose," Red said. "I forgot about going to the store. Soon as he reminded me, I remembered, so I told him."

"Okay, so let's clear this up once and for all," Marlin said. "Be honest with me. Did you go anywhere else on Friday night other than the store?"

"No, sir," Red said immediately, because when in doubt, it was always best to deny everything completely.

Marlin stared at him.

Red did his best to stare back without showing any sign of guilt.

"I'm trying to help," Marlin said. "But you're not working with me. We need to work together."

"I'm doing my best," Red said, "but my memory is sometimes like one of those, uh, whatchamacallits. Can't remember the name for it."

Red heard Marlin's phone vibrate in his pocket. Probably a text. The game warden took a look at his phone and said, "Excuse me for just one minute." He walked twenty yards away and made a call.

"A sieve," Red said to himself. "That's the word."

When Marlin finished with the call to Bobby Garza, he walked back over to Red O'Brien, trying to maintain a poker face. Not easy, because this case was becoming more convoluted and exasperating with each new development.

O'Brien looked at him, open eyed, just waiting.

Marlin didn't rush. He needed to think things through. Considering the new information Garza had just given him, what was the best way to approach this interview?

After a moment, Marlin asked, "Did you have your phone with you all night?"

"On Friday night?"

"Yes."

"I think so."

"You're not sure? Most people would remember if they were carrying their phone or not."

"Okay, yeah, I had it. I remember now."

"So that means you took it with you when you went to Lowe's Market, right?"

"I did, yeah."

"And it was with you when you drove down Miller Creek Loop and Sandy Road and all the other places you went," Marlin said.

"But I didn't go—"

"Come on, now," Marlin said. "Let's not play games. Your phone records give us a pretty good idea where you were."

"My phone records?"

"We got copies of your cell phone records, including location data."

O'Brien was frowning. "How'd you manage that?"

"Got a warrant."

"You got a warrant?"

"Yep."

"Based on what?"

"Probable cause."

"Well, that just ain't right. It's getting where your average citizen don't got any privacy left at all. That ain't the America I grew up in."

Marlin said, "Standard procedure. Again, we were just trying to rule you out."

"You keep saying that, but it sure don't seem like it. Plus, just a minute ago, you said you wasn't trying to trick me."

"And I'm not," Marlin said. "But if I'm going to help you, I need to know exactly what happened. Not just part of the story—all of it."

The curtains parted in one of the windows behind O'Brien. Marlin could see Billy Don Craddock stooping to peek out, grinning. Marlin glared at him and the curtain slowly fell back into place.

"Probably best if I just keep my mouth shut at this point," O'Brien said.

"You can go that route if you want," Marlin said. "Or you can help me set the record straight. Because right now, after that phone call I just took, things aren't looking good."

9

"Okay, well, I said I did not go to Mandy's place on Friday night, and technically that's true," Tino Herrera had said to Bobby Garza twelve minutes earlier. "The truth is, I *started* to go over there, and I even pulled into their driveway, but I turned around."

"Why?"

"Why was I going over there, or why did I turn around?"

"Both."

"Okay, I was going over there because Mandy called me and said she and Dub had gotten into a nasty fight. He said some really mean things to her, which made me mad, so I decided it was finally time for me to talk to him—*mano o mano*—and deal with everything that was going on. I mean, Mandy and me were pretty sure he knew exactly what was going on between us, so why not get it out in the open?"

"You felt that strongly about your relationship with Mandy?" Garza asked, now taking precise notes.

"I don't know if I would put it that way—it's not like I want to marry her—but I care for her and don't want to see her mistreated."

"That's good of you," Garza said. "So then what happened?"

"Mandy said I shouldn't come because she'd had enough drama for the night, and by the time I got there—or almost there—I'd cooled off enough that I decided to listen to her."

"Any idea where Dub was at that point?" Garza asked.

"No."

"So you just turned around and left? You never got out of your car or went inside?"

"No, I never did. Just backed out of the driveway and left."

"Did Mandy know how close you'd gotten to their house?"

"She did, yes. She saw my headlights. I called her and said I'd changed my mind, and she was glad."

"Did she say where Dub was?"

"No."

"Were they still arguing?"

"I couldn't hear anything. I think he must've already gone outside. But this isn't why I'm calling."

"You have something else to share?"

Tino took a breath and Garza waited.

"When I was leaving, going back to town, this old red truck went zooming past me on the county road. I think it was a Ford."

19

"SPEAKING OF TRICKING ME, that's the oldest trick in the book," O'Brien said. "Trying to act like you just got some important piece of information I should be worried about. I've seen that in the movies."

"Name one time I've ever lied to you," Marlin said.

O'Brien didn't answer right away. He finally said, "First time for everything."

Marlin was thinking, *You just can't help some people.* He said, "Here's the situation: Sheriff Garza got a call a few minutes ago from a man named Tino Herrera. You know him?"

O'Brien hesitated before saying, "I know who he is."

"Tino has a relationship with both Dub and Mandy, and he happened to be near their home on Friday night. He told the sheriff he saw you in your truck about half a mile from Dub's place that evening. He said you were driving fast—like you were fleeing the scene of a crime."

O'Brien's face went bright red in an instant. "That's a damn lie! It was the other way around."

He stopped talking abruptly, realizing he'd said too much, but he also knew there was no use in continuing to deny where he'd been on Friday night.

"Tell me what really happened," Marlin said. "I'm still trying to help you out."

O'Brien shook his head, like *Damn, what a mess.* He said, "Okay, fine. Might as well get this over with. What happened was, I was minding my own business, parked on the side of the road, when he went hauling ass past me in that little blue car of his. My headlights lit him up and I got a good look at him."

"Think he saw you?"

"I got no idea, but I figure he got a good look at my truck. So now he's lying about it."

g

"The red truck was going toward Dub's place?" Garza asked.

"Yes," Tino said. "For a moment, I thought he was going to hit me head on. That's how fast he was going. I didn't think he'd be able to stay on his side of the road."

"What time was this?"

"I cannot say for sure. After I got off work, but before I went over to Conrad's. Maybe close to ten o'clock."

"Did you get a look at the driver of the red truck?" Garza asked.

"I did, yes, a very good one."

"Would you recognize him if you saw him again?"

"Absolutely," Tino said. "And I *did* recognize him, yesterday, because he showed up at my restaurant."

Tino paused. Garza said, "The same man you saw on Friday night?"

"Yes, sir."

"And what happened?"

"The man I saw on Friday night arrived with another man—a really big man—in an old vehicle. I think it's called a Ranchero. They came inside and sat in one of the booths. I knew I'd seen the smaller man on Friday night, but I hadn't had any reason to wonder why he was driving on that road in his truck. I found out pretty soon, because when I walked past their booth, the smaller guy stopped me—and he threatened me. It scared me, but I finally decided I needed to tell you."

g

"Why were you parked on the side of the road?" Marlin asked.

O'Brien looked like he'd swallowed a mouthful of sour milk, but he didn't reply. It was obvious what he'd been doing, but he didn't want to admit it, least of all to a game warden.

"Never mind," Marlin said. "Doesn't matter. The point is, you're saying you were parked and it was Tino who went flying past?"

"Exactly," O'Brien said. "He lied to the sheriff."

"Unfortunately, it gets worse," Marlin said.

"Well, whatever it is, it's a lie."

"I hope so," Marlin said, "because Tino is saying you and Billy Don were in his restaurant yesterday—the Dairy Queen in Fredericksburg. And he said…well, let's stop there for a second and deal with that part.

Is it true that you were in the Dairy Queen?"

O'Brien surprised Marlin by saying, "Yeah, we were there. So what?"

"What happened?"

"Nothing happened. What's he saying?"

"He told Sheriff Garza you threatened him."

"That's bullshit!" O'Brien said. "Pardon my French, but that's pure BS."

"He said you told him he'd better keep his mouth shut about seeing you on Friday night."

"Jeez, that's a damned lie, from start to finish. You can ask Billy Don. I don't even *know* what happened on Friday night. Want me to call Billy Don out here?"

"Not right now. Just tell me what you said to Tino."

"Nothing at all! We never even talked to him, and he never came nowhere near our booth."

"Then give me your side of the story," Marlin said.

"I will, because what he said is all a load of crap," O'Brien said. "When we went into that Dairy Queen, we didn't even know who he was. What I mean is, we *did* go in there looking for Tino, because we'd heard that Mandy and him have been fooling around, and so I've been investigating him, but I didn't know he was the same guy I saw on the county road. When I recognized him, we left."

"You've, uh, been investigating him?" Marlin said.

"Well, kinda. Seems like he had a real good reason to hurt Dub, so I was checking him out. I figure my best chance of clearing my good name is if the real criminal gets caught."

"What was the extent of your investigation?" Marlin asked. He had to refrain from making quotation marks with his fingers when he said the word "investigation."

O'Brien said, "That's about it—going to Dairy Queen to see this kid Tino. That's as far as it went. But if you want my opinion, the fact that he's lying about me shows he had something to do with Dub's disappearance. Why else would he lie? He's trying to blame it on me so you won't know he did it. Or maybe Mandy did it and he's covering for her. Or maybe they did it together. Whichever way it happened, it damn sure wasn't me."

O'Brien appeared agitated and nervous and indignant—and completely truthful.

Marlin said, "Part of the problem is that you don't have anyone to back up your story—because you were alone all night."

"And it sucks," Red said. "Wish I did."

"You didn't have anybody with you?" Marlin asked. "Now would be the time to come clean."

"Nope."

"You didn't run into anybody at any point who might be able to verify any parts of your story?" Marlin asked.

"Just the cashier at Super S," O'Brien said. "I mean Lowe's Market. It was the new guy. The one with really big teeth. You know who I'm talking about?

"I'm afraid I don't."

"Tall guy. Big teeth. You know that cartoon donkey from *Hee Haw*? Ha. That would be a good nickname for him. 'Hee Haw.' I'll have to remember that."

"I'm sure he'll be flattered," Marlin said.

"Probably so," O'Brien said. "That's a famous donkey. Anyway, he saw me. He knows I was there. Does that help?"

"Not much," Marlin said. "What I need is—"

O'Brien's face lit up. "Oh, and then there was Dickie Loftin and some other guy."

"I'm sorry, what?"

"I saw Dickie Loftin on Friday night. Billy Don didn't believe me, but it was him."

"You saw Dickie Loftin where?" Marlin asked.

He was remembering what Skeet Carrasco had told him—that Dickie Loftin would've approached Carrasco's ranch from the west, which meant Dickie wouldn't have traveled the portion of road where Dub Kimble was hit, between the ranch and eastward toward Johnson City. Maybe that wasn't true after all.

"In the parking lot of the Super S," O'Brien replied. "Damn it, I mean the Lowe's Market."

"On Friday night?"

"Right."

"What time?"

"The same time when I was buying beer. I saw Dickie riding in one of them Hummers, and I went over to talk to him, but some big guy came along and ran me off. Then they stopped for gas."

"Start at the beginning," Marlin said.

9

Creed Loftin finally realized he was dealing with a madman when they were grabbing some lunch at a Tex-Mex joint in Johnson City called El Agave and Bricker suggested they should go to the hospital in Austin and finish Danny Ray Watts off.

"Before he wakes up," Bricker said. "Shut him up for good, before he has a chance to talk."

Creed wasn't even sure where to start.

"You realize a place like that will have security cameras all over the place?" he finally said.

"Yeah, but we'd wear disguises," Bricker said.

Jesus Christ, did this lunatic think this was some kind of high-school drama class? Was he talking about fake mustaches, wigs, that sort of thing? Creed couldn't even bring himself to ask. "I think we need to keep thinking," he said.

"He could wake up any time," Bricker reminded him.

Creed was ready to discuss the idea he'd had in the shower, if for no other reason than to stop Bricker from compounding the mistakes they'd already made.

"Let's talk about that for a second," Creed said. "Let's say he does wake up, and the first thing he says is that two dudes did it, and one of them was Dickie Loftin's brother. Where does it go from there?"

"Prison, most likely," Bricker said. "Cellmates again." He grinned at the irony.

"Not necessarily," Creed said, keeping his voice low. "What if we come up with a story?"

"Like what?"

"What if we say Watts almost ran us off the road, and when we chased him down, he took out a gun and fired a shot at us?"

"And we fired back?" Bricker said.

"Exactly. Paint it as self defense."

"Not bad," Bricker said.

"It could work."

Bricker ate some chips and thought about it.

He said, "Problem there is, they'll say we're lying, especially when they see we both have a record. Since when do cops believe guys like us?"

Creed was encouraged that Bricker was even considering it. He said, "We'll hire a lawyer to do the talking for us, so we don't have to worry about screwing it up. You won't ever say a word to anybody but the lawyer."

"I ain't got money for a lawyer," Bricker said.

"I'd take care of it," Creed said. "Me and Dickie. You wouldn't have to pay a penny. And the beauty of it is, it doesn't matter if the cops believe us or not, because the bottom line is, they've got to *prove* we did something wrong. The lawyer would keep them away from us and guide us through it. We'd hire the lawyer before we even talked to the cops."

Bricker took a long drink from his bottle of Corona and thought about it. Creed waited patiently, but he was wondering what there was to think about. This was a way out. Why wasn't he taking it?

"There's still one big-ass problem."

"What?"

"Who did the shooting?" Bricker asked. "Me or you?"

"What do you mean?"

"Would we say I shot Watts?"

"Well, yeah," Creed said. "Because, you know, that's accurate. That's the way it happened. Best if we stick as close as possible to the actual facts."

"But, see, that's a deal-breaker right there. You know I ain't supposed to have a weapon on me. They'd violate my parole and I'd be back in the slam for at least ten years."

"Same thing is true for me, though," Creed said. "Besides, the lawyer can work a deal on that."

"Well, then, you say you did the shooting and get him to work that magic for you, not me, 'cause if you think I'm putting that kind of trust in a goddamn lawyer, you're flat crazy. Ain't no way. Lawyers is the reason I already spent half my adult life locked up."

Maybe being a serious fuck-up had something to do with it, Creed thought.

He said, "They're not all like that. Gotta hire the right one."

"No way," Bricker said. "Ain't an option."

So the idea—his best idea, his *only* idea—was scuttled entirely. Creed had let himself get excited by the possibility of making Watts the bad guy, but now he was back to square one.

"What do ya think?" Bricker asked, still waiting on Creed's reply.

Creed shook his head in frustration. He couldn't hold it in any longer. "Honestly, I'm kind of lost."

"How so?"

"What are we doing here?"

"Huh?"

"We've got no plan. We don't know what we're doing. It's like we're waiting around for some big idea to pop into our heads, but there is no big idea. There can't be."

"Whose fault is that?" Bricker said.

It's yours, you flaming psycho. You shot Watts and started all this.

"It's nobody's fault," Creed said. "It is what it is. We just need to come up with a solution."

Bricker leaned in close and it made Creed nervous. "I already told you what we should do. Go up to the hospital and take care of Watts for good. And we still gotta take care of Billy Don Craddock."

"I'm gonna be honest," Creed said. "I don't think either of those are good ideas. Not right now."

Bricker stared at him for a long moment. It made Creed's skin crawl.

Finally Bricker leaned back. "Hey, whatever. You make the call, boss. I'm just the hired help. Don't make no difference to me."

20

RED WENT BACK into the trailer and stood in the center of the living room for a moment, pondering the conversation he'd just had with John Marlin. Strange turn it had taken there at the end.

Billy Don was sunk into his usual spot on the couch, drinking a Keystone Light tall boy. He said, "Shit's hittin' the fan now, huh?"

"Maybe, maybe not. You was listening?"

"To some of it, until I got bored."

Billy Don had the TV tuned to *Rehab Addict*, which, contrary to its misleading name, was one of those home-remodeling shows. They liked to watch those shows and point out all the mistakes and stupid choices the so-called experts made. It didn't hurt that some of the hosts, like the lady on this show, were damn nice looking. Red figured those women wouldn't know how to build a proper outhouse in real life. They were just hired to wear tight tank tops and bend over a lot, while pretending they knew how to spackle or install a toilet or whatever.

"You hear the part about Dickie Loftin?" Red asked.

"Uh-uh."

"I mentioned seeing Dickie in town and that sure got his attention."

"Got Dickie's attention?"

"No, Marlin's. How could that have gotten Dickie's attention? That don't even make sense."

"Maybe not, but following one of your stories is like watching a dog chasing a butterfly."

Red figured Billy Don had heard that line somewhere and had been saving it up for a special occasion.

"You wanna hear this or not?" he said.

"I get a choice?" Billy Don asked.

"I said I saw Dickie on Friday night, and he was all like, 'Oh, really? Tell me more about that.' It was weird. Don't you think that's weird?"

"Maybe he's a Dickie Loftin fan."

"No, it wasn't that. He wanted to know every last detail."

"Unlike me," Billy Don said.

9

"Somebody is lying," Marlin said. "Tino or Red. The question is who. Then you throw in this new stuff about Dickie Loftin and...I don't know what to think."

He and Garza had decided to regroup in the small conference room at the sheriff's office. The door was open and Marlin could hear staff members going about their business in various parts of the building. Jean, one of the dispatchers, was talking to someone on the phone, but it was only a low murmur. The coffee maker in the kitchen around the corner beeped to signal a freshly brewed pot. Air hissed gently from the nearest AC vent.

"Playing devil's advocate, Loftin might have a simple explanation," Garza said. "He might say, 'Oh, right, we went into Johnson City after Skeet's party because we needed more beer.' Or food, or whatever."

Marlin was skeptical. Skeet Carrasco was the kind of host who would have everything you could possibly want.

"You're not buying it?" Garza said.

"Sorry, no."

"I don't blame you. I'm having trouble with it myself," Garza said.

According to Red O'Brien, on Friday night at the Lowe's Market, Loftin had climbed into the passenger side of a black Hummer and refused to open his door when O'Brien approached. Then a large man—Creed Loftin, based on the description—had exited the store and told O'Brien to get away from the vehicle. O'Brien explained that he was merely saying hello to Dickie and didn't mean any harm, but the man denied that anybody was in the vehicle at all. O'Brien told Marlin "it was an all-around disappointing 'sperience, what with me being a big Dickie fan and everything. Big Dickie. Can't believe I just said that."

What's more, when O'Brien told his skeptical friend Billy Don Craddock what had happened, Craddock had posted a comment on Dickie Loftin's Facebook page, but the comment later disappeared. Strange, but Marlin had to wonder if that was user error on Craddock's part. Perhaps he hadn't actually posted the comment, but thought he had.

Garza said, "How long do you think it takes to get from Skeet's place to town?"

Marlin thought about it. "You could probably make it in seven or eight minutes."

"So if you go inside and buy something—and then stop at the gas pumps—you could theoretically get there and back in about twenty minutes."

"I would say so, yeah. Probably less if you drove fast."

"Okay, then maybe Dickie did exactly that—ran into town for something—and Skeet never knew he was gone."

Marlin thought about that possibility.

"Or maybe Skeet did know he was gone, but he chose not to mention it, because he didn't want to implicate Dickie, even if Dickie is totally innocent."

"I guess that's a possibility," Marlin admitted. People lied for all sorts of reasons. "The gas can is kind of weird. Why was Creed Loftin carrying a gas can?"

Garza didn't have an answer.

"I need to call Dickie Loftin again," Marlin said. "On second thought, you should call him. Maybe he'd be more likely to respond to a sheriff."

"I'll do that," Garza said.

"In the meantime," Marlin said, "I'll talk to Skeet Carrasco again and see if his story changes. Maybe it's time to hold his feet to the fire and see if he knows more than he's telling."

"Maybe so," Garza said. "Car dealers have been known to stretch the truth now and then."

"What about Tino?" Marlin asked. "Or maybe it's time to question Mandy again."

"Let's wait and see what we might learn from Skeet and the Loftins. Give it the rest of the day."

Marlin nodded.

"If nothing budges, maybe I'll talk to Tino again in the morning," Garza added.

Deciding how and when to question a particular individual was part experience and part gut instinct. Sometimes it paid to go after someone aggressively from day one, if only to keep an investigation from stalling. Other times it was advantageous to wait—to gain more facts to use as leverage during an interview.

Marlin drained the last bit of coffee in his mug. "Heard anything else from Henry?"

"Not yet," Garza said.

It had been two days since Henry Jameson had processed the crime scene and Dub's truck, and he had also collected a few of Dub's personal items for DNA samples. Marlin found himself impatient for those results, but he knew some law enforcement agencies had to wait weeks or even months to hear back on those kinds of tests.

"Thinking I'll lighten his load and try to identify that car part myself," Marlin said. "He sent it to the DPS lab, and they're always backlogged. Probably won't hear back on that for at least a week or more."

"Probably worth a shot," Garza said, "but when you say you're going to try to identify the part yourself..."

"I'm going to call Jett Anderson," Marlin said.

"Good idea," Garza said. "Want to grab some lunch?"

"You bet," Marlin said.

"Leave in ten minutes?"

"Perfect," Marlin said. He went to his office to check his email and found that the cell phone records for Dub Kimble and Mandy Hammerschmitt had finally arrived. He quickly scanned through them and saw that they were basically useless.

Dub hadn't made any calls or sent any texts on Friday evening.

Mandy had called Tino Herrera once, and he had called her once, which matched what Tino had told Garza. Mandy hadn't made any other calls or sent any other texts.

Dead end.

9

"Hang on a sec," Marlin said a few minutes later from the passenger seat of the sheriff's SUV.

Garza stopped with his hand on the door handle. They had just parked outside El Agave. Marlin had already told him about Dub's and Mandy's disappointing cell phone records.

"See that big guy right there?" Marlin asked, pointing.

"Yeah?"

"I think that's Creed Loftin," Marlin said. He had seen Creed's mug shots.

"No kidding," Garza said. "That's interesting. Why is he still hanging around? And who's he with?"

Marlin pulled out his phone and snapped a couple of quick photos, before Creed Loftin—if it was in fact him—and the smaller man with him walked between two trucks and continued north.

"I'm not positive that's him," Marlin said, "but I'm pretty sure. Wish he hadn't been wearing sunglasses."

He was tempted to suggest they should jump out of Garza's vehicle and go speak to the two men. See how they reacted to a sudden encounter with a sheriff and game warden. But that would probably be an unwise move in the long run. If Creed Loftin was involved in Dub's disappearance, Garza and Marlin had the advantage of knowing he was still in town—or back in town—without him knowing they knew.

Garza was certainly thinking all of the same things. "Bet they're going to the Best Western," he said. "Maybe you should take a peek, to be sure."

"Be right back," Marlin said, exiting the SUV.

He followed from a discreet distance as the men passed in front of the used-car lot next to the restaurant, then turned into the motel, just as Garza had guessed. Marlin turned the corner and stopped near the motel's office door—ready to duck inside, if needed—and watched as the two men went to a room near the back of the motel. They went inside and closed the door.

Marlin took out his phone again and snapped a photo of the black BMW parked outside the room. There were no other vehicles nearby, so Marlin assumed it belonged to one of the two men. Marlin was tempted to go inside and ask the motel clerk if the man in question was Creed Loftin, but the clerk might later alert the two men that Marlin had been asking about them. Not worth the risk.

Marlin returned to the sheriff's vehicle, where he found Garza talking on the phone.

"—and I appreciate that," Garza said.

The other person was talking now, but Marlin couldn't make it out. Sounded like a male.

"I don't think that at all," Garza said. "I just appreciate you setting the record straight. If I have any other questions—"

The person spoke again, briefly.

"Okay, perfect," Garza said. "Thanks, Conrad. I'll be in touch."

Garza ended the call and the expression on his face said that Conrad had just shared something important. "Okay, get this. Even after Tino admitted he drove over to Dub's place on Friday night, he still insisted he went over to Conrad's place after that and stayed until about four-thirty in the morning. Conrad backed that up the other day—but now he's saying he's pretty sure that was Thursday night instead."

Marlin could only shake his head. "Is nobody telling us the truth about anything?"

Garza said, "Conrad was worried I would think he might've been lying earlier."

"And?"

"I figure he probably was. I bet Tino talked him into saying it was Friday, but then he got cold feet and decided to say he was mistaken."

The problem, as Marlin and Garza both well knew, was that innocent people who were worried about appearing guilty often told lies that, ironically, made them appear guilty. Even if Tino asked Conrad to lie for him—though it reflected poorly on both of them—it didn't mean Tino was guilty of anything else. Could be that Tino simply wanted an alibi and Conrad was willing to give him one.

"Did Tino call or text him before going over there?" Marlin asked.

"No, just dropped in, according to Conrad."

That meant there would be no cell phone records to verify which night Tino had visited Conrad. How convenient for both of them.

Marlin said, "How about if we run this plate real quick, then continue this conversation inside?"

21

I'M SO WHITE TRASH, I have more appliances on my porch than in my house.
Trite. Been done so many times.

I'm so white trash, one of my eyes is lazy and the other is unemployed.
That wasn't bad. Would people get it?

I'm so white trash, I can get hours of entertainment from an electric bug zapper.

Wait a second. Didn't Jeff Foxworthy do a line like that? Or was it about a fly swatter? Dickie couldn't remember for sure. Either way, it was too close. That was something he had to avoid—accidentally lifting one of Foxworthy's lines. Dickie already had enough critics without giving them more ammo.

He set the notepad down and took a break. Still had writer's block. Too distracted.

When Dickie and Creed left the Big Ram Ranch on Saturday morning, they'd agreed it would be better if the two brothers didn't contact Skeet for the time being. That way the cops couldn't say they'd been working on their stories or keeping each other up to date on what the cops were asking them. But Dickie finally couldn't stand it anymore. One call to Skeet wouldn't hurt.

Apparently Skeet was equally eager to talk, because he immediately said, "The game warden came out yesterday morning and he—"

"He left me a message yesterday," Dickie said. "Why a game warden?"

"Because there's a hunting angle to it, I guess," Skeet said. "You call him back?"

"Not yet."

"You gonna?"

"Don't know. Maybe later today or tomorrow."

"You can get away with blowing him off," Skeet said.

"Yeah, that's what I think, too. Or maybe I'll get Creed to call him."

"That'd work," Skeet said. "And just say you don't know anything, which is what I told him. Haven't heard from him since."

"And not the sheriff either?"

"Nope. I did have to tell him you were here, but we knew they'd learn about that eventually anyway. I didn't mention Creed. I can always say he slipped my mind if I hear from them again, but honestly, at this point, I'm starting to think we're in the clear."

Dickie was thrilled to hear Skeet's assessment.

Both men were quiet for a moment. Dickie was tempted to tell Skeet the parts he didn't know, namely the fact that Creed was in Blanco County right now, dealing with the two men who'd seen Dickie in Johnson City. Skeet didn't know about any of that. But what purpose would it serve to tell him? Besides, Dickie didn't know much about that himself, because Creed wasn't staying in touch.

Instead, Dickie said, "I guess they haven't found anything, huh?"

"Nope. I let them search the ranch right after you left, and they were searching all of the adjoining properties, too. It was a big production—dogs, a helicopter, the works. They finally gave up yesterday afternoon. From what they said on the news, they're assuming he's dead, for sure."

They hung up a few minutes later and Dickie was feeling a little better about the situation—until the sheriff of Blanco County left a voicemail five minutes later.

9

Jett Anderson, who graduated from Lyndon B. Johnson High School one year behind John Marlin, stole his first car, a Mazda RX-7, when he was 17. He and a buddy got away with it clean, but later that night Jett managed to high-center it on a concrete barrier in a strip-club parking lot in Austin. They left it where it sat and thumbed a ride back home to Blanco County.

A month later, Jett went to San Antonio and stole a Camaro—but he got caught with it two days later when a state trooper pulled him over doing 103 miles per hour.

When the judge asked him why he'd done it, Jett said simply, "I guess I just like cars too much, your honor. I'm a car guy."

He hadn't been sassing the judge. He *was* a car guy, more than anyone Marlin had ever known.

Jett had further run-ins with the law—some minor, some not so minor—but when he was trying to go straight, he worked at auto parts stores, repair shops, used-car lots, and even on a pit crew for a Texas-based NASCAR driver back in the late eighties.

When Jett hit middle age and settled down a bit, he began offering his services as a shade-tree mechanic, running an unlicensed and uninsured shop from his small cabin on nine acres west of Round Mountain. Now, instead of stealing cars, he offered his customers a fair price and quick turnaround on an extensive range of repairs—very often using stolen parts he'd bought on the black market. Or that was the rumor, anyway. Hard to prove. Ask to see his receipts and he'd reply that he wasn't that great at paperwork, and besides, didn't you need a warrant for that?

Marlin couldn't think of anyone who might have a better shot at identifying the bumper fragment based on sight alone. He had a phone number for Jett, but it was from years earlier and was now out of service. Marlin called a couple of other locals who might have good contact info for Jett, but none of them answered either. Marlin decided to drive out to Jett's place.

The gate—closed, but not chained—had five NO TRESPASSING signs on it, along with one promising an armed response. Marlin tapped his horn a couple of times, then opened the gate, pulled through it, and closed it behind him.

He proceeded along a rough, winding caliche road to the rear of the property. Dense groves of cedars prevented him from seeing the cabin until he was almost upon it, and when it came into view, it was unchanged from the last time Marlin had been here, several years earlier. Jett might've been a car guy, but he certainly wasn't a house guy. The cabin—really more of a glorified shack—was wrapped in Tyvek, but it was tattered in places, revealing the plywood underneath. If Jett had made any additional progress on the cabin, Marlin couldn't see where. Maybe he'd been focusing on finishing the inside.

To the right of the cabin, in an area worn grassless by countless tires, more than a dozen cars, trucks, and SUVs were parked in a surprisingly orderly fashion. A couple were dirty enough that Marlin assumed they were non-running, but most appeared fairly new and in decent repair. Further right of the vehicles was a small metal barn—Jett's repair shop. The large rolling door was closed and padlocked.

Marlin stopped in front of the cabin and tapped his horn three more times. Best not to surprise a man like Jett, who often wore a 40-caliber semi-automatic holstered on his hip.

Marlin waited a moment. Would be disappointing if he'd driven out here for nothing. He could leave a note, but Jett might never call him back.

Just as Marlin was stepping from his truck to look around, Jett's front door swung open.

g

After leaving a voicemail for Dickie Loftin, Bobby Garza began returning a long list of calls that had come in from potential witnesses who'd seen the article in the *Blanco County Record* that morning. Asking for leads was occasionally fruitful, but it could be a colossal waste of time.

Amazing how many of the callers wanted to point out that Dub Kimble used to have a thing going with Kelly Rundell, and because of that, maybe Claude Rundell had done something to Dub. Or maybe Lester Higgs had done it, because he was currently seeing Kelly. It was all so salacious. So tawdry. One woman said the Devil had yet again reared his ugly head in Blanco County, and that the investigators should ask the Lord for guidance, but she didn't have anything more specific than that.

Garza took a break and simply sat for a moment, thinking.

No return call from Dickie Loftin yet, but it had only been an hour. Garza had been hoping his tone of voice would make Loftin drop everything and call back immediately, but he certainly hadn't been counting on it. People like Dickie Loftin did things on their own schedule. Or they hired attorneys to deal with these kinds of situations, even if they were innocent.

Garza picked up his phone again and started to call Tino Herrera, but he decided to wait until tomorrow.

He went back to the list of callers.

g

Jett Anderson studied the printed photo for less than five seconds before he grinned and said, "Boy, are you gonna feel dumb."

"Probably no more than usual," Marlin said.

"Of course, I remember you from school," Jett said. "You ain't dumb at all. All I meant was you're gonna feel dumb right now."

They were standing in front of Marlin's truck. After Marlin had explained the reason for his visit, Jett had appeared eager to help. Anytime a law-enforcement officer showed up without questions about Jett's questionable shop was probably cause for an elevated mood.

"What am I going to feel dumb about?" Marlin asked.

"I'd say that's part of a fender, all right," Jett said. "But it's from a four-wheeler."

Marlin didn't know whether or not to be disappointed. He hadn't considered the possibility that the part wasn't from a car or truck. If it were from an ATV, there was a good chance it was unrelated to the disappearance of Dub Kimble. Just a random piece of debris.

"I guess it could be from one of them brush guards they put on the front of those things," Jett said, "but I'm about ninety percent sure it's from a fender, probably the rear. Definitely ain't from a car or truck, though. Where'd you find it?"

"Along the side of a county road."

"Probably some kid riding in the ditch. Popped a wheelie and drug his ass end on the ground. Tore his fender up and didn't know it until later."

Jett handed the photo back to Marlin.

"Hate to ask this," Marlin said, "but are you sure?"

"I'd bet my left nut on it," Jett said. "And I lost my right one years ago."

22

IT WAS LATE in the afternoon—as they were drinking bourbon and swimming in the motel pool, and Bricker began to flirt with a couple of teenage girls, leering at them at first, then sidling closer and asking where they were from and what they were doing in Blanco County—when Creed finally came to the conclusion that Bricker would have to die.

To be more specific, Creed would have to kill him.

That was the only way out of this mess. There was no way around it.

Creed had been wracking his brain, trying to think of some other solution, but he'd come up empty.

Even if Danny Ray Watts died without telling the cops what had happened on that county road, killing Bricker was the only reasonable long-term solution—the only way to ensure that Creed could wipe his hands clean of everything that had happened and know for sure it wouldn't come back later to bite him in the ass.

See, that was the thing—even if he told Bricker that he was calling this operation off right now, and even if he paid him a lot of money for what he'd done, what about the months and years to follow? Bricker would be out there, doing who knows what, and always carrying the knowledge around with him. Able to squeal on Creed if he got into a tight spot and needed to bargain with a DA.

Creed had to kill him. And then he'd have to dispose of the body.

Make it look like Bricker had gone on the run. Maybe he'd fled the country.

Then Creed could tell just about any story he wanted to tell. Nobody could contradict him except Watts, if he lived, and Creed could still use the road-rage story. Far from ideal, but the only choice he had. Dump it all in a lawyer's lap and see what happened.

He was working on the details in his head, getting comfortable with the idea, which wasn't easy, when Bricker pushed through the chest-high water, Coke can in hand, and leaned against the side of the pool, next to Creed.

"Christ, what's that look on your face? You look fuckin' grim."

"Nothing. I'm fine."

"Got a couple of live ones," Bricker said quietly, nodding toward the two girls, who were stretched out on lounge chairs, soaking up some September rays. Clear skies and eighty-two degrees. The Coke can in Bricker's hand had a generous amount of booze mixed in, same as Creed's. No alcohol allowed at the pool. Had to hide it.

"How old're they?" Creed asked.

"Shit, I don't know," Bricker said. "Old enough."

Damn liar. Creed heard earlier when the girls said they were eighteen, which meant they were probably seventeen, or maybe even sixteen.

"That blond one was saying she thinks you're good looking," Bricker added. "Said she likes your muscles."

Which might've been true. Creed hadn't heard everything they'd said. He'd stayed over on this side of the pool when Bricker decided to make the moves on a couple of possible minors. What was the age of consent in Texas? Creed couldn't remember. He'd never *had* to remember before.

"Where're their parents?" Creed asked.

"Not here, so who cares?"

"They're staying at the motel alone?" Creed asked. Maybe they *were* eighteen after all.

"They're not staying here at all. They used to live here in town and the clerk lets 'em swim whenever they want. What's with all the questions? You wanna get laid or not?"

Creed could hardly keep the disgust off his face. A man like this—a predator—needed killing. Creed would be doing the world a favor. Dads everywhere would pat him on the back for doing it. Cops, too.

Creed drank some more bourbon. Thirty minutes passed.

The girls got into the pool and splashed around. Creed could tell that they were aware they had an audience—and they liked it. There was no denying they looked damn good in their bikinis. So young and toned.

"Think they're really eighteen?" he said quietly to Bricker.

Bricker laughed, like *Oh, that's what's holding you up?* He said, "Pretty sure they are. Just started college, is what they said earlier."

Creed nodded. If they were in college, he'd feel better about the situation. College kids were basically adults, right? Young, but still adults. Besides, what was he supposed to do—ask for ID? Maybe he should just roll with it and have some fun. He'd been under such pressure lately.

"Y'all want some bourbon and Coke?" Bricker called out.

"Absolutely," one of the girls responded immediately.

"Not too much, though," the other girl said. "I don't like my drinks too strong."

"Since when?" the first girl said, laughing.

The second girl splashed some water at her.

Of course, Creed would still have to kill Bricker. Tomorrow. Or the next day.

Soon, though.

9

Debbi and Amye.

Amye and Debbi.

At first, Creed had a hard time remembering which was which. Debbi was the brunet in the red bikini. Amye was the blond in the blue bikini.

They'd spent their entire lives in Johnson City, but—just like some stupid movie cliché—they'd always said they'd get out of this small town as soon as possible and find something better. It was a big world out there, you know, and all that stupid shit. They'd even made a pact to leave together. Corny as hell. They'd graduated high school four months earlier, and now they were going to Texas State University in San Marcos. *Big fucking deal*, Creed thought. *Going from Johnson City to San Marcos? Way to really break free.*

"What is that, forty-five minutes away?" Creed asked.

Creed and Bricker and the girls were clustered in a group now, just the four of them, early evening, the sun starting to set on the other side of the highway, their faces cast in shadows. The girls were obviously in no rush to leave. Getting sillier and louder. The bourbon was doing its job.

"More like an hour," Debbi, the brunet, said. Earlier, she'd made sure to emphasize that there was no "e" at the end of her name—like it could possibly matter. "It's, like, so totally different from living here, though. There are kids from all over the place. I have a girl in one class from *Norway*."

"Wow," Creed said. "That's pretty exotic."

He was teasing her, and Bricker kicked him underwater, but Debbi didn't pick up on it, partly because the girls were so buzzed.

"It's just so cool to kind of get away from the whole small-town mentality," Amye said. She'd also pointed out that her name was not spelled the traditional way. Debbi chimed in, saying her missing "e" had somehow wound up at the end of Amye's name. Wasn't that crazy? And they laughed like it was the funniest thing. It would be so nice if they'd stop with that stupid laughing.

"If you wanted to get away," Creed asked, "why are you here now?" Bricker glared at him.

"I had to pick something up at my parents' house," Debbi said.

"Yeah, a check," Amye said.

"Whatever," Debbi said. She turned toward Creed. "Besides, it's not like we said we'd never come back at all. Most of our friends are still here."

"The coolest thing about college," Amye said, "is that you can totally set your own schedule without anyone telling you what to do."

"And if you miss a class or something, it's no big deal," Debbi said.

"Exactly," Amye added.

"Like, I have a class at nine tomorrow, but..." Debbi looked at Bricker and gave him a coy smile.

The message was obvious. This stupid, drunk girl was planning to sleep with Bricker later. She had no idea what she was dealing with. Creed didn't give a damn at the moment, though. Didn't care about anything, really. The booze had wiped his cares away, and why should he be bothered with what Debbi did? She was an adult. Could make her own choices.

"Yeah, we probably won't make that one," Amye was saying, and now Creed noticed she was smiling at him in that same way.

"There's like a hundred people in that class anyway, so the professor won't notice, and we can just get the notes later," Debbi said. "Going to class is actually a waste of time on some days."

Creed felt a foot under the water again, but this time it wasn't Bricker kicking him. It was Amye rubbing the inside of his calf. Was that on purpose?

"Neither of us ever went to college," Bricker said. "But we done all right for ourselves."

"What do y'all do?" Debbi asked.

"For a living?" Bricker said.

"Yeah."

"This and that," he said. "I used to be an underwear model."

"What?" Debbi exclaimed. "Liar."

"You don't think I could be an underwear model?" Bricker said.

"I didn't say that."

"Wait 'til you see what's inside the underwear," Bricker said.

"Oh, God!" Debbi screamed. "You are such a perv. Control

yourself!"

But Creed could tell she was loving every minute.

"Okay, I'm jerking your chain," Bricker said. "But both of y'all could be models, though. Seriously. Swimsuit models. Like the gals in *Sports Illustrated*."

Which was heavy-duty bullshit. The girls were cute and everything, and they had decent bodies, but swimsuit models? Not a chance. Even if they each lost ten or fifteen pounds, they simply weren't in that league. Nowhere close.

Amye seemed to know that, because she said, "Like I would stoop to anything that demeaning. Besides, I like to eat more than a cucumber sandwich every now and then."

Creed slid his hand along Amye's outer thigh and she didn't object. It was cool that they were all standing around in a circle, close enough to talk, but in the darkness, none of them could see what was happening under the surface of the water.

"They've had some heavier girls in that issue lately," Debbi said. Then she added, "Not that you're heavy, Amye! I didn't mean it to sound that way. I think I weigh more than you do, probably."

"And it's all up here," Bricker said, cupping his hands in front of his chest like breasts.

"You're terrible!" Debbi said. "And it's so not true. I wish my boobs were that big—like as big as Amye's."

"I bet y'all have seen each other naked, huh?" Bricker said. "Being such good friends and all."

Creed had to admit that Bricker had a pretty good line of bullshit. He managed to say some outrageous stuff without pissing the girls off. Walked a fine line.

"We'll never tell," Amye said.

"Hey, I have an idea," Bricker said. "It's nice and private out here. Why don't you two gals take your tops off?"

"Ha," Debbi said. "No way. If anybody saw us—"

"Who's gonna see?" Bricker asked.

"Forget it," Amye said. "Not out here."

"So maybe inside?" Bricker said.

"We're not making any promises," Amye said.

The conversation lulled for a moment, and then Bricker said, "Creed, tell 'em what you do for a living." Before Creed could reply, Bricker said, "This guy right here is Dickie Loftin's brother."

"No way!" the girls said in perfect unison.

Creed should have been furious. What the fuck was Bricker doing? Weren't they supposed to be flying under the radar on this little expedition? But he liked the way the girls were looking at him with a new respect. They were almost awestruck. Creed had seen that expression plenty of times, but generally it was directed at Dickie, and Creed had to stand to the side and watch.

Creed just shrugged, like *What's the big deal? Dickie Loftin is my brother. So what?*

"That is amazing!" Amye said.

"So amazing!" Debbi agreed.

And then, of course, they asked a million questions, and Creed answered them, making it clear that Dickie's career would fall apart without Creed's guidance and management. He was the brains behind the scenes. He told them he was the one who originally came up with the "white trash" concept, and that he'd written most of those lines.

He even went so far as to tell them about being busted for cocaine several years back, and how he had taken the rap for Dickie, who had shoved the blow at him during a traffic stop. Not a small amount, either. Eight goddamn grams Dickie had bought just thirty minutes earlier at a party. In hindsight, Creed wished he'd let Dickie take the fall himself. Would've worked out fine. Hey, look at Tim Allen. Got nailed for possession of 650 frigging grams and went on to become a huge star.

"Do you know Tim Allen?" Amye asked.

"Oh, sure. He's a good guy."

The girls were eating it up, and Bricker was grinning at Creed. *You owe me one, buddy.*

"How long were you in jail?" Amye asked.

"Nearly three years," Creed said.

He noticed that Bricker wasn't mentioning that they'd met in prison. Creed let it slide.

"That is wild!" Debbi said.

"So wild!" Amye said.

Now Amye reached over in the darkness and began to rub the inside of Creed's thigh with her hand. He felt himself beginning to stiffen in his swimsuit.

At that moment, all of his troubles seemed so far away. Maybe they should just party tonight, and then go home tomorrow and see what happened. Maybe they'd never hear from the cops again. Maybe Creed had been worrying for nothing. Maybe there was no need to kill Bricker—to take him off the board. That was too drastic. He could always do it later, if it became necessary.

"Who wants another drink?" Bricker asked.

"I'll take one," Debbi said.

"Me, too," Amye said, her eyes locked on Creed's.

23

SKEET CARRASCO RETURNED Marlin's call at nine-thirty that evening.

"Sorry for the delay," he said. "I'm branching out and buying a Kawasaki dealership up in Dallas, and it was crazy all day, dealing with lawyers, accountants, and on and on. What can I do for you?"

Marlin was torn. Ask questions now, when he had the chance? Or wait to do it face to face?

"I just need to clarify a few things with you, Mr. Carrasco. You mind if I come out to see you in the morning?"

"I'm afraid I won't be here," Carrasco said. "I have to run up to Dallas. Leaving first thing."

"What I need you to do is postpone that meeting so we can talk. You mind doing that for me?"

"This is about that missing man, I guess? Dub Kimble?"

"It is, yes."

"Honestly, I wish I could help, but the sad fact is, I already told you everything I know."

Marlin remained quiet for a moment to see what Carrasco might say next. The silence stretched.

Finally Carrasco said, "I'd be happy to answer any questions you have right now."

"I guess that'll have to do," Marlin said. "The other day, you gave me a guest list from Friday night. Did you happen to accidentally leave anyone off that list?"

When Carrasco replied, his tone suggested that he knew Marlin already had an answer to that question.

"I don't think so," he said. "What I did was look at some pictures from the party and some emails and write everyone's name down. Did I miss someone?"

"Creed Loftin."

"Oh, right. Creed. Dang it, I'm sorry about that. Now that I think about it, I don't believe he ever came inside, which is why he slipped my mind."

"Why would he do that—stay outside when there was a perfectly good party a hundred feet away?" Marlin asked.

"Well, Creed isn't a real sociable guy, that's all. At least, not when he's running in Dickie's circles. I think there's probably a little bit of sibling rivalry there, if you want my opinion. So if Dickie likes someone or something, Creed tends to have a different opinion. It can get pretty tense around the two of them, because they argue all the time. Just petty stuff, though. Typical brother bullshit. You got any brothers?"

"No, sir."

"Well, take my word for it. On the one hand, you bicker, but on the other, there's nobody more loyal than a brother."

A text from Bobby Garza popped up on Marlin's phone.

Henry called. DNA from blood on road matched D. Kimble.

No surprise there. Would've been more surprising if it hadn't matched.

Marlin said, "Last time we talked, you mentioned that Dickie spent the night in your house. I'm assuming Creed did, too."

"Yes, that's right, but he never came inside until later, after the party."

"Do you know if Dickie ever left your property on Friday night?" Marlin asked.

"Not that I know of."

"So he might have?"

"I can't imagine why he would. Everything he'd need, we'd have right here at the house."

"But he could've slipped away at some point?"

"I suppose it's possible. What did Dickie say about it?"

"He hasn't called me back. I left voicemails, and so did the sheriff."

"Man's always hard to reach."

"Do you have any security cameras on the premises?"

"Only inside the house, but they turn off when I'm home. It's all automatic—connected to my phone."

"Can you give me Creed Loftin's phone number, please?" Marlin said.

"Sure thing." Skeet Carrasco recited the digits and Marlin wrote them down. "You're not thinking Dickie or Creed had anything to do with the missing man, are you?"

Marlin said, "I just need to ask them both some questions, same as anybody else who was in that area on Friday night."

"By all means, if I talk to Dickie, I'll tell him to return his damn calls," Carrasco said with a laugh.

"I would appreciate that."

"Hey, you happen to know a man named Lester Higgs?" Carrasco asked.

"Yes, I know Lester."

"I figured you did. Well, I don't mean to repeat gossip, but my understanding is that he used to see a woman that this man Dub Kimble was seeing recently. A married woman, apparently. I don't know if there's any truth to it, but I figured I'd better pass it along, in case that's something you want to check out. Seems like there could've been some bad blood between Lester and Dub, or between Dub and the woman's husband."

"Who told you about that?" Marlin asked.

"Honestly, I can't recall. That was a few weeks ago. I don't really know Lester all that well, but I do know his boss, Mack Hawley, which is the only reason the rumor stuck in my head."

Marlin wasn't sure what to make of all this. Was Skeet Carrasco trying to steer him away from Dickie and Creed Loftin? Or was he genuinely trying to be helpful?

"Mr. Carrasco, thanks for your time."

"Please call me Skeet."

9

Later, in the motel room, they turned the lights off and each couple pretended they had privacy and couldn't see or hear what the other couple was doing ten feet away.

Amye pushed Creed onto his back and climbed on top, guiding him inside her, and sweet Jesus it felt good. He fondled her breasts and almost lost it immediately. Had to pace himself. He grabbed her by the hips and slowed her down. That was better. He could last longer at this speed.

He turned and glanced at the digital clock to distract himself. 11:26. How long could he last? He was going to aim for ten minutes, knowing that was probably out of the question. The pleasure was too great. The build-up had been too intense.

After a few minutes, she leaned down and placed her torso flat against his, her breasts rubbing his chest, and whispered in his ear. "You can go if you want to."

"Not yet," he said.

He was vaguely aware that he could hear Bricker snoring already.

"Does it feel good?" Amye asked.

He nodded. "But slow down," he said.

"I don't think so." Teasing him. Proving she was in control.

"I'm gonna lose it," he said.

"That's the point, isn't it?"

He held on. Held on.

"Slow down," he said again.

She shook her head and didn't slow down. She kept moving at the same rhythmic speed and Creed could hardly stand it. He was afraid to even move or he'd be done.

She gently grabbed his earlobe with her teeth, and then began to kiss his ear.

"Oh, Jesus," he said.

"Don't worry about me," she said. "You go."

He shook his head.

"You're stubborn," she said.

He ran his hands along her back and down over her buttocks. Great body. Firm.

She kissed him hard, then slipped her tongue inside his mouth.

He crossed the point of no return.

9

He woke and the clock read 2:13.

Something wasn't right.

Had he heard something? Had it been a dream? Someone in an adjoining room?

"Stop it!"

A woman's voice, hissing.

There was a woman beside him. That's right. Amye.

"I said I don't want to."

But it wasn't Amye's voice. She was asleep. Unmoving. Creed was groggy. Trying to figure it out.

"Quit!"

It was Debbi. The brunet with Bricker.

"What the fuck's your problem?" Bricker said.

Debbi cried out in pain and Creed woke fully in an instant.

He sprung out of bed, still naked, still drunk. It was dark in the room now and he couldn't tell exactly what was happening. He stumbled toward the door and flipped the light switch just as he heard a slap.

Debbi shrieked.

The next twenty seconds was chaos. Debbi crying and yelling at Bricker. Creed asking what the fuck happened. Amye quickly gathering their things, wrapping Debbi in a blanket, and taking her out the door. Slamming it closed behind them.

Creed looked at Bricker, who was still in bed, propped on his elbows.

"Well, shit," Bricker said.

"What'd you do?" Creed asked.

He heard a car door slam somewhere outside. Then another.

"Nothing, man," Bricker said. "That bitch is uptight. Good riddance."

"What did you do?" Creed said, his teeth clenched.

"I told you. Nothing."

"You fell asleep on her earlier—"

"Shit if I did."

"—and when you woke up just now, you wanted to prove you—"

Squealing tires interrupted him, and then everything was silent.

"Did you slap her?" Creed asked.

Bricker shook his head—not denying it, but more like it wasn't worth talking about.

"Did you fucking slap her or not?" Creed asked.

"You heard her freaking. She deserved it."

Creed didn't think about what he was about to do, he just did it. Took two big steps over to Bricker's bed and drove his right fist square into Bricker's face. Creed could feel the impact of his knuckles on flesh and bone, and he liked it. Bricker let out a grunt and tried to raise his hands to defend himself, but Creed was already driving his fist downward again, this time catching Bricker in the bridge of the nose. It was a heavy blow and it knocked Bricker out cold.

Creed towered over him, breathing rapidly, his heart hammering. He could feel a sharp pain in his right hand, just below the wrist.

He stood quietly and listened for ten seconds. He heard nothing. There was a chance nobody else in the motel had heard anything, considering that air conditioner units were running hard in every room, masking outside noises.

Bricker was still limp. Unmoving. It was like he was dead.

Like he was dead.

Creed realized this was the opportunity he needed, handed to him by two drunk college girls. Wasn't it? How long should he think about it? He'd been thinking too much. Time to act.

He placed one knee on Bricker's bed and wrapped both hands loosely around Bricker's throat. It felt good. It felt *right*, as if everything that had happened so far had been leading up to this.

Creed began to squeeze, tighter and tighter, and he didn't stop until Bricker was gone.

9

He waited thirty minutes, just in case anyone else in the motel had heard the commotion and was sitting by their window, waiting to see what might happen next. Unlikely, but why risk it? Longest half-hour of his life, knowing that Debbi and Amye might've called 911. Cops could show up at any minute.

But they didn't.

Did that mean the girls weren't going to call it in? Possibly. Whatever Bricker had tried with Debbi, she'd stopped him. Now they'd just want to put the whole sordid episode behind them. Calling the cops meant all their friends and family members would eventually learn what they'd done—banging two older guys in a motel room. What decent, God-fearing small-town girl would do that? No, Creed was betting they'd already made another pact—to never tell another soul what had taken place in this motel room.

Bricker's body was right where Creed had left it on the bed. The surprising thing was that his eyes were closed. Creed always figured eyes stayed open when someone was dead.

"You brought it on yourself," Creed said.

Bricker didn't reply.

"I think I broke my hand, thanks to you," Creed said.

Bricker remained silent.

Creed knew he had to move the body before daylight. Couldn't wait until tomorrow night.

Think. Don't blow this. Don't do anything stupid.

He got dressed and quietly exited the room, closing the door behind him. Stood on the sidewalk. Looked left, then right. No security cameras that he could see.

Everything was quiet. No lights showing from any of the rooms. Just a few security lights along the sidewalk and in the parking lot.

The motel was L-shaped, and his room was in the lower part of the L. The office was at the top of the L, near the highway.

He walked to his left, then made a right turn and approached the office.

Now he saw it. One exterior camera, aimed at the swinging glass door to the office. Probably another camera inside the office, but that didn't matter. What mattered was that there were no other cameras aimed at any of the rooms, or at the parking lot.

Perfect.

He went back into the room and sat on the edge of the bed, thinking.

How would he do this? Wrap the body up in a sheet and carry it to the BMW as quickly as possible? Dump it in the trunk? It might be his only choice, given the limited resources inside the motel room—but what if someone in another room just happened to glance outside when he was doing it?

He could think of one other option, but it was almost too gruesome to consider. Carry the body to the bathtub and cut it into pieces. Arms. Legs. Torso, with head attached. Creed had butchered deer before, and he had a strong stomach, but Jesus Christ, he couldn't do it to a human being.

And now he thought of a third option. Leave the body right where it was and call the cops. Tell them he'd reacted in the heat of the moment, after Bricker had tried to force himself on Debbi, and he must've punched him harder than he intended. Or even say Bricker took the first swing. Would they believe him? He'd have the girls to back him up. But would the cops eventually connect him and Bricker to Danny Ray Watts?

He needed to think it through just a little. He had time.

9

When he woke up, slowly, not remembering yet what had happened, he realized the room was much lighter than it had been before. Past sunrise. He could hear people talking right outside his room.

Then panic shot through him like an electric current.

He'd fallen asleep.

He sat up straight in bed, still dressed in the clothes he'd put on last night, and looked to his left.

"Oh, Jesus," he muttered. "No fucking way."

It couldn't possibly be true.

Bricker's bed was empty.

24

WHAT DID it mean?

Where was he now?

Bricker was still alive, obviously. The choking hadn't worked.

Creed felt fortunate that Bricker hadn't killed him in his sleep. He could've done exactly that, with ease. Stick that big knife between Creed's ribs and give it a twist. Or slit his throat.

Creed rose carefully from the bed and listened. His heart was beating like a goddamn tractor piston. Was Bricker in the bathroom? Creed took two quiet steps on the carpet, and now he could see that the bathroom door was open and the light was off. He forced himself to look inside, including behind the shower curtain, and it was empty.

He went back into the room. Now he realized that all of Bricker's belongings were gone. No wallet or cell phone on the nightstand. No big knife in its leather holster.

This was crazy.

Where was he?

Creed had another moment of instantaneous dread. What about the BMW? He quickly crossed the room and peeked through the curtains. Oh, thank God. It was parked right where they'd left it. He didn't see any flat tires or broken windows.

What time was it? He turned and saw the clock. Almost nine in the morning.

Creed had no idea what to think. Or what to do.

His phone was in his jeans pocket, where he'd left it for nearly 24 hours without checking it, just to avoid Dickie. Now he didn't have any choice but to take a look, and sure enough, there was several texts from his brother. All of them were asking Creed to call him. Some of them sounded urgent.

There was also several voicemails waiting. The first one was from

Dickie, and he'd left it last night at 6:23.

Hey, I wish you'd call me back, or at least text me, but I guess you're tied up with something. Listen, you remember hearing about that man that went missing near Skeet's place when we were there this weekend? The sheriff—guy named Garza—called to ask me some questions about it, but obviously I don't know anything about it, so please give him a call, would ya? He probably wants to talk to you, too, since you were there. I think they're calling everybody who was at the party. Guess they haven't found the guy yet. Anyway, please take care of that for me, because I'm busy writing all day for the Houston show and don't really want to deal with it. Okay, thanks. Later, bro.

Everything about his tone was strange, and Creed knew exactly what it was. Dickie was speaking as if he knew that anything he said might be heard by the cops at some point. They might get a warrant for the voicemails, so he was trying to sound casual. And innocent. Also, Dickie never called Creed "bro." And he never asked politely for Creed to complete various tasks, he bossed him around like an asshole. Rarely said "please" or "thanks."

Right after that, there was a message from Skeet Carrasco at 9:45.

It's Skeet, and I wanted you to know I just gave your phone number to a game warden here in Blanco County. He's working with the sheriff's department on finding that poor guy who went missing last Friday night, and they still haven't found him, so they're wanting to talk to everybody who was at my place. Just routine, but I guess they haven't talked to you yet, so somebody will be calling, and I think they've already tried to reach Dickie. I know y'all get a lot of calls and you're busy getting ready for Houston, but if you see a call from the 830 area code, you might want to take that and help them out. Well, I guess you can't really help them out, but let them ask their questions so they can move on with their investigation. Anyway, that's what's going on. Hey, it was good seeing you, by the way. We need to get together more often. Come see me. Wish I could make it to the Houston show, but I'm tied up with this deal I'm working in Dallas. I'll talk to you later.

Same weird tone of voice that Dickie had. Not being himself. Playing for an audience.

Creed had several other voicemails, some from numbers he didn't recognize, but all of them were business related, not from a game warden.

And none from Bricker. Creed had almost been hoping Bricker had left a message, so Creed would at least know what he was up to. It was worse to know that Bricker was out there, royally pissed off, and probably planning some sort of revenge for what Creed had done.

What would Bricker do?

Was there a chance he would do nothing at all?

Possible, but not likely. He was a little fucking maniac. Those types didn't just fade into the night. A guy like Bricker might—

Creed's phone rang in his hand and made him jump.

Another number he didn't know, and yes, it was from the 830 area code. Probably the game warden or someone from the sheriff's office.

Creed didn't answer. Not right now. No damn way. He needed to get his shit together before he could even think about talking to a cop.

He went to get some ice for his aching hand.

g

"I'm gonna get me one of the Ultimate Meat and Cheese Breakfast burritos," Billy Don said.

"Just one?" Red said.

"Okay, three," Billy Don said. "Want anything?"

"Yeah, I guess."

They were back at the Sonic in Fredericksburg, in the parking slot the farthest away from the restaurant itself, hoping to talk to the red-haired carhop again. They'd driven for 30 minutes—in Billy Don's Ranchero again—just to see the carhop. Red had been craning his neck to watch out the back window, but he hadn't spotted her yet.

It would be a real hassle if the redhead wasn't here. What was her name again? He wanted to ask her something. He wanted to ask her to *do* something. To help him out of this bad situation.

"Oh, you should try the Pancake on a Stick," Billy Don said. "Looks like a corndog, but it's actually a pancake wrapped around a link of sausage."

"That's fine."

"Or the French Toast Sticks."

"Either one. I don't care."

Billy Don pushed the red button beneath the menu.

"Want me to ask for her?"

Lydia. That was her name.

"No, that would be kind of weird," Red said. "But if she doesn't bring our food, we can ask the gal who does. Seems more casual that way. Like 'Oh, hey, is Lydia working today?'"

"Thanks for the acting lesson," Billy Don said.

Welcome to Sonic. May I take your order?

g

Tino Herrera knew he should tell the truth—the *full* truth—but he wasn't prepared to do that just yet. That would mean he and Mandy would both be in trouble, and he didn't want to get her into trouble. She was too sweet. And she had such spectacular feet. He wanted to continue to fondle those feet on a regular basis. Yes, there were other women available, many with adorable feet, but Tino ranked Mandy's feet right up there with the best he had ever had the pleasure to caress.

At the same time, Tino knew he had put himself in the middle of a bad situation, and it unnerved him enough that he'd hardly worked up enough enthusiasm to flirt with the lovely middle-aged ladies who had walked in a few minutes earlier, just after Tino had unlocked the doors. Both of the ladies had rings on their fingers, which never deterred Tino. What did stop him was the sight of the Blanco County sheriff, Bobby Garza, pulling into the parking lot.

Maybe it was a sign. Maybe it was time to spill it all.

Tino waited, watching from behind the counter, until the sheriff exited his SUV. Now Tino felt an urge to duck into the rear of the restaurant and avoid Garza altogether, but Tino's car was parked out front, so what was the point?

Instead, Tino did the opposite. He greeted the sheriff enthusiastically the moment he walked through the door.

The sheriff said, "Let's talk outside for a minute."

So Tino followed him. What choice did he have? They stood beside the driver's door to Garza's vehicle. Tino wondered if perhaps the sheriff had chosen this spot on purpose—right out front where anyone passing by on Main Street could see that Tino was being questioned by the police.

"Mr. Herrera," Garza said, "I wanted to say I appreciated the additional information you gave me yesterday—about seeing that red truck near Dub's place on Friday night, and about the threat he made."

"Have you talked to him?" Tino asked. He almost slipped and called the man by name. Red O'Brien. But Tino wasn't supposed to know that name. He was only supposed to know that he saw a man in an old red truck on Friday night, and that same man had shown up at the Dairy Queen and threatened him. It was true, he *had* seen the man, but Tino had been the one fleeing. Mandy had told him who the man was and about the dispute between that man and Dub.

"We're still looking into it," Garza said. "And that's why I feel the need to tell you something. I've been in law enforcement for a damn long time. I've seen just about everything, and I've talked to thousands of people over the years. What amazes me, over and over again, is how many people think they can make up stories without getting caught. But they rarely do. You follow me?"

"I think so."

"The changes in technology alone make it harder for anyone to be less than honest," Garza said. "Cell phones, GPS, all that stuff."

"Yes," Tino said. "I understand. That's why, the first time we talked, I told you that Mandy once fired a shot at Dub. Because I am honest and wanted you to know the truth."

The sheriff had no way of knowing that Tino and Mandy had agreed, even before the cops had approached Tino, that it would be better for him to share that information—because all of Dub's friends knew about that incident, and they would certainly tell the police about it. It would look better coming from Tino. It would make him appear trustworthy.

"I appreciate that, but I'm not positive you told me everything," the sheriff said.

He stared at Tino.

Tino wondered what Garza had learned.

"I did tell the truth," Tino said, and his voice sounded weak.

Garza shook his head, as if disappointed. "This is the last chance you're going to get. You can correct what you've already told us, and add what you've left out, and then walk away from this in good shape. But after this conversation, all bets are off. I won't cut you any slack. If you have information and you don't share it, I will come after you hard."

"I understand."

"You were with Conrad on Thursday night, not Friday night."

So that's what it was. Conrad had turned on him. That bastard. Tino tried to appear confused. "That doesn't sound right."

"But it is. And now I have enough probable cause to get your cell phone location data and prove it. Same with Friday night. You said you drove over to Dub's place, pulled into the driveway, and then left immediately. But the data will tell us if you were there longer. You see where this is going?"

"Yes, sir."

"Then tell me what really happened," Garza said.

"My memory isn't always great," Tino said. "I worked on Thursday and Friday."

"How long did you stay at Dub's and Mandy's on Friday night? You didn't turn around in the driveway, did you? You parked and stayed longer than that."

"I can't remember," Tino said.

"Come on, Tino," Garza said. "You need to tell me what really happened. You got out of your car, didn't you?"

"I think instead I would rather not talk to you anymore," Tino said. "Not without an attorney."

25

LYDIA WAS RUNNING LATE, but she would be here any minute. That was according to the girl who'd brought Red's and Billy Don's food. So now they were eating slowly and waiting for her to arrive.

Red was still thinking about the strange visit from the game warden the morning before. Why had John Marlin been so interested in hearing about Red's encounter with Dickie Loftin on Friday night? He'd had one idea, and it seemed crazy, but was it possible the comedian had something to do with Dub Kimble's disappearance? Ultimately, Red had dismissed that idea, because a rich guy like Dickie Loftin could just buy his way out of trouble. It was the American way. Rich people hardly ever had to pay the price for—

"There she is," Billy Don said.

An older brown Toyota had just pulled into the lot, with Lydia behind the wheel, and now she was parking in a spot back near the dumpster, in a row where the employees parked.

When she stepped out, Red said, "Hey, Lydia."

She didn't hear.

"Lydia!" Red hissed louder.

She still didn't look this way.

So Billy Don laid on the Ranchero's horn.

"Way to keep it subtle," Red said.

"She's looking, ain't she?"

First thing that morning, Marlin had contemplated the idea of driving to Stephenville and attempting to locate Dickie Loftin's Hummer. Check it for front-end damage. But that very well could be a waste of time. What were the odds he could actually get a look at it? If

138 | BEN REHDER

the Hummer was damaged, Loftin would have it tucked away somewhere, and Marlin would need a warrant to see it. Besides, the hefty grill guard meant Loftin could hit something fairly substantial—a deer or pig or a human being—and not sustain any damage. Blood could be wiped away.

Call Creed Loftin again? Wouldn't do any good.

So Marlin chose a different option. He went into his office, shut the door, and turned out the lights. Took a seat behind his desk and closed his eyes. He needed some quiet time. Let his mind wander over all the possibilities, because he knew the answer was out there. It almost always was.

At this point, he had no idea whether the apparent death and disappearance of Dub Kimble was an accident or not, but there had certainly been a cover-up, which included moving the body.

But who did it? The list of prime suspects was now fairly short. Four people.

Mandy Hammerschmitt made the list because she'd fought with Dub that night, and she'd taken a shot at him—or at least tried to scare him by shooting in his direction—in the past. Plus, Dub had cheated on her, and Mandy herself had a secret boyfriend, and that sort of domestic discord often led to violent behavior. Mandy had appeared genuinely distraught when they'd questioned her, but her emotions could've been the result of fear—concern about getting caught.

Tino Herrera was higher on the list. Equally plausible, too, if not more so. Tino was the angry secret lover who decided to confront the abusive boyfriend. He'd lied about his whereabouts that night, and he'd tried to create an alibi that didn't hold up. And now Marlin wondered if Tino had been trying to divert attention away from himself when he'd told Marlin and Garza about the shot Mandy had fired at Dub. Perhaps Tino cared for Mandy enough that he had been willing to stand up to Dub, but when it came to the possibility of prison, well, she was on her own, then. That was a solid theory. Same reason Tino had mentioned seeing Red O'Brien—to offer alternative suspects.

Then there were the Loftin brothers. They were suspects simply because they'd been in Johnson City Friday night, and Skeet Carrasco hadn't mentioned it. Skeet had also left Creed off the guest list, which could have been an oversight, but what if it wasn't? Had he been trying to hide the fact that Creed was in the area that night? Was that why he had brought up Lester Higgs? And the fact that neither Dickie nor Creed had answered or returned any phone calls didn't make them appear any more innocent. Could one of them—or both of them, together—have hit Dub with the Hummer? Why had they gone into Johnson City? Was

Skeet covering for them?

Marlin could hear other people moving around outside his office in the sheriff's department, but he remained blessedly undisturbed. No ringing phone. No knocks on his door.

Skeet Carrasco. Big-time car guy. Maybe there was something in the fact that Carrasco had a small automotive empire at his disposal. If Dickie or Creed Loftin damaged the Hummer on Friday night, Carrasco could've had it repaired good as new the next morning. Make some calls and employees would hop to it. They'd bring the appropriate tools and materials and get it done immediately, right there at the ranch.

Interesting, but there was no indication the Hummer had been damaged. Just an ATV. Probably unrelated.

And now Marlin remembered something. He opened his eyes and sat up straight. Skeet Carrasco had said on the phone that he was buying a Kawasaki dealership. Kawasaki manufactured ATVs. So Marlin had to wonder: Did Carrasco own a blue four-wheeler?

9

"I'm hoping you might do a favor for me," Red said from the Ranchero's passenger seat, and he wasn't surprised when Lydia looked at him with suspicion.

"Depends on what it is," she said, standing just outside his window. "And please don't even ask if it's, like, weird."

Red liked this girl. She could handle herself. Had an attitude.

"Ever hear of a guy named Dub Kimble?" he asked.

"Don't think so," Lydia said. "Hey, what size engine does this have in it?"

"Got a 351," Billy Don said from the driver's seat, with his mouth full.

"Tryin' to show everyone your breakfast?" Red asked.

"Nope," Billy Don said. "Just you."

"Sweet ride," Lydia said. "Restore it yourself?"

"Dealer did."

"Oh, God, is that an eight-track player?" Lydia asked.

"Yeah, and *that* I put in myself," Billy Don said.

"That is so awesome. Old school."

"Found it on eBay and—"

"Dub lives west of Johnson City," Red said. "Except he went missing on Friday night."

"Oh, I think I heard something about that," Lydia said. Her phone chimed with a text and she checked it. "Oh, God, Jerry, keep it in your shorts. My manager is watching me, wondering what I'm doing out here." She began to type a reply. "He's had a big stick up his butt ever since he got promoted. He's like twenty-three years old and suddenly acts like a cranky old man."

Billy Don chuckled about that between bites of his third breakfast burrito.

"So," Red said, "on this thing with Dub Kimble, did you hear that Tino is a suspect?"

Lydia looked up with wide eyes, grinning. "No way!"

"It's true," Red said.

"Oh, my God! That's why the cops were there the other day! He told everybody it was about an unpaid speeding ticket. What a jerk."

"Not just a jerk, a suspect, because supposably he was sleeping with the girlfriend of the guy who went missing."

"That doesn't surprise me at all. He'll sleep with anybody, whether they're married or not, as long as he likes their feet. I'm surprised he hasn't been shot. Jeez, he is such a friggin' slut."

"I've been wondering about that," Billy Don said. "Guys can be sluts?"

"Sure they can," Lydia said. "Why should that word apply only to females? Why is there a double standard?"

Billy Don laughed, until he realized she was waiting for an answer. He said, "Hey, no argument from me. If you say Tino's a slut, he's a slut."

"Can we just focus for a minute?" Red said. "On the favor? Please?"

"Which is what, exactly?" Lydia asked.

"Wish I was a slut," Billy Don mumbled.

"Okay," Red said. "Well, the other part of the equation that you should know is that I'm a suspect too, because the missing guy was maybe gonna sue me."

"Oh, this is good," Lydia said. "So much more interesting than the regular boring crap around here. Did you kill him?"

"What?" Red said. "Of course not. They don't even know for sure he's dead."

"How long has he been missing?" Lydia asked.

"Since Friday night," Red said.

"Then he's probably dead," Lydia said. "Gotta be. Unless he ran off for some reason."

Now Red liked Lydia even more, because she was a quick thinker. He'd never pondered the possibility that Dub had run off. Red didn't think it was likely, but he couldn't rule it out, either.

"Whatever it was," Red said, "I didn't do it, and I don't know nothin' about it."

"Why was he gonna sue you?" Lydia asked.

"He was helping me build an elevated home—"

"Tree house," Billy Don said.

"—but he fell and hurt himself," Red said. "Blamed it on me instead of the dozen beers he'd drunk that afternoon."

"Better all around if you don't let your work crew get inebriated," Lydia said.

"Or drunk," Billy Don added. "Just saying."

"And so now the cops think you killed him because of that?" Lydia asked Red.

"Red's paranoid," Billy Don said.

"Oh yeah?" Red said. "Then why have they come out to talk to me twice?"

"One of them times was a game warden," Billy Don said, "so that don't hardly count."

"Game wardens are real cops!" Red insisted. "They can arrest you and take your guns and stuff. You know that as good as I do."

By now Lydia was eyeballing them as if she wasn't sure what to think.

"Back to the matter at hand," Red said. "Tino's a suspect and I'm a suspect and there's a couple other people that're suspects, but since I saw Tino near Dub's place on Friday night—"

"Wait, tell me about that," Lydia said.

So Red did—the full story, from start to finish, leaving nothing out and being completely honest. No reason to keep anything from her.

When he was done, she was just about to say something when her phone chimed again and she checked it.

"Jerry again?" Red said.

"Yeah."

"I'll take care of this," Billy Don said. He pushed the red button, and when a man asked for his order, Billy Don said, "Lydia just talked me into getting ten more breakfast burritos."

Lydia giggled.

"Ten? Really?" the man asked.

"That's Jerry," Lydia whispered.

"You bet. She's quite a salesman," Billy Don said.

"Saleswoman," Lydia said.

"Okay, they'll be right out," Jerry said.

Billy Don looked at Red and Lydia and shrugged. "I can freeze 'em. Breakfast all week."

"Or two days," Red said. "Anyway, back to the favor…"

"Spit it out, dude," Lydia said.

"I want you to talk to Tino, if he'll talk to you—"

"Oh, he'll talk to me," Lydia said.

"And then maybe you could try to get him to tell you anything he might know about—"

"I'm in."

"I haven't finished."

"You want me to find out if Tino had anything to do with that guy going missing, or if he knows anything about it."

"Exactly."

"You want me to be a spy."

"Kind of, yeah."

"I will totally do it."

"You will?"

"Absolutely." It was obvious that Lydia was thrilled with the idea. She wanted to pay Tino back for jilting her at the prom.

One thing Red had learned growing up in Johnson City—and he figured it was the same in every small town in America, including Fredericksburg—was that people had a hard time keeping their mouths shut. If some juicy piece of gossip was floating around, you could be certain that it would spread faster than butter on a hot skillet. If Tino wasn't directly involved with Dub's disappearance, there was a good chance he knew who was.

"Might all of us get into a little trouble," Red said to Lydia, because he felt he should warn her of the risks. "Cops don't like sovereign citizens poking around in this kind of stuff."

"Doesn't matter," Lydia said. "Count me in. Totally."

26

SURE ENOUGH, the call from the 830 area code was from the game warden, and he left a message, but it was short and to the point.

This is Blanco County Game Warden John Marlin calling. Please call me back as soon as possible. It's important. Thanks.

Creed deleted it.

He had more important things on his mind. Chiefly Bricker. No sign of him after an hour. No calls or texts. The tension was fucking unbearable. Creed knew he'd have to look over his shoulder for a long time to come, waiting for the moment when Bricker would come for him. Or, worse, he might send someone else instead. A total stranger might walk up and bust a cap into Creed's forehead. Could happen tomorrow. Or a year from now.

Shit.

Creed had no idea what to do, so he packed up his stuff and left the motel. Took a right out of the parking lot and headed north, planning to start the drive back to Stephenville. Then he noticed he needed gas, so he turned around and went back into Johnson City.

Just as he pulled into the Exxon on the east side of Highway 281, he saw Bricker walking south out of the parking lot.

9

Johnson City was a surprisingly busy little town. Lots of traffic flowing through all the major intersections, and plenty of vehicles parked in front of every business that appeared to be open on a Tuesday morning.

Bricker had to be patient, waiting outside the Exxon gas station and convenience store, even though he was seething. About to totally lose it. Go on a goddamn rampage and make the national news. Blaze of glory. Tempting as hell. But if he did that, he wouldn't have a chance to pay Creed back. And there would be payback. Total and complete annihilation. He'd almost shot Creed in the head while he was sleeping, but that wasn't good enough, and it would've been sloppy. High risk. So he'd resisted the urge.

He'd walked over here just minutes earlier, needing a cup of coffee and some aspirin, because his head was pounding. The alcohol, yeah, and the fucking sucker punches. One cheek was swollen and his eye was starting to bruise. Plus, his neck was aching, like maybe Creed had throttled him when he was unconscious. Bastard.

Bricker finished the coffee and tossed the cup in a nearby trashcan.

He needed a vehicle, obviously. Problem was, he had about sixty bucks in his wallet. Should've insisted that Creed pay him up front, or at least half of it. Five thousand dollars would've done the trick.

He walked south—away from the Exxon, and away from the motel. Passed another little motel, a barbecue joint that wasn't open yet, and an antique store. Kept walking along a chain link fence with a bunch of trees on the other side. Came to the Lowe's Market, which had a Subway sandwich shop beside it, and a Dollar General, and a bank out front, and directly across the highway was the sheriff's office, which meant he should keep walking.

Passed an RV park, and then a Laundromat, and then a self-storage facility, and that was about it. Edge of town.

He looked across the highway again and saw a place called Whittington's Jerky. He and Creed had passed it several times in the past few days and it was always crowded, as it was now. Too crowded. Too many witnesses.

He turned and went back the way he had come—passed the self-storage facility and the Laundromat, and the RV park—and then he veered right into the parking lot toward the Lowe's Market. Then he veered further right, past the gas pumps near the highway, angling toward the Subway shop and the Dollar General. He needed a goddamn ride.

Dollar General was open, and the timing couldn't have been any more perfect, because as Bricker approached the store, he passed a green Nissan—and he noticed that the keys were hanging in the ignition. The owner had gone inside and hadn't considered the possibility that someone like Bricker might be hanging around.

9

Creed was trying to be inconspicuous while keeping tabs on Bricker.

Where would he go? What would he do? One thing was for sure: Keeping Bricker in sight felt so much better than not knowing where he was.

After spotting Bricker, Creed had pulled out of the Exxon and crossed the road to the Dairy Queen. From there, Creed could see down a long, straight section of road, and he watched with binoculars until Bricker was almost out of sight. Just as Creed had prepared to pull out of the DQ and move further south, Bricker had turned around and begun walking back in this direction. Then he took a right into the parking lot of the Lowe's Market, on the other side of the highway.

Creed drove slowly south, past the sheriff's office, and pulled into a small propane store directly across from Lowe's Market. Stopped in a shady area that offered a little bit of concealment.

Raised the binoculars and saw Bricker again. What the hell was he doing? Stopping at a green car. Then Bricker casually climbed into the car…and drove away.

He'd stolen the car, just like that.

Creed watched as Bricker crossed the parking lot, about to enter Highway 281.

Please take a left. Please go south.

Bricker waited for traffic to clear, and then he took a left.

Creed let out a sigh of relief.

It appeared Bricker was going home, back to Austin. At a minimum, he wasn't going to Stephenville. Not right now.

Was he giving up? Or was he simply regrouping? Biding his time? A moment later, the Nissan was nothing but a dot way down the highway. Then it was gone.

Creed didn't see any benefit in following. He pulled onto the highway and went north.

27

IN TEXAS, all-terrain vehicles were titled, but not registered. That meant there was no database Marlin could search to determine if Skeet Carrasco owned any ATVs. So he decided to do it the most direct and old-fashioned way. He called Carrasco, who answered on the first ring.

Marlin said, "Mr. Carrasco—"

"Please, call me Skeet. How ya doing this morning, John?"

Marlin could tell that Carrasco was using the hands-free features inside a moving vehicle, which matched Carrasco's claim that he had a meeting in Dallas today.

"I'm doing just fine. Mind if I ask you a question?"

"What's up?"

"Do you own any ATVs?"

"Uh, well, sure. When you own a ranch, they're a necessity, especially when you've got hunters coming out."

"What make are they?"

"Kawasaki. Great ATVs, which is why I decided to branch out with the new dealership."

"The model?"

"Let's see. Brute Force 300."

"What color are they?"

"Uh, sort of blue."

"All of them?"

"Yes. They're identical."

"How many do you own?"

"How many?"

"Yes, please."

"I believe it's three."

"You're not certain how many you own?"

Carrasco chuckled. "That sounds terrible, doesn't it? Man can't even keep track of his own possessions. Reason I say that is, I know I owned four at one point, because I got a good deal for buying in quantity, but I believe it's just three now."

Marlin could feel a tingle on the back of his neck. He was onto something.

"What happened to the fourth one?" Marlin asked.

"Karl told me the engine seized up, so I told him to scrap it or sell it for parts or whatever. He hauled it off."

Karl Hines was Carrasco's part-time employee—not a full ranch manager, but someone who took care of odds and ends a few days a week. Marlin had met Hines on a couple of occasions—a tall, taciturn man who didn't readily cooperate with government officials. He had two bumper stickers on the rear of his truck—one for the National Weapons Alliance and one that read AMERICA FIRST.

"The engine just seized up?" Marlin said. "Without any warning?"

"Yeah, it got a sudden oil leak when a guest hit the oil pan on a rock. Funny how that happens. He didn't know any better and kept riding it."

"Expensive mistake."

"You got that right."

"When was this?"

"Pardon?"

"When did Karl haul away the ATV?"

"Couple of weeks ago—or at least that's when I asked him to do it. Don't know when he got around to it. May I ask what this is all about? Why the interest in my four-wheelers?"

"Just background information," Marlin said. "Who was the guest?"

"Who?"

"Right. The guest who was riding the ATV when it seized up. Who was it?"

Carrasco had been doing his best to appear unflappable as he answered Marlin's questions, but now he took a long pause, and then he said, "All due respect, I've been trying to cooperate since Friday night, but I'm not one of those people who gives in to intimidation, even by law enforcement. You're not going to bulldoze me. I'm too stubborn for it."

"I wasn't trying to—"

"You were badgering me," Carrasco said. "I know it when I see it, and I don't appreciate it. If you were one of my salesmen, that would get you fired *muy pronto*."

Carrasco was creating a phony excuse to end the interview. Feigned umbrage. Marlin needed to head it off.

"Well, if it came across that way, I apologize. I was just trying to—"

"I'm afraid I've had enough for today."

"Skeet, if you'd just let me—"

"You can call me Mr. Carrasco. Better yet, don't call me at all."

He hung up.

Marlin quickly opened the address book on his computer and found Karl Hines's phone number, but when he dialed it, his call went straight to voicemail. Hines was probably talking to his boss at that very moment.

Marlin jumped online and searched for *kawasaki brute force 300*.

He clicked on a page from a dealer out of Austin and saw that the Brute Force 300 was in the middle of the spectrum as far as price. About five grand apiece on the low end, and up to nine grand with all the bells and whistles. So Skeet Carrasco had spent a total of at least $20,000, and maybe up to $36,000, for ATVs that were likely no more than toys for his guests.

Marlin opened the photos he'd taken of the ATV fender fragment he'd found along the county road, and he began to compare them to photos of the Brute Force 300 on the dealer's site. He studied the part from all possible angles.

Granted, most ATV fenders looked somewhat similar, but from what Marlin could tell, the fragment he had found along the county road perfectly matched the fender of a Brute Force 300.

Outstanding.

Marlin called Karl Hines a second time, and then a third, leaving messages each time, but Hines didn't call back.

Marlin jumped into his truck and started toward Hines's place, a small brick home on Avenue Q, on the west side of Johnson City. As he drove, he called Bobby Garza, who was on his way back from Fredericksburg. Marlin quickly described his conversation with Carrasco, including the abrupt ending.

Garza said, "We need to press Carrasco and Hines as hard as possible—see where it leads."

"On it," Marlin said.

"Funny thing is, Tino just shut down on me, too. I told him I was getting a warrant for his cell phone and that was the final straw. No more questions without a lawyer."

Marlin had to remind himself that innocent people sometimes behaved in ways you wouldn't expect—such as refusing to answer questions—and maybe that's what Tino and Carrasco were both doing.

"I want to get a warrant to see Carrasco's ATVs, and another one to search Karl Hines's place for the missing ATV—this afternoon, if possible," Marlin said

"I'd guess the judge is going to be hard to convince on that one," Garza said. "But it can't hurt to try."

"I figure Hines has—or had—the ATV, or Carrasco totally made that up on the fly and now he's scrambling to get Hines to play along with it."

"That possibility right there is why the judge probably won't grant your warrant," Garza said. "In fact, maybe we should hold off on that, because if we get a warrant and the evidence gets tossed later…"

Garza had a good point. If they found the ATV under a warrant that was later deemed faulty, it would be like they hadn't found it at all, and they wouldn't have the chance to find it a second time. Skeet Carrasco would make sure of that.

"Going to ask Hines some questions and see where that leads," Marlin said as he turned onto Avenue Q. Hines's home was on a small lot with no fence and few trees.

Garza said, "Hang on a second. Lauren is on the other line. She's at the hospital with Danny Ray Watts."

"I'll hold," Marlin said.

As he neared Hines's place, he saw no vehicles parked out front. The home had no garage, just a little carport, currently empty, so it appeared nobody was home. Marlin pulled to the side of the road and stopped directly in front of the residence, intending to make his presence immediately visible.

Where was Hines?

Marlin stepped from his truck and walked to the front door. Knocked twice, waited, but got no answer. Knocked again. Went back to his truck and circled the block. From Avenue O, he had a clear view into Hines's backyard. A small shed occupied one rear corner of Hines's lot, and parked directly behind that shed was an ATV—a Kawasaki Brute Force 300. Was it damaged? From this distance, Marlin couldn't tell. He grabbed his binoculars and scoped it out.

"Yes," Marlin said quietly.

The right rear fender had a large chunk missing—the piece he'd found beside the county road—but there was also damage to the front end, including a bent cargo rack and a flat tire. Just then, Garza came back on the phone. Marlin had forgotten he was on hold.

The sheriff said, "Hang on to your britches, because Danny Ray Watts just came around and you won't believe what he told Lauren."

28

BEFORE MEETING TINO, Lydia had never thought much about her feet. Sure, she painted her nails occasionally, usually a fun, vibrant color, and she was satisfied in general with their appearance. Her feet weren't unusually long or wide or hairy. Her toes tapered nicely from the largest to the smallest. But were her feet sexy? Would guys notice them the same way they drooled over boobs or butts or legs? That hadn't been her experience. Guys weren't into feet.

Then she met Tino.

The first thing he'd ever said to her, while she was sitting in a booth at Dairy Queen, had been, "Ooh, I love your Candie's."

It had taken her a moment to realize he was referring to the cherry-red wedge sandals she was wearing. With matching toenail polish, of course.

"Oh, thanks," she said, totally thrown by his comment, because how often did men in Fredericksburg, Texas, notice the shoes a girl was wearing?

Was it just a line? A way to set himself apart? Maybe, but she didn't care, because he was hella cute. They continued to make small talk, and all the while, Tino kept stealing quick glances at her feet. At first she thought it was a nervous tic —he was looking downward because he couldn't maintain eye contact—but, no, he was definitely checking out her feet.

Okay. Whatever. Maybe he just liked shoes. Nothing wrong with that. It would be her little secret that she'd bought the Candie's for seven dollars at Goodwill.

Then he asked her out, and she jumped at the chance. This guy was so unlike the other men in town.

On their third date, after they'd gone dancing, he offered her a foot massage. What girl doesn't like a foot massage? His hands were so skilled—strong, but gentle—that it wasn't long before she was letting out little grunts and moans of pleasure. Ten minutes later, in a move that totally caught Lydia off guard, Tino wrapped his mouth around one of her big toes and began to gently suckle.

For the first few seconds, she thought it had to be a put-on. She almost giggled. But he kept sucking, with his eyes closed. Then he began to do a little moaning of his own. And here's the thing—it really felt kind of good, and why should she care if his turn-on was a little off the mainstream? She had never been a judgmental girl. Whatever floats your boat, as long as it was all consensual, right? One thing was for sure— now she understood why Tino preferred open-toed footwear.

In the weeks that followed, he did things to and with her toes and feet that she never even discussed with her closest friends. There were long sessions of tender foot care that involved lotions and creams. Tea tree oil. Heel balm. Callus removers and pumice stones. Battery-operated massagers and rolling foot files. For a girl who was on her feet all day, it was, quite frankly, heaven.

As for the kinky side of it, the truth was, she didn't mind broadening her own horizons. What she *did* mind was that when they were out on a date, Tino was frequently distracted by the feet of passing females. No question about that. Constantly checking out their "tootsies." She was amused, at first, until she realized it was no different than him scoping out girls' racks. She called him on it a few times, and he would apologize, but he kept doing it. Fine. Whatever.

Then came prom and that son of a bitch totally ditched her without warning. Never showed up, even though she was waiting in a nice chiffon dress and a dazzling pair of Vince Camuto Peppa sandals in gold leather, another Goodwill score.

She'd waited. And waited. And called. No Tino.

Turned out that lowlife scumbag had gone to the prom with some tramp in Kerrville, thirty minutes southwest of Fredericksburg. Lydia had been furious—murderous, even—but eventually she put it behind her. He wasn't worth it, was he? Most guys weren't.

But somehow talking with those two rednecks had dredged it all up again. Made her remember how mad she'd been. Made her remember what a dog Tino was. Apparently, he hadn't changed, still catting around, using his silver tongue, and wasn't it time for someone to put him in his place?

So, not long after the two rednecks had asked her to spy on Tino, she told Jerry she was having a "female emergency" and rushed home to change clothes. Ten minutes later, she strutted into the Dairy Queen—a place she hadn't entered in two years—wearing her tightest jeans and a low-cut blouse. And her cherry-red Candie's, of course. She'd seen Tino's car parked out front, so she knew he was working.

He was behind the counter when she walked in, and he literally did a double-take. Glanced at her for a split second, looked away, and then looked again with wide eyes, like he was either surprised or scared.

Then his gaze dropped to her feet.

She approached the counter.

"Hey," she said.

Her smile and her body language were doing all the work—telling Tino that everything was cool now, after all this time.

"Hey," he said back, walking over to her.

Fortunately, the place was almost empty and the other employees were gathered together, chatting on the other side of the pass-through window from the kitchen, so they wouldn't be able to hear Lydia's conversation with Tino.

"How's it going?" Lydia asked.

"Great," Tino said. "Is, uh, everything okay?"

Puzzled by her sudden appearance. Not suspicious, though, and that was good.

"Yep, I'm doing great," she said.

"You look great," Tino said. "I mean really great."

"Thanks."

"Love your Candie's," he said, grinning, in an obvious reference to that day they met two years earlier.

"Why, thank you," she said. "They've always been my favorite."

"Mine, too. You, uh, want to order anything?"

"No, not really. Just came in to say hi."

"To me?"

"Yeah, why not?"

"That's, uh…"

"Great?" she said.

The conversation was awkward, but that would have been the case even if she hadn't had a hidden agenda.

"Yes, definitely," he said. "It's great."

She leaned in closer, giving him a good look down her shirt, and his eyes dropped to her cleavage. He had his foot fetish, but that didn't mean he was oblivious to the other parts of a woman's body.

"You know I used to be really mad at you," she said quietly.

He raised his eyes to meet hers. "Yes, I know, and you had every right. I was such a jerk. I'm so sorry about that. Do you know that it still keeps me awake sometimes?"

Ha. What a frigging liar. Same old Tino.

"Aw," she said, "that's sweet that you care that much. But I'm past it now. You can let yourself off the hook."

"That's good to hear," he said.

"It took awhile," she said, "but bygones and all that. And it was high school, you know?"

"I'm so happy to hear that."

She was surprised he wasn't being more aggressive, so she said, "In fact, I was kind of thinking we should get together sometime."

"Oh, wow," he said.

"If you want to," she said.

"Oh, I want to," he said.

"So…"

"The thing is, I'm going away."

"What?"

"I'm going away. For a while, at least."

"Why?"

"It's kind of complicated," he said.

"But where are you going?"

"We're—I'm not sure yet."

We're?

"When?" she said.

"Tonight," he said.

"Oh," she said, trying to sound mildly disappointed, but her mind was spinning. The two rednecks in the truck were right. Something was going on with Tino. Was he running from the law? Did that mean he was guilty? Why would he run if he were innocent?

"But…" he said.

"Yeah?"

"I get off work at eight," he said. "I don't have to close tonight."

What a dog. Hoping to get laid before he left town. She wanted to slap his face, but she also wanted to pay him back for being such a weasel—especially if he was somehow involved in the disappearance of that man.

"So…you want to meet up when you get off work?"

"Yes," he said. "Yes. I would like that. Right when I get off."

Sleazebag. Slimeball. Cheating bastard.

29

"LET'S HEAR IT," Marlin said.

"Watts says he was driving down Kendalia Road, minding his own business, when two men in a BMW started hollering at him, saying he had something stuck underneath his truck. So he pulled over, and when he got out, he recognized one of the men as Creed Loftin. Turns out Watts had also seen the Loftin brothers in Johnson City on Friday night."

Marlin was again parked in front of Karl Hines's house, and now a silver GMC truck slowly passed Marlin's truck and turned into the driveway.

Garza said, "Apparently, just like Red O'Brien, he had an unpleasant encounter with them, which involved Watts yelling a friendly hello at a stoplight, which got him a rude gesture from Dickie in response. This was right around ten o'clock, which would mean it was probably right after they'd run into O'Brien in the Lowe's Market parking lot."

This was extremely valuable information—an impartial witness corroborating O'Brien's claim.

The silver GMC truck reached the end of the driveway and parked under the carport.

"So," Garza said, "after Watts pulled over on Kendalia Road, he says Creed Loftin told him he wanted to apologize for that ugly little incident, and then he said they were thinking about shooting a TV show in this area—and that he was hoping Watts would keep quiet about seeing Dickie, because it was all hush-hush for the time being."

"Which is total BS," Marlin said. "He didn't want word to reach us that they were in Johnson City on Friday night."

Karl Hines stepped from the GMC and stood behind it, staring in Marlin's direction. Hines would have to wait a few minutes.

"Yup," Garza said. "Watts basically told Creed Loftin to shove his apology, even though they were offering him five grand to keep quiet, and then there were some words back and forth. Then the little guy with Creed pulled a gun and shot Watts. No warning whatsoever—went straight from angry words to the shooting. Watts fell to the ground and played dead, and he could hear the little guy bragging about the shot he'd made, and saying Watts was nothing but trouble and deserved it. Then the little guy started asking Creed if he wanted to leave the body or haul it off. Creed started freaking out, asking the little guy why he'd done it, and saying he didn't know the guy'd been carrying a gun."

So Creed Loftin was not a willing participant in the shooting. Good to know.

Hines began walking slowly down his driveway.

Garza said, "And Creed said the guy's name. Watts said it sounded like 'Bricker.'"

"Bricker?"

"Right. Or something close to it."

"Fantastic."

"Yep. Shouldn't be too hard to figure it out. Anyway, this guy—Bricker—asked Creed again if he wanted to leave the body or move it. Creed said leave it, because they had to get the hell out of there before anyone else showed up. Then Watts heard them drive away. A minute or so later, he tried to get up, but he lost consciousness, and he doesn't remember anything else except a few random moments in the ambulance."

Marlin felt the familiar adrenaline rush that came with making quick, significant progress on a case.

Hines reached the street and walked toward Marlin's truck, stopping just in front of the bumper. Marlin made eye contact and gave him a just-a-minute gesture. Hines glared at him in return.

"What's your next step?" Marlin asked Garza.

"Get an arrest warrant for Creed Loftin and round him up. I figure putting Creed in a cell overnight might encourage him to answer some questions, especially if he thinks he can cut a deal. In the meantime, I'll get someone—probably Ernie—to try to ID this Bricker guy so we can get a warrant for him, too."

It was a complicated situation. On one hand, Creed Loftin had a good reason to come clean about the Watts shooting and seek a plea bargain. On the other hand, Creed Loftin wouldn't want to explain why he and Bricker had approached Danny Ray Watts in the first place. That would involve admitting he and Dickie were in Johnson City Friday night.

"Hey, Karl Hines is standing right outside my truck," Marlin said.

"Let me see what I can get out of him."

"Keep me posted," Garza said.

"Will do."

Marlin disconnected and opened his truck door.

"Mr. Hines?" he said, stepping forward and offering his hand, which Hines shook reluctantly.

"Help you with something?" Hines asked.

"I need to talk to you about that four-wheeler parked in your backyard," Marlin said.

"That's what I figured. Mr. Carrasco said you'd been hassling him about it."

Bad start.

"Just wanted to ask him some questions," Marlin said. "He told me it was in your possession, so I need to—"

"Hassle me, too?" Hines said.

"Not at all. Think I can take a quick look at it?"

"The ATV?"

"Yes, sir.

Hines was a reticent man with an adversarial demeanor about him, at least right now. "I don't believe so."

"I can't look at it?"

"Nope."

"That's disappointing," Marlin said, grinning, trying to be as non-threatening as possible.

"Life's a bitch," Hines said.

"Don't I know it," Marlin said. "Mind telling me how it got damaged?"

"Did you go into my backyard?" Hines snapped.

"No, sir, I could see it from the next street over," Marlin said. "I could see the damage. How did that happen?"

"I wrecked it."

"*You* wrecked it?"

"Yes, sir."

"When was this?"

"Couple days ago."

"Where?"

"What's this all about?"

"Skeet didn't tell you?"

"He said you wanted to see the ATV, that's all."

"Did he ask you to say you wrecked it?"

Hines didn't bat an eye. "Nope. It's just the truth."

"So you're going to stick with that?"

Hines simply stared at him.

"What about the oil leak?" Marlin asked.

"What about it?"

"Did it have an oil leak?"

"Yep. Some moron hit a rock out at the ranch, lost all the oil, and the engine froze up. I brought it home, fixed it, and then I wrecked it, like a dumbass."

"You got a receipt?"

"For what? I said I fixed it myself."

"For the parts," Marlin said. "You had to have bought some parts for an engine that badly damaged."

Hines shook his head, showing his temper. "Of course I did, but I'm having a hard time understanding how this is any of your damn business."

"Because I'm investigating a crime," Marlin said.

"Then get a warrant. Isn't that how things work?"

"You can let me see the ATV without a warrant, if you want. Unless there's a reason you don't want to let me see it."

"Mr. Carrasco owns it, so you'll have to ask him."

It appeared Hines wasn't going to budge, so Marlin decided to press harder.

"Karl, I hate to see you get mixed up in a bad situation," Marlin said, "but I'm afraid that's about to happen. Skeet is using you, and you probably don't even know why. I can assure you it's a mistake to get caught up in this mess."

"I ain't getting caught up in nothing. Just exercising my rights."

"You're trying to protect your boss and I understand that," Marlin said. "But I need you to tell me the truth about that ATV. Tell the truth now and I'll forget about any little fibs you might've told me already."

"You calling me a liar?" Hines asked.

Marlin was doing his best to remain calm and patient, but Hines's body language was sending some bad signals. It was probably just posturing, but Marlin began to prepare himself for anything stupid Hines might do. Marlin also decided that, if Hines wasn't going to cooperate, why not try a different approach? Poke the ant bed with a stick.

"Actually, yeah," Marlin said. "I think you're lying to me, so I guess that makes you a liar."

A tense moment followed, with Marlin wondering if Hines might try to throw a punch, but finally Hines said, "In that case, I got nothing more to say."

He turned and walked back to his house.

9

Marlin drove around to Avenue O again and knocked on the door of Hines's back-fence neighbor, an elderly man Marlin had known for years.

"Mr. Easley, you mind if I get into your backyard?" Marlin asked.

Easley looked at the camera in Marlin's hand and said, "I got poachers hiding back there, Johnny?" His eyes were twinkling with humor.

"Not as far as I know," Marlin said. "Your neighbor has a four-wheeler parked in the back of his lot and I need to get some pictures of it."

"Karl Hines?" Easley asked.

"Yes, sir."

"He done something wrong?"

Easley seemed hopeful that the answer was yes.

"I'm not sure," Marlin said. "But it sure would help me out if I could get back there."

"Oh, you bet," Easley said. "Come on through the house."

Less than a minute later, Marlin was standing beside the chain link fence at the rear of Easley's property, snapping photos of the ATV. Karl Hines was nowhere to be seen.

Easley, standing ten feet behind Marlin, said, "Is it stolen or something?"

"No, nothing like that. Wish I could tell you more, but that's about it."

"I understand," Easley said. "Never have warmed up to that man. Not the friendly sort at all."

Marlin snapped several more photos from another angle. He wasn't seeing any additional damage, but he was getting great documentation of the damage he had seen earlier.

"About a month ago," Easley said, "my daughter was over here with her dog—cute little sucker, but he likes to bark at squirrels. He ended up limping and it turned out someone had shot him with a pellet gun. Vet bill cost her a hundred dollars. Only one around here with a pellet gun is Hines."

Marlin stopped for a moment and turned around. "Anything like that ever happens again, you call me, okay? Anytime, day or night."

"You can bet your butt on that."

"In the meantime, if you should happen to see him out there messing with that ATV—"

"You want me to keep an eye on it?"

"Well, I'm not expecting you to spend a lot of time on it, but if you—"

"I got no plans today," he said, obviously giddy with the idea of helping Marlin catch Karl Hines in whatever crime had been committed. "I can sit in the chair in my back bedroom and listen to the Astros game."

"That would be great," Marlin said. "But if he does start to move the ATV, or to remove any parts, please don't talk to him. Just call me, okay?"

"You can count on it."

30

RED WAS RELAXING in his recliner with a cold beer, a can of mixed nuts, and an episode of *Rehab Addict*, when Billy Don returned from a trip down to the mailbox and dumped several envelopes into his lap, including one right on top from Mandy Hammerschmitt. It didn't have a stamp or a postmark on it, just Red's name, which meant Mandy must've placed it in the mailbox herself. Red tore it open and found a handwritten note. As he read, he almost choked on a Brazil nut.

> *Red,*
>
> *I been thinking about this situation with Dub falling out of your tree house. The lawyer told us we could probably get mid six figures, but considering that Dub is gone now, I figure the income he would of earned is lower. Thats why I'm willing to strike some sort of deal. This way we won't have to hassle with a bunch of lawyers and judges and all that crap. Here's the offer....you pay me $20,000 in cash and we'll call it square. I'll drop everything and we can get on with our lives. The only thing I ask is that we get this settled by eight oclock tonight. I think thats plenty fair and hope you do to. Call me and I'll come get the money. I'll give you a receipt and everything.*
> *Mandy*

She had written her phone number at the bottom.

"Is she out of her ever-lovin' mind?" Red asked.

"She has nice handwriting," said Billy Don, who had been reading the note over Red's shoulder.

"But seriously," Red said. "Has that gal totally lost her shit?"

"They say good penmanship means you're smart," Billy Don said, "but see the way she crosses her t's real low? That means she's insecure."

"What are you babbling about?"

"Saw it on my phone the other day. I'm learning all kinds of

LAST LAUGH | 161

int'resting stuff lately."

"I'd say 'interesting' is a stretch. All I know is, she's friggin' illusional if she thinks I'm giving her twenty grand."

"Or maybe it's a sign of being nervous," Billy Don said. "I could look it up."

"Please don't," Red said.

Billy Don lowered himself into his usual spot on the couch, where he sank so low his knees and shoulders were at the same level.

"Why is she in a rush to make a deal all sudden-like?" Red wondered.

Billy Don took a big drink from the beer can he'd left on the cable-spool coffee table earlier.

"And why by tonight?" Red asked.

"Bet she's planning to haul ass," Billy Don said.

"Huh?"

"She's gonna run and she needs cash to do it. Maybe you was right about her killing Dub."

Red thought about that for a moment. "Makes perfect sense, just like I said all along. I'm usually right about these things."

"Except you wondered about Tino, too, and Lester Higgs, and Claude Rundell, and even Kelly. Hell, you even wondered about Dickie Loftin last night."

"So what?"

"If you name that many people as the person who mighta done it, it ain't real hard to be right."

"But I figured it was probably Mandy right from the start. She was my number one choice."

"Ain't the way I 'member it."

"Would you stop arguing about everything?"

"One thing's for sure, she knows you got money to spare," Billy Don said. "Hell, everybody knows, 'cause you've told that story to everybody in town, most of 'em twice. And everybody knows how you feel about banks."

"Yeah, but I got it in a safe," Red said.

"Whoop-de-doo," Billy Don said. "Remember that time we stole that safe out of that old man's house?"

Red remembered it well. They'd used a dolly to cart it out, and then they'd eventually had to use dynamite to blow the damn thing open. What was inside? Nothing of value. Waste of a felony.

"Mine's bolted down," Red said.

"If we was trying to steal a safe what was bolted down, think we'd figure out a way to do it?" Billy Don asked.

Red thought about it. The answer was clearly yes. Maybe it was time to cave in and put his money in a bank, despite the fact that banks were about as trustworthy as your average congressman. But he couldn't get sidetracked by that right now. Right now, he had to think about Mandy. Red didn't like being pressured for the money, even if it would make a troublesome situation go away.

"Hey, I just thought of something," Red said. "If she's planning to run away from the cops, don't you figure she'll run even if I don't give her the money? I mean, what other choice does she have?" He sat up a little straighter. "Plus, hey, once she's gone, that'll mean the threat of the damn lawsuit is gone, too, even if I don't give her any money. Right?"

"You're the legal expert 'round here," Billy Don said, possibly being sarcastic.

"I'm pretty sure it would be," Red said. "I mean, 'cause how could she sue me if she's on the run? There's something called habeas corpulence that means you can't sue somebody unless you show up in court to do it."

"I don't think it—"

"This just might be a blessing in disguise. No lawsuit, plus, if she runs, the cops'll stop thinking I'm a suspect."

"They don't think you're a suspect."

"They do, and that's why I say, let her run. I'm not gonna give her a dime, and she'll run anyway, and then all my problems will be solved."

But Billy Don was already distracted by the TV show lady, who was wearing a particularly clingy top in this episode, and she'd managed to get it damp while installing a new sink. Oops. Red and Billy Don had discovered, watching these home-improvement shows with all these pretty ladies in them, that there were all kinds of great jokes to be made about nailing and screwing and getting wood. Witty stuff.

Red watched for a few minutes himself, enjoying the break from all the crap, but then a commercial came on, so he turned his attention back to the situation with Mandy. Then Red had another thought. If Mandy was taking off, would she have told Tino?

He grabbed his Korean cell phone and painstakingly typed a text to Lydia.

Got reasson to think Dubs girlfriend is going on the run tonight, shes coming over later, trying to get money out of me, wunder if tino knows anything

Lydia sent a reply in less than a minute.

OMG! I talked to him a few minutes ago and he said he was leaving town tonight! We're supposed to meet when he gets off work!

Red must've made some sort of sound, because Billy Don said, "Huh?"

"Hang on," Red said. He typed a reply. *Think they is running away together.*

As usual, he forgot the question mark, but Lydia answered him anyway.

Absolutely. Should we tell the police?

No point, Red said. *They r still sovverin citizens an r free to leave town.*

She said, *Then what should we do?*

He said, *Let me think.*

She said, *K.* Then a minute later, she added, *I have an idea.*

Red said, *Lets hear it.*

9

It took some doing, but after searching parking lots all over north Austin for an hour, Bricker found a Ford Explorer that appeared to be as old as his was, and the same color—red, bordering on maroon. The SUV was parked in the outer reaches of Lakeline Mall. There were plenty of spots near the SUV, but Bricker parked a few rows over and sat for a moment, checking nearby vehicles for occupants—maybe a husband waiting in the car while a wife ran inside to exchange an item. He didn't see anybody. He noticed a security camera mounted on a nearby pole, but nobody would have any reason to review the footage, and he doubted there was a person monitoring the live feed. Chance he was willing to take.

He got out of his SUV with a screwdriver in hand and quickly removed his front and rear license plates. Then he carried them over to the matching SUV and swapped the plates in less than two minutes. Nobody saw him, as far as he could tell. The person who owned this SUV might drive around for weeks or months without noticing the plates were wrong, or they might not find out until their next yearly inspection.

Bricker went back to his own Explorer and put the new plates on. That should buy him some time if the cops started looking for him. Maybe they already were. Between the Watts shooting and the girl in the motel room, Bricker had really been on a tear. At this point, he figured he didn't have much time left.

31

"HIS NAME IS Alan Bricker," Garza said, standing in Marlin's office doorway.

"That was fast," Marlin said.

"And we have Creed Loftin's parole officer to thank for that," Garza said. "He told Ernie that Loftin and Alan Bricker shared a cell several years ago. Apparently Bricker has been a frequent flyer at facilities all over the state."

Garza placed a printed mug shot on Marlin's desk. Looked like a million other mug shots—the offender staring the camera down, attempting to appear tough and unruffled.

"Was this at his Mensa acceptance ceremony?" Marlin asked.

"If it was, he doesn't look too happy about it."

"We got an address?" Marlin asked.

"An apartment complex in northeast Austin," Garza said. "Ernie called the manager there and she verified that Bricker is indeed a tenant and she saw him less than an hour ago, but now his SUV is gone. Ernie's going to visit Danny Ray Watts in the hospital right now to see if he can pick Bricker out of a line-up. If he can, we'll be able to get a warrant for him, too."

"How's the warrant coming for Creed Loftin?" Marlin asked.

"Just finished writing the affidavit," Garza said. "The judge said he'd see me in ten minutes. Then we'll just need to track Loftin down. Lauren is over at the motel right now in her personal vehicle watching for him, but no word yet. I'm guessing Loftin has left town, in which case we'll just go get him, as soon as we know where he is—back home in Stephenville or wherever."

Marlin gave Garza a one-minute overview of his encounter with Karl Hines and summed it up by saying, "He might know something or he might just be doing what Skeet asked him to do. I couldn't even guess."

"You push him hard?"

"Yep. The man has a poker face and a bad attitude. Emmett Easley thinks Hines shot his daughter's dog with a pellet gun."

"I've seen men get beaten like a rented mule for less than that."

"Me, too," Marlin said.

"Bet you can get a warrant for that ATV now," Garza said. "Since you've seen it firsthand and can confirm it is damaged."

"What I'm working on right now," Marlin said. "Would love to haul it off this afternoon before Karl Hines can do anything with it. Mr. Easley is keeping an eye on it right now."

Garza grinned. "Oh, yeah?"

"He's not real fond of Hines, as you can guess," Marlin said.

Garza nodded and took a sip from his mug. "Get the feeling we're about to break this one open?"

"Man, I hope so."

9

Mandy didn't answer, so Red left a voicemail. "Got your letter, and I gotta admit at first I thought you was a crazy bitch. But I been thinking about it some more and I figure we might be able to reach a reasonable compromise. So gimme a call and let's work out the details."

She called back in three minutes, which wasn't a surprise, and Red put it on speakerphone so Billy Don could hear.

"Compromise?" Mandy said.

That was the word Lydia had suggested when she'd told Red her idea.

Red said, "Yeah, it's when you work out some kind of agreement that you both—"

"I *know* what a compromise is," she said. "But that's the thing— what I said in my letter *is* a compromise. A damn good one. I ain't making no damn compromise on top of my compromise."

"Well—"

"Twenty grand is a whole lot less than I might get if we go to court," Mandy said.

"But you probably can't even sue me," Red pointed out, "since you and Dub wasn't married. You ain't got what they call legal standing."

Lydia had suggested that phrase. She was pretty dang smart.

Mandy said, "Anybody can sue anybody for anything. That's how it works."

"Even so, you could sue me and get nothing. Ever thought of that?

And you'd still have to pay your vultures. I mean lawyers."

Red had nothing to gain by arguing, but he simply couldn't resist. He didn't like this floozy pressuring him for cash.

"Look," Mandy said. "This ain't negotiable. It's a take-it-or-leave-it kind of deal. If you wanna leave it, fine, but I'm warning you the lawsuit ain't gonna be pretty."

Red opened his mouth, about to unload a massive stream of four-letter words and world-class insults on her, but Billy Don began waving his arm around, which meant *Stop! Stick to the plan!*

Damn it. Billy Don was right.

"Fair enough," Red said, gritting his teeth. "Twenty thousand dollars just because Dub fell out of a tree like some kind of moron."

"Cash," she said. "Not a check."

"At least you're not pushy or anything," Red said.

"I can be there in twenty minutes," she said.

"I'm sure you could," Red said, "but contrary to the blabbermouths around town, I don't keep that kind of money in the house. I need some time to get it."

"From the bank?"

"Ain't none of your business," he said.

"I could meet you there—at the bank."

"Why the big rush?" Red asked, again unable to resist the temptation. "How about we get together tomorrow or later this week?"

"Because I got a lot of bills stacking up," she said.

Yeah, right. No question about it—she was planning to skip town.

"Okay, well, best I can do is have you come over here at about seven o'clock," he said.

"Really? You can't get it any—"

"Seven o'clock," Red said. "That's my part of the compromise. Take it or leave it."

"Fine," she said. "Take it."

9

Sheriff Bobby Garza, with a freshly signed warrant in hand, parked his marked unit in a spot directly in front of room 115, where the housekeeper's rolling cart was just outside the open door. Creed Loftin's BMW was nowhere to be seen. Deputy Lauren Gilchrist pulled up next to him in her truck. They both stepped out of their vehicles, but Garza sensed they were out of luck.

It was Lauren's investigation, so Garza stayed a few steps behind her as she stopped in the open motel room doorway. Looking past her,

Garza noted the absence of any personal items in the room.

The housekeeper was in the bathroom and gave a small yelp of surprise when she came out and noticed Lauren and Garza waiting.

"Sorry about that," Lauren said. "They gone?"

"Yes, ma'am."

"How long ago?"

"I'm not sure. I got here at ten and they were already gone."

"You find anything unusual?" Lauren asked.

"Like what?"

"Blood on anything. Towels, washcloths."

The housekeeper's eyes widened at that comment. "I'm sorry, no, and I'm almost done with the room."

"Will you let us know if you see anything like that?"

"Of course."

"And don't touch it."

"I won't."

"Thanks a lot. Sorry about spooking you."

They walked over to the office and found a young man with a shaved head and a hoop earring behind the counter. Garza hadn't seen him before. Not a local. Probably drove over from Dripping Springs or Fredericksburg, or maybe he lived somewhere in between.

"Morning," Lauren said, and they introduced themselves. The young man's name was Simon. "Creed Loftin already checked out?" Lauren asked, making it a foregone conclusion that they knew Loftin had been there. Therefore, Simon wouldn't be breaching a customer's confidentiality.

"Yes, ma'am."

"You get the name of the man who was staying with him?"

"I never even saw him," Simon said.

"Were you here when they checked in?"

"No, ma'am."

"Who was?"

"Hang on a sec." He clicked some keys on his computer. "That was the manager, Cindy. She isn't here right now."

Garza had noticed a security camera outside, covering the doorway into the office. It would be good to have footage of both Creed Loftin and Alan Bricker, if they'd both entered the office.

"How long do you hold the video from the camera outside?" Garza asked.

"I'm not sure. I think it stays in the cloud for thirty days."

"Who would know for sure?" Garza asked.

"Also Cindy."

"Can you access the footage?"

"Sorry, I can't. What I mean is, I would, but I don't have the password to get onto the website."

"Do you have a cell number for Cindy?" Lauren asked.

The young man wrote it on a piece of paper and handed it to Lauren. "I should tell you that Cindy doesn't answer her phone much on her days off. I don't think she even checks voicemail."

"Simon, we really appreciate your help," Lauren said.

"Sure thing."

Outside, Lauren tried Cindy's number and got voicemail, just as Simon had predicted. She left a brief message asking Cindy to call back as soon as possible.

Then Garza placed another phone call to Creed Loftin, but it also went to voicemail. Garza left a longer, more detailed message.

"Mr. Loftin, this is Sheriff Bobby Garza. I understand our local game warden called you earlier and now I'm calling. I'm afraid we've both reached the limits of courtesy and I want to be real clear at this point. You need to call me back immediately. Better yet, if you're still in Blanco County, come on over to my office right across from the motel where you were staying and ask for Lauren Gilchrist or for me. Won't take long and then you can be on your way. But either way, I need to talk to you, and I don't mean tomorrow or next week. I expect you to call me as soon as you get this message. Thank you, sir."

32

WHEN CREED WALKED into the game room, Dickie, seated on the couch, looked up at him, "Jesus effing Christ, it's about time. Where the hell've you been?"

Creed had gotten into Stephenville around noon, but he hadn't been ready to face Dickie just yet, so he'd stopped at a strip club to have a few cold beers and brace himself. Now it was nearly two o'clock.

"Yeah, I know," Creed said. "I'm sorry. We need to talk."

"I *know* that! The sheriff called me," Dickie said. "And so did a game warden. And Skeet says—"

"Just settle down for a minute," Creed said. "And we'll—"

"Settle down? You drop off the radar for more than twenty-four hours—not returning my calls—and now you're telling me to settle down?"

"I had to do it that way," Creed said. "But now I need to tell you everything. And you're not gonna like a lot of it."

"What happened?"

"Let me get a drink first," Creed said. "Want one?"

"No, I'm good."

"I think I'd better get you one anyway."

"That bad?"

Creed didn't answer. Instead he walked over to the bar and filled a couple of crystal tumblers with ice. Poured three fingers of Garrison Brothers bourbon into each one. Handed one to Dickie.

Then he sat down, took a long drink, and told his brother everything. The shooting of Danny Ray Watts. The girls at the motel. Choking Bricker. The stern voicemail from the Blanco County sheriff not twenty minutes ago. Creed didn't leave a single detail out, because if they were going to stay out of prison, they needed to work on a story together. They would need to be consistent.

When he was done, Dickie appeared dazed and defeated—as if he were having a hard time comprehending what he had just heard. Finally he simply said, "That's crazy."

"I know."

"What did you do? You shot a guy?"

"It wasn't me, Dickie. I just told you. It was Bricker."

"But you trusted him. You brought him into all this."

Creed shrugged. He didn't know what to say.

"That's the dumbest thing you've ever done," Dickie said.

"I know, Dickie. I know. He's a damn psycho, but there's nothing I can do about it now. Only thing we can do is try to figure out a solution."

"Solution?"

"Yeah."

"I can't imagine what we could do to avoid the freight train of bullshit heading our way."

"There has to be a way. We just have to think of it."

"What happens when the guy you shot wakes up?" Dickie asked.

"I didn't shoot him," Creed replied.

"But you were there, Creed, and that's basically the same thing, from a legal standpoint."

"He might not wake up."

"But he might, and on top of that, you've got the two girls. What about them?"

"I stopped him, okay? I stopped Bricker from slapping her around."

"Was he raping her?"

"I don't know what he was doing, but whatever it was, I made him stop. I'm the good guy here."

"Who's gonna believe that?" Dickie said. "And you think those girls are gonna say, 'Oh, that one guy was a jerk, but the other guy, Creed, he was a real sweetheart'? You're talking about two college girls getting laid in a motel room by a couple of convicts they just met."

Dickie's bleak attitude was bringing Creed down. Okay, so maybe Dickie was right, but Creed wasn't ready to give up just yet.

"You talk to Skeet lately?" he asked.

"Yesterday. He's hanging tight."

"Well, of course he is."

"The game warden came out to see him on Sunday morning, but Skeet said he didn't know anything and you and me didn't either."

Creed felt his phone vibrating in his pocket, so he checked the caller ID, worried that the sheriff was calling again. But it was worse. "Oh, shit."

"Who is it?" Dickie said.

"It's him. It's fucking Bricker."

Dickie didn't say anything and neither did Creed. They both just waited as the call went to voicemail, and then there was a pause of a solid minute before an alert popped up showing that Bricker had left a message. Creed didn't want to listen to it. He wanted to throw his phone in a lake instead.

"Play the damn voicemail and let's see what we're dealing with," Dickie said.

9

"I brought you a six-pack," Deputy Ernie Turpin said, using the nickname for a photo lineup that featured six possible suspects.

"Man, I wish," Danny Ray Watts said, grinning from his hospital bed. "I could use a cold one about now. Or six."

"I bet. Looks like you're doing pretty good."

"I can't complain, considering."

Turpin was genuinely surprised by how healthy and vigorous Watts appeared after having been shot in the chest just two days earlier.

Turpin moved beside the bed and said, "Okay, so here's the reason for my visit today. I'm going to show you a set of six photographs—and please keep in mind that it is just as important to clear innocent people as it is to identify any guilty parties."

"I understand."

"The people in these photos may not appear exactly as they did on the date of the incident—two days ago—because their features can change. I'm talking a different hairstyle, different length, mustaches, beards, and things like that."

"Got it," Watts said, plainly anxious to see the photos.

"The person who committed the crime may or may not be in these photos," Turpin said. He himself did not know which one was Alan Bricker, if Bricker was even included. Sheriff Garza had created the lineup and given it to Turpin to present. Research showed that fewer false IDs occurred when the person presenting the photos didn't know the identity of the suspect.

"Yeah," Watts said.

"And even if you don't make an identification, rest assured that we will keep investigating."

"I appreciate that."

"You understand everything I've told you?"

"I do."

"No questions?"

"Nope."

"Okay, good."

Turpin arranged the six photos on the wheeled table that patients used for meals. Then he swung the table so that it was positioned over Watts's lap.

"That guy right there," Watts said in less than five seconds, tapping a photo.

"Where do you recognize him from?" Turpin asked.

"He shot me on Sunday. He was with Creed Loftin on Kendalia Road. They pulled me over, just like I told the sheriff, and then this little son of a bitch shot me."

Turpin jotted some quick notes, including quotes from Watts.

"How certain are you that the man you identified is—"

"One hundred percent," Watts said. "No question at all. I recognized him immediately."

"Okay, I'm going to ask you to sign and date that photo," Turpin said.

Watts did as he was asked, and then he said, "It was him, right? I mean, I know it was, but I want you to confirm it for me. If you don't mind."

"Hang on," Turpin said. He pulled out his phone. Earlier, Garza had emailed him a single photo—the one of Alan Bricker—for Turpin to check *after* the lineup. He opened the email and saw the same photo Watts had just selected.

9

Bricker was a few miles south of Lampasas, not quite halfway to Stephenville, when he thought of a nice twist.

First things first, though. He hadn't eaten since yesterday, so he was hungrier than a goddamn stray dog. He pulled into a little drive-in burger joint called Storm's. Asked for the Storm's Special with double cheese, plus a side of fried okra and a strawberry shake. Funny, why did it feel like he was ordering a last meal?

He realized there was still time to change the course he'd set. Just bail out and move on with life. Might be facing prison time for all the crazy shit he'd pulled in the past few days, but so what? He could handle prison like a boss. But that didn't feel right.

He'd always assumed he'd go out in a big way, and this was probably it, right? It would make headlines across the country. Around the world, even. And it wasn't like he was going after innocent people. Creed fucked up in a big way. The bruises on Bricker's throat were proof of that. Creed had tried to *kill* him. So full steam ahead.

The food came and he ate every last bit. Tossed the trash on the floorboard. Then he pulled out his phone and made a call.

33

CREED HIT THE BUTTON and heard Bricker's voice—raspier than it usually was.

Hey, man. I don't know what the hell happened last night, but I figure I probably got out of line with one of them gals. Fuck it, you know? Shit happens when you're wasted. Guess I don't blame you for kicking my ass. Anyway, in case you're wondering, we're good, you know? Well, my throat isn't so great, as you can hear, but don't sweat it. As far as the money you owe me, we can deal with that later, after we see how things shake out. So, tell you what—I'll call you in a couple days and we'll sort it out. Okay, amigo? Talk to ya later.

Dickie had a relieved expression on his face, like, *Whew. We dodged a bullet on that one.*

But Creed played the message a second time, just to make sure he heard everything right.

"What?" Dickie said afterward.

"I don't know."

"Don't know what?"

"If it's legit."

"What are you saying?"

"That he might be suckering us."

"Jesus Christ, just how crazy is this guy?"

"Crazy enough."

"You saying he might be coming after you?"

"Not just me. Us."

"Son of a bitch!" Dickie said. "Does this lunatic know what happened on Friday night?"

"Absolutely not," Creed lied.

"You're sure?"

"Definitely. He didn't need to know any of that. I just wanted him along in case I ran into trouble."

"And look how that worked out," Dickie said.

Creed could tell that his brother was on the verge of losing it. He was running his hands through his hair, a nervous tic he'd had since childhood.

"You have to stop it. *We* have to stop it. No more arguing. Okay? We have to figure something out—some kind of explanation for everything that has happened so far."

"Like what?"

"Right now, I got no idea. But let's think."

9

An hour later, they had a plan. Kind of. It was loose, and it might have to evolve, and a big part of it revolved around Creed's best guesses as to how Bricker would react. But they could push Bricker in the direction they wanted him to go.

Creed started by sending Bricker a text. *Got ur voicemail, don't call me anymore, u r lucky you arent in jail.*

They waited ten minutes and got no response.

So Creed sent a second message. *U r a rapist and a murderer. I'm not getting nailed for ur stupid actions.*

Another ten minutes passed with no reply. That was fine. Creed wasn't really expecting one.

Next step. The Blanco County sheriff.

Creed took a deep breath and made the call, while Dickie sat there beside him listening.

Please don't answer, Creed thought. *Please go to voicemail. Please, please, please.*

No such luck.

"This is Sheriff Bobby Garza."

"Hey, it's Creed Loftin returning your call."

Creed was doing his best to sound friendly and casual.

"Mr. Loftin, where are you right now?"

"Pardon?"

"Where are you?"

"At home."

"In Stephenville?"

"Yes, sir."

"When did you get back there?"

"Earlier today."

"What time, exactly?"

Creed figured the sheriff was trying to determine whether Creed had left Johnson City *after* the sheriff had left his voicemail, which would indicate that Creed had intentionally avoided him.

"I wasn't paying a lot of attention to the clock, to be honest," Creed said. "Can you tell me what this is all about? I know there was a man who went missing the other night near Skeet's place..."

"That's right, and I need to—"

"The thing is, I don't know anything about that, and neither does Dickie. He said you called him, too, and I don't want to waste your time with—"

"It wouldn't be a waste of time," Garza said. "We need to speak to everyone who was in the area that night, and so far you and Dickie are the only ones—"

"Wait, in which area? I heard you were searching mostly to the east of Skeet's place."

"That's true."

"But that's not the route we took."

"You're talking about the county road from Skeet's place to Johnson City?"

"Isn't that what we're talking about?"

"You're saying you never traveled that portion of the road on Friday night?" Garza asked.

Creed's chest was tightening up. This was the decisive moment. He could either lie or tell the truth. Or take the third option.

"Why does it sound like you don't believe me?" Creed said.

"We've got witnesses that saw you and Dickie in Johnson City on Friday night," Garza said. "Are you saying you weren't there?"

Creed was breathing heavily.

"I'm not sure what to say at this point," Creed said. "I've already told you that we don't know anything about the—"

"It's a fairly simple question," Garza said. "Were you in Johnson City Friday night?"

"Sheriff," Creed said. "I understand there must be a lot of pressure to figure out how the poor guy died, but I—"

"Mr. Loftin?"

"Yeah?"

"Who says the man died?"

"What?"

"You just said he died, but we don't know that's true. We haven't found him."

Oh, fuck. Dickie was sitting nearby, listening, and looking like he wanted to puke.

Creed said, "I just, you know—he's been missing for, what, three days now? Four days? It just seems like he's probably dead. I don't mean to sound insensitive, but don't you figure that's true?"

Creed knew he was stammering. The sheriff didn't reply for a long moment, and Creed began to wonder if the call had been disconnected.

Then Garza said, "We need to sit down and sort all these questions out. Me, you, and your brother. What are y'all doing tomorrow morning?"

"I'm not sure what—"

"Around ten o'clock," Garza said. "I'll drive up to your place and we can talk. Won't take long. You and Dickie live in the same house, right?"

"Yeah. It's a temporary arrangement."

"Will Dickie be around?"

"I think so. Wait, he has a show in Houston tomorrow night."

"What time is he leaving?"

"Probably around two. Both of us. I'm driving him."

"That gives us plenty of time. We'll talk in the morning and we can put this behind us."

"That's fine," Creed said, trying to sound cooperative, and knowing there was no way he was going to follow through.

"Then I'll see you tomorrow morning at ten o'clock," Garza said. "I need you to be home when I get there. Both of you."

"We'll be here," Creed said.

9

John Marlin was proofreading the affidavit he'd just finished writing, hoping to get a search warrant for the ATV at Karl Hines's place in the next thirty minutes, when Bobby Garza stopped in his office doorway again and said, "Wanna ride with Lauren and me to arrest Creed Loftin?"

"Absolutely. He still in town?"

"Stephenville," Garza said. "He thinks we're meeting for an interview in the morning, but I want to sneak up there now and grab him before he changes his mind or lawyers up."

"You ask him about Alan Bricker?"

"Not yet. Didn't want to scare him off, and I'd rather see his face when I drop that name. Right now, he thinks the conversation will be about Dub Kimble, not about Danny Ray Watts."

"You're a devious man."

"Thank you."

"When are we leaving?"

"Ten minutes," Garza said. "That work?"

Marlin would ask Ernie Turpin, who had just gotten back from Austin, to present Marlin's affidavit to the judge and confiscate the ATV while he was gone, assuming the warrant was granted.

"You bet," Marlin said.

g

Like many cities of its size in Texas, Stephenville had a Walmart, located on the southwest side of town. Bricker pulled into the parking lot and checked his phone. He'd heard a couple of incoming texts a few minutes earlier, and now he saw that both were from Creed.

As Bricker read them, he clenched his teeth so tight he could taste blood.

That son of a bitch was going to turn on him. So predictable for a loser like Creed. Didn't surprise Bricker in the least. It wasn't like it actually mattered, but it confirmed for Bricker that he'd been right not to let the whole thing go.

He found a spot and went into the Walmart, which was crowded with all kinds of subhumans blocking the aisles with as much intelligence in their eyes as cattle.

Bricker had a shopping list in his head, and he started with the most basic item, which would be back in sporting goods. Ammo. Hundreds of rounds. He might not need it all, but better to have it and not need it than the opposite. Not just .380, but also nine-millimeter rounds for his TEC-9.

Then he'd grab some rope or zip ties or even some chain. No, none of that crap. Duct tape instead. Hard to beat duct tape. Just in case he needed it.

He grabbed a few more items, then found a canvas duffel bag to carry everything in. Put it all on his credit card. Wouldn't matter if the cops eventually traced him to this store. By then it would be all over. And it wasn't like he was ever going to pay the bill, right?

g

Garza kept it at a steady eighty miles per hour—and nearly ninety when they reached wide-open stretches of highway with no traffic—and the miles flew past quickly. It was five-thirty and they were thirty minutes outside of Stephenville when Marlin got a call from Emmett Easley.

"I see somebody back there looking at the ATV right now," Easley said.

"Is it Karl?" Marlin asked.

"No, somebody else. I can't see real good. Dadgum, I need to clean these windows."

"Is it a deputy?" Marlin asked. "Maybe Ernie Turpin?"

"Hang on a minute," Easley said. "I need to put the phone down."

Easley was probably reaching for binoculars. Marlin figured it might be easier just to text Ernie, but Mr. Easley had been so helpful, Marlin was willing to wait. If it was Karl Hines moving the ATV, there wasn't much Marlin could do about it—not until the warrant was served.

Thirty seconds passed.

"Well, I can't tell if it's Ernie," Mr. Easley said, "but it's a deputy, all right. He's rolling the ATV toward the gate."

"That's perfect, Mr. Easley. Thanks for letting me know."

34

"YOU REMEMBER HOW to use it?" Creed asked, holding a .40 caliber Beretta PX4 Storm out for his brother.

They'd done some target shooting a few years earlier, when Dickie had first bought the gun. But, as far as Creed knew, the semi-automatic had been collecting dust in Dickie's nightstand ever since. Dickie wasn't a gun guy. Creed wasn't either—not compared to the real gun nuts—but he went hunting every few years, and occasionally shot a pistol for fun.

"Yeah, you pull the trigger," Dickie said.

"If there's one in the chamber, sure, but right now, there isn't. You have to be sure there's one in the chamber or the gun won't fire."

"You think I'm an idiot?"

"No, but if you—"

"Give it to me," Dickie said.

Creed handed him the gun, carefully keeping the barrel pointed toward the floor. Treat every gun as if it were loaded.

Dickie racked the slide and chambered a round.

"I remember this little lever right here is the safety," he said. "It won't fire right now."

"Right. Good."

"And I remember that when I shoot, I need to keep my wrist firm or it won't cycle the next bullet properly."

"Excellent."

"And if you're gonna shoot somebody, aim right smack in the middle of their torso."

"Perfect."

Dickie carefully placed the gun onto the coffee table, then took a drink of bourbon. Creed wanted to suggest that he put the booze down, but a little bit might not be a bad thing under the circumstances.

"We really gonna do this?" Dickie asked.

"Unless you got a better idea," Creed said. "Besides, I'm probably wrong. He probably won't even show."

Creed could tell that Dickie didn't believe him, and Creed didn't believe it himself. Not after he'd sent those texts. Bricker wouldn't be able to resist doing something about that.

"We should get into position," Creed said. "It might be a long afternoon."

9

Dickie Loftin lived in Los Rancheros, the nicest neighborhood in Erath County, which wasn't saying much, but it was gated, which would present a problem for an overenthusiastic fan seeking an autograph.

But it wouldn't be a problem for Bricker. He'd been to Dickie's house a couple of times with Creed, and he'd heard conversations, and he knew the guard in the little shack at the entrance was the only guard on duty at any given moment. That meant it wasn't a big deal to hop the fence in some out-of-the-way spot and cut between houses to the main road, because all of the houses were on at least five acres, and some were on ten or even twenty, like Dickie's house.

House.

Hell, it wasn't a house, it was a mansion. Maybe they wouldn't call it that in Hollywood, but by North Texas standards, it was a mansion for sure. Living like a goddamn king. Five thousand square feet. Huge pool around back. Tennis court that he never used. Even a helicopter pad, although he'd sold the chopper after a year. Didn't feel safe in it.

The hell of it was, this wasn't even Dickie's only home. He had an apartment in Los Angeles, plus an oceanfront home in Panama City Beach, Florida, also known as the Redneck Riviera. Bricker figured that nickname alone drove Dickie's decision to buy a place there. Playing up the whole redneck angle. Riding on Jeff Foxworthy's coattails like a son of a bitch.

Not for much longer.

Bricker had a hard time understanding why Dickie even owned a place here in Stephenville. He grew up here, but so what? Other than that, what was the attraction? Bunch of nothing around here. Why hang around?

He parked at a strip center half a mile from Dickie's neighborhood and struck out on foot, dressed in blue jeans, work boots, and a basic white T-shirt. He was carrying the canvas duffel bag. As he was walking, he pulled an item out of the bag—a bright-orange safety vest, designed for hunters, but similar to the kind that road construction and utility crews wear.

He donned the vest as he turned onto a street that took him into a neighborhood just north of Los Rancheros. Then he cut across an empty lot and hopped a four-foot fence to the greenbelt that ran between the two neighborhoods. Fortunately, there were plenty of trees in the narrow strip of land—a natural privacy barrier between the two neighborhoods—so there was cover to conceal Bricker's movements.

The fence on the south side of the greenbelt—the perimeter wall of Los Rancheros—was seven feet tall, stone, with ornamental iron spikes at the top. Fortunately, the spikes were placed twelve inches apart and they weren't all that sharp on top. What kind of security expert would recommend that kind of bullshit? Basically worthless.

Bricker started walking along the greenbelt.

If anyone asked—and nobody would—Bricker would say he was conducting a routine inspection of the easement for any potential threats to underground utilities. Tree roots could really cause problems, you know? Same with erosion. Couldn't have exposed cables, could we?

The greenbelt curved gently to the southwest and less than one hundred yards farther, Bricker was directly behind Dickie's estate. Bricker hadn't heard any barking dogs or spotted a single person in the backyards to his right.

He was prepared to jump up, grab one of the iron spikes, and hoist himself over the wall, but he got even luckier. A small oak tree grew less than two feet from the wall behind Dickie's house. Almost as good as a ladder. Hadn't Creed ever checked back here to see if there was a vulnerable point? Apparently not. No wonder Dickie gave him shit on occasion. Creed was a slacker.

Bricker removed the safety vest, wadded it up, and stuck it in his pocket. Then he slung the duffel bag over his shoulder and climbed the tree, planted one foot on top of the fence between two of the spikes, and dropped effortlessly to the ground on the other side.

Not as many trees over here, because Dickie had removed the cedars years ago, but there were still enough oaks that Bricker couldn't see the rear of the house from here. That meant he couldn't be seen.

He moved slowly, quietly, stopping behind larger oaks on occasion to simply wait and listen. After he'd covered fifty yards, he caught his first glimpse of the house. He moved to his right and now he could see the area around the swimming pool.

And he saw Dickie sitting by himself poolside, unmoving, with a glass of amber liquid cradled in one hand. Bourbon. Dickie loved bourbon. Often drank on stage, during a performance, and Bricker knew for a fact that it was the real deal, not tea or some shit like that.

The situation couldn't be any better.

Bricker stood perfectly still for several minutes, and in that same time, Dickie didn't so much as twitch. Was he sleeping? Passed out? Didn't really matter, did it?

Was anyone else inside the house? Bricker could hear a faint voice, but he was pretty sure it was music coming from the poolside speakers.

g

Creed was watching from a window in a rear bedroom on the second story. Starting to get bored and fidgety, and beginning to think he was wrong—and then he saw movement. Just a quick flash. Way in the back of the property. Could be a bird or a squirrel.

There it was again.

Creed grabbed his binoculars and took a long look. Was that an arm jutting out from behind an oak tree? He tried to hold the binoculars as steady as possible, but now he was trembling.

Leaning in a corner within arm's reach was Dickie's Sako .270—another impulse purchase that had sat unused for several years—but Creed was wondering if he'd be able to make an accurate shot. Didn't matter how good the rifle was if he couldn't stop shaking.

And right then Bricker stepped out from behind the oak tree, carrying a weapon of his own.

g

Dickie Loftin lived in a gated community, complete with a security guard stationed in a little hut. Didn't see that often, even in the wealthy neighborhoods west of Austin. Garza pulled up to the hut and lowered his window just as the guard slid his own window to the left.

"Afternoon," Garza said.

"How's it going?" the guard said. Young guy, which was what Marlin expected. Probably nineteen or twenty. Finished high school and wasn't sure what else to do with himself.

Garza said, "I'm Sheriff Bobby Garza from Blanco County. Can I get your name?"

"Uh, Tony Hays."

Tony was no more than five-seven and maybe 145 pounds.

"Okay, Tony, thanks. How long have you been on duty?"

"Since ten o'clock this morning."

"Any breaks?"

"Well, I mean this job isn't very busy, so breaks just kind of happen all day."

"Have you left your post?"

"No, sir."

"Okay, great. Can you tell me if Creed Loftin has left since you've been here?"

"No, sir. I mean, yes, I can tell you, and no, he hasn't left."

"Perfect. The thing is, we need to get in to see him, and I need you to keep it under your hat. That means no letting him know we're coming."

"Wow," Tony said. "Is he, like, in trouble?"

"I can't tell you that," Garza said, "but I bet if you guessed, you'd get it right. That's between you and me, right?"

"Yes, sir."

"I appreciate that. Do you know if his brother is home?"

"Dickie? I don't really know. I know he was yesterday."

"Is there anybody else at the house, as far as you know?"

"I don't think so." He quickly consulted a computer inside the hut. "He hasn't had any visitors all week."

"Is there anybody there like a lawn crew or housekeeper or anyone like that? Pool guy? Anybody?"

"Not as far as I know. Nobody has been through today. It's been pretty quiet."

"Okay, great. Tony, we appreciate it. You mind opening the gate for us?"

"Oh, sure. You, uh, need any help?"

The kid grinned, joking, but Marlin could tell he really wanted to join in the action, or at least get a chance to watch it.

Garza said, "Actually, it would be helpful if you stayed right here and kept the gate closed, and if anybody should show up wanting to go to the Loftin house, don't let them in until we get back. Can you do that for us? Shouldn't take long."

"Yes, sir. Sure can." He was thrilled to have a task to do.

The kid pushed a button and the gate rolled open to the right. Garza gave him a solemn nod and drove through.

35

CREED MADE THE CALL, and he could see Dickie below, poolside, picking up his phone.

"Yeah?"

"He's coming," Creed said. His voice sounded unusually high—almost like a different person.

"From where?" Dickie asked.

"Near the back fence."

"This is fucking crazy," Dickie said, almost in a whisper. "You sure he won't just shoot me?"

"Not a chance. He'll want more than that. He'll want to turn this into a long, drawn-out deal. Besides, he wants me, not you."

But Dickie had the Beretta stashed under a towel on the table, just in case.

"Where is he now?"

"Coming your way slowly."

"How far?"

"Maybe sixty yards. You'll see him in a minute."

"I can't do this," Dickie said.

"Yes, you can. Stick with the plan."

"But why shouldn't I go inside?"

"That won't work. We talked about this."

Sweat was beginning to trickle from Creed's hairline and run down his forehead and temples.

"He's going to shoot me," Dickie said.

"I promise he won't. I guarantee it."

Creed was about eighty percent sure he was right. He was still watching Bricker closely and the psychopath had not raised his weapon yet. Looked like a TEC-9. Bricker had bragged about owning one, but Creed had figured he was bullshitting.

Creed had never even seen a TEC-9, since they hadn't been manufactured in more than two decades. It was basically a semi-automatic pistol, except that it was capable of accommodating a 50-round magazine, and Creed could see that Bricker's had one. Looked wicked—some people referred to it as an "assault pistol"—which was why so many TV producers had made it the weapon of choice for terrorists, drug dealers, and gang members back in its heyday. And in real life, it had been used in plenty of mass shootings, street fights, and other violent crimes.

"I can't believe I'm doing this," Dickie said.

"I'm watching him," Creed said. "You're fine."

Bricker was still making his way slowly toward the house, doing his best to move quietly, without being heard or seen. Creed had given Dickie the choice to be sitting in the second-floor window instead, and Creed would've sat by the pool, but Dickie hadn't had the stomach for it. He wasn't sure he could shoot a person.

"He's about to step out from the trees," Creed said. "And then he'll move quickly."

"Fuck," Dickie said softly. "If he kills me, you kill him, okay?"

"You got it, bro. But he won't."

Creed set the binoculars aside and grabbed the rifle. He could tell that it was a well-crafted piece of equipment that would be deadly in the right hands. He worked the bolt and slid a bullet into the chamber, smooth as silk.

Creed's heart was thundering now. Hands still trembling. He had to calm down. This was no big deal. He'd read about a Canadian sniper in Iraq who killed an ISIS member from more than two miles away. Two goddamn miles. Incredible. This shot here would be about forty yards. Piece of cake.

Everything happened quickly.

Bricker stepped from the trees and walked quickly toward Dickie, now with the TEC-9 raised.

Creed slipped the barrel of the .270 through the four inches of open window, his heart flopping and thumping like a fish out of water.

Bricker was yelling something at Dickie—Creed could hear it through the window and over Dickie's phone—but he couldn't make it out. Didn't matter.

Dickie sat perfectly still, just as he was supposed to. Following the plan.

Now Bricker stopped less than ten feet from Dickie, aiming the weapon at Dickie's chest. Creed could clearly hear him say, "Don't you move unless you wanna get shot."

"I won't," Dickie said.

"Where's Creed?"

"He's not here."

"Bullshit!"

"He's not."

"Anyone else inside?"

Creed looked through the Redfield scope and found Bricker in the crosshairs. The problem was, Bricker was standing on the other side of Dickie. If Creed shot too low, he ran the risk of hitting his brother.

"Nobody," Dickie said.

"You remember me?"

"You're Creed's friend. You shared a cell."

"Remember my name?"

"It's Bricker."

"Surprised you got it right."

The security camera on the back porch was recording all of this—Bricker pointing the weapon, threatening Dickie. That was a key part of the plan. Get it all on video. And the timing had to be right. Creed needed to wait another 15 or 30 seconds, so enough time would have elapsed that he could later claim that he had seen what was unfolding outside and then run for the rifle. If he shot too soon, the cops might figure out that he'd been waiting in the window, rifle at the ready.

"No, I remember," Dickie said. He sounded reasonably calm and collected, considering the situation. Creed had to give him props for that. "I have to admit I'm not crazy about having a gun pointed at me."

Bricker was squinting—the low evening sun getting in his eyes—and he took two steps to his right. Now Creed had a clean shot, and he knew he should take it. But he still wasn't steady enough.

9

Bobby Garza maneuvered his SUV slowly along Dickie Loftin's long, winding driveway. They passed a wooded area near the front of his acreage, and then the home came into view, centered on the twenty acres. Gorgeous place built from sandstone. Marlin guessed it was six or seven thousand square feet.

Closer to the home, the driveway split in two: the branch to the right went to the side of the house, likely to a garage, and the branch to the left delivered visitors to a circular drive in the front of the house. No vehicles were parked there except for a Gator utility vehicle. Probably what Dickie and Creed Loftin used to show visitors around the acreage.

"Place looks deserted," Lauren said from the front passenger seat.

She was right. Marlin didn't see any movement anywhere. Then again, maybe they simply expected the home of a hard-partying celebrity like Dickie Loftin to be teeming with people, including friends, business associates, and assorted hangers-on. But they saw nobody, and every last window in the front of the house had blinds or curtains drawn tight.

Garza brought the SUV to a halt in the circular drive, with a clear view of the front door, and killed the engine.

There was no need for conversation at this point. They were all seasoned veterans, and they'd discussed earlier how they would approach the situation. Garza and Lauren would go to the front door, while Marlin would go around back, just in case.

Creed Loftin didn't know an arrest warrant had been issued and he had no idea they were coming, but even if he'd known, they didn't consider him a flight risk. No, instead, Creed would immediately hire a high-dollar attorney—or perhaps his brother would hire one for him—and Creed would be bonded out shortly thereafter.

All three of them stepped from the SUV, and Marlin said, "Give me two minutes to get around back."

Garza nodded.

There was a line of shrubs extending from the left side of the house, so Marlin went around the right-hand corner instead, walking slowly. He noted that all the windows along this side were also blocked by curtains or blinds, which was a little unusual, because massive pecan and oak trees cloaked the house in shade.

He passed an HVAC condenser unit humming loudly as the fan spun, preventing him from hearing anything or anyone inside the house. He kept moving. Five more yards. Then ten. And twenty. And now he began to see the pool area behind the house—first a pump house, then the right-hand edge of the concrete apron around the pool, with chairs scattered here and there, and then the edge of the pool itself.

The AC unit behind him shut off abruptly and now Marlin heard a voice.

And another voice. A conversation. The place wasn't abandoned.

Marlin couldn't make out the exact words. He took a few more steps, almost to the rear corner of the house. He could see most of the pool now, but he couldn't see the far-left apron.

Right about now, Bobby and Lauren would be knocking on the front door. Was Creed Loftin one of the voices Marlin was hearing? Talking to Dickie? Or was it somebody else?

Marlin took another step, and another, and he reached the corner. He peeked around it and saw two men. Dickie Loftin was seated. The other, Alan Bricker, was standing—and holding Dickie at the end of a TEC-9.

9

"Guess Creed hasn't told you what's going on," Bricker said.

Creed could hear the conversation clearly on his phone.

"Not really," Dickie said. "We haven't talked much since Saturday."

"Well, here's the deal," Bricker said. "He kinda went nuts on me down in Blanco County."

"How so."

"Got into a road-rage situation and ended up shooting some poor guy right in the chest—"

That son of a whore!

"—and then, later on, he tried to force himself on this young lady in our motel room. What I mean by that is, he tried to rape her."

Damn liar!

Creed placed the crosshairs on Bricker's sternum, but he had a hard time holding it still. The original plan called for Creed to shoot Bricker in the leg, but he'd changed his mind. This deviant deserved far worse. Creed wanted to shut him up for good.

"And when she put up a fight," Bricker said, "he smacked her across the face."

Such bullshit!

"Now, I don't know how you was raised, but in my neck of the woods, we don't treat women that way. I think your brother is—"

Creed couldn't stand it anymore. He jerked back on the trigger.

9

Marlin flinched at the sound of the shot and instinctively recoiled, pressing his back against the side of the house. Where had the shot come from? He'd been watching the two men by the pool and it was clear Bricker had not fired his weapon. The shot had come from somewhere else.

Had Bricker or Dickie Loftin been hit?

Less then one second after the shot had been fired, Marlin took a quick glance around the corner of the house. Dickie Loftin had rolled out of his chair and flattened himself on the concrete, protectively cradling his arms around his head. Cowering, basically.

Alan Bricker, who was equally surprised by the shot, did the opposite. He ran, TEC-9 in hand. The bad news was, Bricker was heading directly toward the corner of the house where Marlin was waiting.

Marlin had one immediate thought: *He's going to think I fired the shot. At him.*

And how would Bricker react when he saw Marlin? He would open fire—with a weapon capable of tearing a man to pieces in short order. Marlin couldn't justify gunning Bricker down—he was simply fleeing from gunfire. That left Marlin with one option.

He turned and ran, hoping to round the front corner of the house before Bricker saw him and opened fire.

He'd only made it halfway when he heard a shot behind him and knew he'd run out of time. He would never make it to the corner.

He dove for the closest cover—the HVAC condenser unit. He hit the ground hard and scrambled behind the large metal box, just as three more shots rang out in rapid succession.

36

AT PRECISELY SEVEN O'CLOCK, Mandy Hammerschmitt bounced her way up Red's long caliche driveway in an old green Toyota truck that squeaked and groaned in protest. Red and Billy Don waited on the front porch, drinking beer and seated in faded lawn chairs.

When Mandy killed the engine and got out of her truck, Red said, "You need new ball joints."

"What do you think it is, Christmastime?" she replied.

Billy Don let out a little ambiguous snort.

"Dangerous driving around like that," Red said.

He couldn't help noticing she was a little unsteady on her feet, possibly because she was wearing high-heel shoes. Eye-catching shoes with a Texas theme—mostly red, with a white star centered in the glittery blue portion on the top of her foot. Like something a Dallas stripper might wear on July Fourth. Mandy's toes were peeking out the front of the shoes, with the nails painted a matching red. She was also wearing a blouse unbuttoned just enough that Red had a hard time keeping his eyes up where they belonged. The woman had a nice pair.

"You a mechanic?" she asked.

"I know a bad ball joint when I hear one."

"Well, I'll fix it right up the next time I hit the lottery. Speaking of which, you got the money?"

"You cut right to it, don't ya?" Red said.

Or maybe she was unsteady because of the contents inside the large lidded travel mug in her hand. Red could hear ice rattling around when she took a drink.

"Look," she said, wiping her mouth with the back of her hand. "I'm not trying to be a hard-ass or take no more than I deserve. I figure it's a good deal both ways. Sorry if you don't agree, but Dub fell out of your tree 'cause he was trying to help you. He was being a friend and he hurt his back in the process. Did you know I had to take him to the 'mergency room the next day?"

Red hadn't known that.

"I bet he never mentioned it," Mandy said, "because he didn't want to make no big deal out of it. Then it got where he couldn't get out of bed, even with pain pills and all. I ain't making this shit up. He finally got up and moving again, but he couldn't even lift a case of beer."

This was all news to Red—although he still harbored suspicions that Mandy was lying, or at least exaggerating.

"But why did he have to threaten to sue me?" Red asked.

"Because how else was he gonna make up for his lost wages? Most people have insurance, so it wasn't like you were gonna be paying for it yourself."

"'Cept I don't have insurance," Red said.

"Well, sugar, we all know that now, but Dub didn't know that at the time. Water under the bridge. Besides, I didn't come here to argue. You got the money?"

Red paused for a moment, then said, "What's in your mug?"

"Huh?"

"What're you drinking?"

She looked down at the mug, almost as if she'd forgotten she was holding it. "Orange juice."

"And what else?"

"Little bit of vodka. So what?"

"Why don't you come inside and I'll make you another one? While we're at it, I'll get you the money and I've got a form I want you to sign."

She looked at him suspiciously. "What kinda form?"

"Just something I wrote up that says you ain't gonna sue me 'cause I'm giving you twenty grand. We've gotta have something on paper, don't we?"

"I guess."

"You sign it, we share a drink, and we call it square."

She didn't answer right away, and now Red was wondering if she knew he was up to something.

He said, "Truth is, I'm ready to be done with all this and call a truce. Come inside and sign this form, okay? Then you can go back home…or wherever you're going."

It was a subtle comment meant to reveal that they knew Mandy might be leaving town. Red was offering his support, but Mandy would know that Red could just as easily alert the authorities if she didn't cooperate.

"Yeah, okay," Mandy said. She shook the mug. "I'm almost out anyway."

9

Creed fired the shot at Bricker with the deer rifle, and then he was suddenly flat on his ass with something warm running down the right side of his face. His ears were ringing. He cupped his right cheekbone and drew his hand away. His palm was smeared with blood. He was dazed, but he knew what had happened. The scope had kicked backwards with the shot and cut him. Amateur mistake. He hadn't held the rifle tightly enough.

Didn't matter right now.

He struggled to his knees and peeked out the lower portion of the window. Dickie was flat on the concrete beside the pool, covering his head, and Bricker was hauling ass, almost to the corner of the house down to Creed's right.

The shot had missed. Now all hell was going to break loose.

9

Bobby Garza and Lauren Gilchrist had just mounted the front steps to the Loftin house when they were startled by a shot from behind the house.

"What the hell?" Lauren said.

"Big gun," Garza said, as they descended the stairs they'd just climbed.

"Like a deer rifle. We need to check on John."

"That sounded like it—"

Another shot.

"Different weapon," Lauren said.

"But not a .357," Garza said, because that's what Marlin carried. That meant at least two shooters.

Garza and Gilchrist quickly hustled back to the SUV. They were going to need more firepower.

9

The condenser was far from ideal cover—there was very little inside of it substantial enough to stop a nine-millimeter round—and Marlin saw that at least one of the bullets from Bricker's weapon had exited this side of the unit, just two feet from his head.

Marlin had his .357 in his hand now, and it felt wholly inadequate. Better than nothing, but in this situation, just barely.

Bricker fired two more shots and Marlin heard them slam into the condenser. Then Bricker let out a long shout.

Yeeeehawwww!

He sounded like a lunatic, enjoying himself.

Where was he?

Not close, but not terribly far away, either. Maybe twenty or thirty yards. He might be somewhere along the side of the house, or still to the rear, but with a view down this side.

"What's a matter?" he called out. "Don't wanna shoot back?"

Bobby and Lauren would already be on the way to help him out, but Marlin couldn't just wait for Bricker to fire more shots. He took a quick peek and saw that Bricker was using a pecan tree for cover.

"State game warden!" Marlin yelled. "Drop your weapon!"

Bricker replied by firing another shot that slammed into the condenser.

9

"I know what you're doing," Red said.

"Huh?"

"I know exactly what you're doing," Red said.

"Me, too. I'm sitting on your couch, trying not to stick to anything, and drinking bourbon and Coke, mostly because you didn't have any vodka and orange juice. I'm also waiting for you to give me the money."

"No, I mean later," Red said. He was seated in his recliner, but only on the edge of the seat, with his feet planted flat on the carpet. "Tonight. Probably right after you leave here. I know what you're doing. And with who."

"With who?" Mandy asked.

"You really want me to spell it out?"

"If you can," Mandy said. "Better not use any long words."

"Hey, you don't have to be ugly. At least not personality-wise."

"Listen, asshole, if you don't—"

"Okay, I'm sorry. Calm down for a second. I'm not trying to screw you around. I'm gonna give you the money. And then I guess you and that boy Tino is gonna run off somewhere together. Am I right?"

She said, "I don't know anyone named Tino, and he's not a boy."

Red laughed. "Oops. You hear what you just said?"

"Well, it's none of your damn business, is it?" she said.

"Don't worry. I'm not gonna tell anyone."

"Why are we even talking about this? Either give me the money—right this minute—or I'm outta here, and then you'll hear from my lawyer instead."

"You oughta stop pretending you got a lawyer," Red said.

"You oughta stop pretending you know what I got or don't got."

"You know what? I like you."

"Don't gross me out."

"You're feisty."

"You're gonna see feisty if you don't stop yammering and get my money."

"See, like that," he said. "Feisty. Okay, I'll get your money."

"Then do it."

"But there's one condition," he said.

"Oh, for fuck's sake," she said.

"It's no big deal," he said.

"Yeah, right."

"Not considering that you'll be long gone after tonight anyway."

"It better not involve anything physical," she said. "Unless it's just my hands."

"What? No. Come on. I wouldn't do that."

Mandy didn't reply.

"Unless you want to," Red said.

"Dream on," Mandy said.

"Okay," Red said, losing his concentration for a moment. "I, uh…What I want is for you to tell me what really happened to Dub on Friday night."

Mandy made a face, like Red was crazy, but she didn't say anything right away. She was thinking about it! Then she rattled the ice in her mug, which was empty again, and said, "Gonna cost you another drink."

37

JUST AS GARZA and Gilchrist reached the SUV, they heard two more shots, followed by someone screaming *Yeeeehawwwww!*

Garza handed Gilchrist a short-barreled Remington 870 loaded with seven rounds of buckshot, and he grabbed an AR-15 with a thirty-round magazine.

Someone shouted, "What's a matter? Don't wanna shoot back?"

Then Marlin yelled, "State game warden! Drop your weapon!"

Hearing Marlin's voice gave Garza an enormous sense of relief, until another rifle shot rang out. They had to help him as quickly as possible.

Lauren signaled that she would slip between the shrubs to the left and proceed clockwise around the house. Garza nodded, then he ran to the right, to the front corner of the house, following the same path Marlin had taken.

g

Creed was right. All hell was breaking loose—but not in the way he expected. He thought Bricker might try to find cover and then shoot at Dickie. But Creed, watching from the second-floor window, was confused by what he was seeing instead. Just as Bricker neared the corner of the house, he suddenly stopped, raised the TEC-9, and fired a shot toward the front of the house, followed quickly by a three-shot burst. What in the hell was he shooting at? Or who?

Then Bricker fired two more shots and yelled *Yeeeehawwwww!* like some kind of damn psycho.

Creed could see him ducking behind a tree now, obviously focused on someone Creed couldn't see.

"What's a matter?" Bricker called out. "Don't wanna shoot back?"

Creed had no idea what to think. Who was it? Who would suddenly show up and draw Bricker's attention that way? Those questions were answered one second later when the person shouted a response to Bricker's taunt.

"State game warden! Drop your weapon!"

Creed was thrilled. Bricker would give up now. This fiasco would come to a quick end. Right?

Wrong. Bricker responded by firing yet another shot.

Dickie, still lying flat on the concrete, scrambled to his feet and sprinted for the wooded area to the rear of the property. Smart.

Creed moved from the rear window to a side window. Now he could see the AC condenser down below, and he could tell that someone was prone behind it, using it for cover. Bricker had the game warden pinned down behind the condenser.

From this angle, Creed could no longer see Bricker behind the tree.

He returned to the rear window.

9

Garza reached the front right corner of the house and listened for one moment. He was tempted to call out—to let Marlin know that reinforcements had arrived. But he didn't want the shooter or shooters to know he was there, if he could avoid it.

Garza drew a slow, steadying breath, then took a quick peek, bobbing his head around the corner and immediately pulling it back before anyone could take a shot at him. What Garza saw was not encouraging.

Marlin was prone behind a metal HVAC condenser housing, which was at least thirty feet from the corner where Garza stood—too far for Marlin to make a sudden break for better cover.

Well beyond the condenser, near the rear corner of the house, were several pecan and oak trees, and the person who'd fired at Marlin was almost certainly hiding behind one of those.

But how many shooters were there? That was the key question. Garza was confident he'd heard two different weapons, which would suggest two people. Or more. Scary thought. What the hell was going on here?

Garza keyed his microphone and said, "How many, John?"

They were all wearing earpieces to keep their radios quiet.

"Bricker at the rear corner," Marlin said quietly. "Another in the house. Second floor, I think."

"Lauren, you got eyes on Bricker?" Garza asked.

Two seconds passed.

"Not yet," Gilchrist said. "Too many trees. Give me a minute."

All three of them knew they had only one objective right now: extract Marlin from the dangerous position he was in. That would require Garza and Lauren to lay down some covering fire while Marlin scrambled for safety. Garza was wishing Lauren had the AR-15 instead of the shotgun, so she could engage Bricker from a greater distance.

"I'm right behind you at the corner," Garza told Marlin.

"Stay where you are," Marlin said.

"Copy."

"What are you carrying?"

"The 15."

"Good. I think the subject in the house was shooting at Bricker," Marlin said.

That was helpful information, if it was accurate, and it explained why the person hadn't fired any additional shots.

Gilchrist said, "Got an open window on the second floor, rear corner. Now I'm going silent."

"Key your mike when you're ready," Garza said.

"Copy."

9

The rush was even greater than Bricker had been expecting. Unbelievable. Total exhilaration. Like taking ecstasy. He could feel it in every cell of his body.

But he wanted the game warden to shoot back. Increase the danger. Just keeping the guy pinned down wasn't difficult with the TEC-9. Stupid son of a bitch had nothing but a handgun, and he was too scared to return fire with it. He was probably on the radio, though. Calling for backup. The place would be swarming with cops in five or ten minutes.

Should he stay here or go inside and wait for a big showdown? He could force Dickie inside and use him as a hostage. Keep the cops at bay.

But when he glanced over, he saw that Dickie wasn't lying by the pool anymore. He wasn't anywhere in sight. The little bitch had run away. Well, shit. Bricker realized he should've shot him when he'd had the chance.

That left the game warden. Bricker would probably have just enough time to finish him off before the cavalry arrived.

Bricker stepped from behind the pecan tree and kept the TEC-9 trained on the AC condenser. He squeezed off another round and relished the sound of it slamming into the metal unit. He figured that game warden was soiling himself with every shot.

Bricker fired three more quick shots. He loved the way the weapon felt in his hands. Powerful, but the kick wasn't overwhelming. He hadn't been counting, but he knew he had plenty of bullets left, plus another full magazine in the canvas bag, along with hundreds of boxed rounds.

The one thing he didn't have in abundance was time. He had to get inside soon.

Was the game warden already dead? Some of the bullets must've made their way through that metal box.

"Come out now and I'll let you live," Bricker called out.

9

Garza couldn't stand it—hearing all those shots and not being able to act. But sticking his head around the corner again when Bricker was firing freely would be incredibly stupid. He had to remain calm if he was going to help Marlin.

He heard Bricker say, "Come on out and I'll let you live."

And then, in his earpiece, he heard Lauren keying her microphone.

Oh, thank God.

She'd gotten close enough to see Bricker without him seeing her. Time to put this son of a bitch on the ground.

Garza keyed his mike in response.

He waited.

"Hey, boy," Bricker called. "You dead or what? If you don't come out right now, I'm gonna—"

Bricker's voice was swallowed by the roar of the Remington 870. Such a sweet sound.

Garza immediately turned the corner, the AR-15 braced and ready, and made another split-second assessment of the situation.

Marlin was still flat on the ground, but he'd shifted to his right, just far enough to peek around the condenser and fire his .357.

Bricker was at the rear corner of the house, no longer hidden behind a tree, and he was turning to his right, toward the source of the shotgun blast. His posture—a slight hunch—indicated that at least one round of the buckshot had struck home.

The AR-15 was equipped with a red-dot scope for quick target acquisition, and less than half a second after rounding the corner, Garza had Bricker in his sights.

He pulled the trigger.

g

Marlin was ready.

He knew how Bobby and Lauren would approach a situation such as this one, and he was fully prepared for it.

The moment Lauren had a shot at Bricker with the shotgun within reasonable range, she would take it, and then Bobby would turn the corner—just enough to fire the AR-15 without totally exposing himself.

Marlin waited.

He heard Lauren key her mike, and then Bobby keyed his in reply…

Two seconds later, Marlin heard the unmistakable boom of the Remington 870.

Marlin had moved to the far-right side of the condenser, and now he shimmied even farther right, .357 in hand, all of the anger and fear inside of him replaced by a laser-like concentration.

The boom of the shotgun hadn't even faded by the time Marlin had Bricker in his iron sights. He pulled the trigger, and at the same time he heard Bobby squeeze off a round from the AR-15 behind him, and another roar from the shotgun.

Bricker flinched hard and the weapon slipped from his hands.

Marlin kept firing.

So did Bobby.

As did Lauren.

Alan Bricker jerked and thrashed in response to the gunfire, blood appearing in several spots through his shirt, but he remained standing, his face a grim mask of defiance.

Then he finally crumpled to the ground and did not move.

Three seconds later, Bobby Garza was at Marlin's side, the AR-15 still pointed in Bricker's direction. "You hit? You okay?"

Marlin got to one knee. "I don't think so," he said. He holstered his revolver and quickly checked himself from head to toe. He knew from experience that adrenaline could mask the pain of an injury. But he found nothing. "I'm fine," he said.

The condenser fan attempted to kick on, but instead it made a horrible screeching sound and metal began to slap against metal.

g

At 7:38 p.m., with the sun dropping behind the horizon, a man called 911 and reached the Erath County Sheriff's Office. As soon as the dispatcher answered, the man gave a panicked report.

"My name is Creed Loftin. I don't know what the hell is going on! There was some kind of crazy shoot-out with the cops and Alan Bricker right outside my home. Bricker was holding a gun on my brother!"

"Sir, what is—"

"I'm inside and I just don't want to get shot! And my brother Dickie is still outside somewhere. Tell 'em not to shoot us because we're not the bad guys!"

"What is the address, sir?"

38

RED GAVE MANDY a wave as she began down the slope to the county road.

Billy Don, standing beside Red, said, "So. What the hell happened in there? I didn't hear any hollering or bitching."

"It worked," Red said.

"For realz?"

Mandy's ball joints were complaining just as much going downhill. She reached the bottom of the hill and turned onto the paved county road.

"Yep. Don't sound so surprised."

"She told you what happened to Dub?"

"Yep."

"And it sounded legit?"

That was another word Billy Don had been using a lot since he'd started using Facebook. Legit.

"Pretty much," Red said. "It all made sense."

"So what happened?" Billy Don asked.

Red told him exactly what Mandy had said.

"Huh," Billy Don said when Red was finished.

"Yep."

"That might even be the truth," Billy Don said.

"Maybe. Could be. I think it probably is."

"But we still don't know the full story."

"It's all I could get."

"How come she didn't freak out about the money?"

"She didn't have nothing to freak out about, because I gave it to her."

Billy Don spit out some beer he had just swigged. "Do what?"

"Changed my mind and gave her the money," Red said.

The original idea—Lydia's idea—was for Red to offer the money to Mandy for the information, and then refuse to pay up. What could she do about it?

"You just gave that crazy lady twenty thousand dollars?" Billy Don asked.

"Yep.

Billy Don laughed. "Bullshit."

Red shrugged.

"So you really did it?" Billy Don asked. "You really did?"

"It was worth it. No more lawsuit that way, no matter whether she stays or goes, gets arrested, whatever. And I can afford it."

"But why?"

Red shrugged again. He wasn't sure why he'd done it. He wondered if he might regret his actions later and want that money back. He decided to forget about that for the moment and drink another beer.

𝓰

Mandy navigated the twisting county road back toward town, and she couldn't help but notice how good it felt to have told someone what had happened. Not some bullshit version, but the actual, God's honest truth. Most of it. After all, it wasn't like she *wanted* it to happen the way it did. She never wanted any harm to befall Dub, except for those times when he made her really mad and acted like a general ass.

She rounded a curve a little too fast and the ice rattled inside her mug. When she reached a straightaway, she sent a text to Tino. *Got the money! See you soon.*

He replied immediately. *The sooner the better.* And he added several dollar-sign emojis, plus a kissy face. Such a sweet kid. And she was very well aware that he *was* a kid, and they didn't necessarily have a future together. Not a long one, anyway. But, for now, he'd do. A couple of months, a year, or whatever.

She replied: *Got your car gassed up?*

She had to do that—remind him of things. Same way she'd always had to remind Dub. Maybe it was just men in general who needed reminders.

He replied: *Doing that right now, need anything else before we hit the road? Not a thing, sweetie.*

𝓰

Lydia was waiting in her car.

Tino was running a little late. Just five minutes. No biggie, right? He'd be here. He was so excited earlier at Dairy Queen. Thrilled at the idea of kissing Lydia's perfect feet again.

She waited some more. Now he was ten minutes late. She checked her phone, looking for a text, but there was nothing there. Should she text him? Hell no. That would come across as desperate. She was *not* desperate. She really couldn't care less about the situation. He was the one who wanted to see her, not the other way around. Well, she *did* want to see him, but to spy on him, not for anything else.

Fifteen minutes late.

Tino was probably taking care of some things before he left town. Just running behind. He'd be here any minute. Then she could pry more information out of him. Get revenge. Make him pay.

She double-checked her feet. The toenail polish was perfect. Glossy, without being tacky. No chips or blemishes of any kind. Exactly the way he liked it.

Okay, now he was twenty minutes late. Not cool.

Was he okay? Maybe he'd gotten into a wreck. Or maybe he'd gotten arrested! That was entirely possible, based on everything she'd been hearing.

Maybe she should go ahead and text. Just to see if he was okay. That was reasonable, wasn't it? So she did. *Everything okay? Waiting on you...*

What happened next gave her some encouragement. She saw those three little dots in a talk bubble that indicated he was typing.

Then she waited.

And nothing happened. Apparently he'd decided not to reply.

So she sent another. *You there? Worried about you.*

She waited ten more minutes and he didn't show up. He didn't answer her texts.

She wanted to believe she hadn't been suckered. She really did.

So she waited twenty more minutes. No Tino. Oh, for fuck's sake. It was just like prom night all over again. How could she have been so stupid?

So she sent him another text: *I hate you, you enormous sphincter. You are a miserable excuse for a human being.*

Felt good. Liberating. So she sent another one.

Speaking of sphincters, good luck in prison. A pretty boy like you will need all the luck you can get.

She actually laughed out loud. She normally wasn't one to use the specter of sexual assault as a threat, but in this case, she just couldn't help herself.

The three dots in a talk bubble appeared again and then went away. Fine by her. She was done with that jerk.

She put her phone in her purse, started her car, and drove home.

39

"WHEN WAS THE LAST TIME we fooled around in the middle of the day?" Marlin asked.

"Don't know," Nicole said, "but I recommend that we meet here again tomorrow. And perhaps the day after."

"Works for me."

"It's therapy," she said.

"I'm in."

They were in bed at one-thirty on Thursday afternoon.

Marlin was on administrative leave while the Erath County Sheriff's Office and Texas Rangers investigated the shootout at the Loftin residence. Lauren Gilchrist was also on leave, and coming to terms with the fact that a round of buckshot had pierced Bricker's superior vena cava, a large vein carrying blood into the heart—likely the shot that had killed him, although Bricker had been hit several times by multiple weapons. Lauren hadn't seemed particularly disturbed to be informed she'd made the fatal shot.

Bobby Garza, on the other hand, opted to override departmental policy for himself, because he couldn't very well go on leave at the same time as his chief deputy. Nicole had taken some impromptu vacation time to be with Marlin.

"I need to bring something up that's been on my mind lately," Nicole Marlin said.

"You're going to suggest that I need to stop taking vitamins, because my virility overwhelms you?" Marlin said.

He knew what was coming, though. And he figured he couldn't blame her.

"Remember a while back when you brought up the idea of retirement?" she asked.

"Of course."

"And I was surprised at the time, and maybe I even said some things that made you think I didn't want you to do that."

"That's not the way I took it," he said.

"I'm glad, because I want you to do what you *want* to do."

They lay in silence for a full minute.

He *had* thought about retirement, at least briefly, but at the time, a dangerous man had made some veiled threats to Nicole. Marlin had wanted the ability to stay home more—to defend his woman and his home. A primal instinct driven by fear, but he couldn't help himself. Marlin had later shot that man dead, and there was no denying the relief he'd felt. It had taken him some time to admit that to himself and grow comfortable with it. It had been easier with Alan Bricker. More and more, Marlin had begun to realize that an evil man like Bricker charts his own fate.

"You wouldn't have to actually retire," Nicole said. "You could move on to something else."

"Like what?" he said.

"That's the question, isn't it?" she said. "I got very lucky and found something else I love to do. I wouldn't change a thing. Maybe you could think about what else you might like as much as being a warden. Something where people don't shoot at you as much."

"That's the only part of it I don't like," he said. "The getting shot at."

"Imagine that," she said.

The windows were open because it was unusually cool—only in the low seventies—and a white-winged dove was calling insistently from the limbs of a live oak no more then ten feet away.

"Or we could just stay right here indefinitely," Nicole said. "Have food delivered and left on the doorstep. Get up to shower now and then."

That notion held some appeal, but only for a week or two. Marlin knew he would get restless after that. Right now, for instance, in any spare moment, his mind would quickly return to the Dub Kimble case. There were still a lot of questions, and Marlin knew they might never get the answers. The Loftins and Skeet Carrasco were refusing to answer questions.

Mandy and Tino had disappeared, with the rumor being they'd run off together. That was their right, though. They were free to go anywhere they wanted. They were no longer considered suspects in the Kimble case.

208 | BEN REHDER

A moment passed and Marlin's mind was suddenly groggy and his eyes were closed.

He was surprised to realize he'd dozed off and Nicole was no longer in bed beside him. How long had he been out? Did it matter?

He reached for his phone on the nightstand and saw that he'd missed a call from Bobby Garza earlier, after which Garza had sent a text.

Creed Loftin is coming in with his lawyer to give a statement at four o'clock.

9

"Despite my strenuous objections, my client wants to clear his good name, and his brother's too. He has decided to give a voluntary statement of the events surrounding the night Dub Kimble disappeared, plus the shooting of Danny Ray Watts, and even the shootout at his home two nights ago. But I need to set a few ground rules. He will provide as much detail as he remembers, and when he's done, he *might* answer some questions. But the bottom line is, you will all agree that Mr. Loftin is doing his civic duty as a good citizen to set the record straight, and that the charges against him need to be dropped immediately."

The man speaking was "Boots" Baker, a gray-haired criminal defense attorney known across Texas for his alligator boots, western-cut suits, and the ability to stretch the truth to its breaking point in the hunt for reasonable doubt.

Seated around a conference table in the Blanco County Sheriff's Office were Baker, Creed Loftin, Bobby Garza, and Angelina Vehreg, the district attorney, who'd driven down from Llano for the meeting. Marlin and Lauren Gilchrist were in another room, watching on video, since they were both on leave and couldn't actively participate.

Garza, Gilchrist, and Marlin had all given statements to Erath County investigators in the hours after the shootout—explaining how it likely tied into the Kimble and Watts cases—but Creed and Dickie Loftin had both refused to answer any questions. Erath County deputies had no grounds to arrest or detain the men, but Garza and his team still had the arrest warrant for Creed Loftin, which they executed, bringing Creed back to Blanco County late Tuesday evening and booking him into the county jail.

Boots Baker had bailed him out the next day and Marlin could just imagine that the previous twenty-four hours had consisted of lengthy conversations between Creed, Dickie, Skeet Carrasco, and Baker, weighing the pros and cons of speaking to law enforcement. Then Boots Baker had called Bobby Garza to arrange this meeting.

"We certainly appreciate the cooperation," Angelina Vehreg said.

She was a tall, intelligent woman in her early fifties, with short blond hair and green eyes. Marlin had worked with her on several occasions and was always impressed with her competence. "And we look forward to hearing what Mr. Loftin has to say. I'm hoping his brother Dickie and Skeet Carrasco will also agree to give statements sometime soon."

Baker grinned. "Those boys have both decided they're not interested in talking to nobody about nothing, and I fully support them in that decision. If that changes, I'll be sure to let y'all know." He looked around the table. "Shall we begin?"

Vehreg nodded.

"Creed?" Baker said.

Marlin thought Creed looked nervous as hell, but that was common for people in his situation, innocent or guilty.

"Okay," Creed said. He had several pages of handwritten notes in front of him. "I'll start with Friday night—when we went to the party at Skeet's place."

9

"I been thinking about something," Billy Don said. "If you ain't gonna tell the cops what Mandy told you—"

"And I ain't."

"Which is stupid."

"They'll say I made it up to divest attention away from myself."

Also, the truth was, Red didn't want to send the cops after her, because then she might double-cross him and try to file a suit despite their agreement.

"Well, in that case, you should probably repeat it for me, and I'll record it, before your memory gets all kludgy."

"All what?"

It was two days after Mandy's visit to Red's house and, surprisingly, he still didn't regret giving her the money.

"Kludgy," Billy Don said, taking his usual sunken spot on the couch.

"You making up words now?" Red asked.

"No, it's a real word."

"Lemme guess. You saw it on Facebook."

"Yeah, so what?"

"That just means somebody else made it up. What does it even mean?"

"It means something is all screwed up, or it don't work right. Hey, your plan for the tree house was kind of kludgy. That's a perfect example."

Billy Don grinned at him.

"Your face is kind of kludgy," Red said. He decided he would start using that word on every occasion possible, just to show Billy Don how annoying it was.

"All I'm saying is, before you forget exactly what she said, you should tell it to me again, and I can record it."

"You got a recorder?"

Billy Don held up his iPhone. That was his answer to everything these days.

Truth was, it was a good idea. That way, if it came down to it, the cops or some slick lawyers couldn't say Red wasn't remembering correctly. Red could also include the details of the deal he had struck with Mandy, including her promise that she wouldn't sue him at a later date.

"Let me grab a beer first," Red said, hoisting himself out of his recliner.

"Get me one," Billy Don said.

"Regular or kludgy?" Red said on his way to the kitchen.

"That don't make sense."

"That's the kludgiest thing I ever heard."

40

"WHAT HAPPENED FRIDAY NIGHT," Creed Loftin said, looking at his notes, "is that we decided to do a little publicity stunt. Me and Dickie did. We'd been talking about that for a long time—just doing something a little silly or stupid to keep his name in the news. And the stunt needed to be something kind of white trashy—you know, to tie into his routine—but nothing too crazy. So we decided it might be kind of funny if Dickie got arrested for driving drunk on a four-wheeler around Johnson City late at night. Just driving circles around the courthouse or something. Smoking a cigar and carrying a bottle of whiskey. His fans would eat that up. So we were at Skeet's place for the party, and I was outside in the Hummer with Bricker, and we—"

"Wait a second," Garza said. "Alan Bricker was at Skeet Carrasco's that night? That's what you're saying?"

The skepticism in the sheriff's voice was obvious.

Creed looked at Boots Baker, who nodded.

"Right," Creed said. "He rode along with me for grins. But we never went inside. I don't think anybody else knew he was there."

"Let's hold any other questions until the end, please," Baker said. "Creed, go on ahead."

Creed said, "Okay, so, Dickie went to the party and hung around for a while, mingled and all that, and then later, after everybody left, we decided to go ahead with it. Dickie got one of the four-wheelers from the barn and then we followed him in the Hummer. Bricker was driving. I was in the back and Skeet was in the passenger seat."

g

"Dub was being an asshole," Mandy had told Red earlier. "First he made fun of my biscuits, and then we started arguing about the, uh, extra-curricular activities both of us had been engaging in, and it went downhill from there. He said some really hateful shit, so I went into the bedroom and came back out with my thirty-eight."

"Whoa," Red said, but with admiration. He liked a woman who stood up for herself.

"By the time I come out, he was already outside, taking a leak beside his truck. I ain't proud of it, but I aimed above his head and fired a shot."

"And you accidentally hit him?" Red asked.

"No, I'm a pretty good shot, even with a cheap-ass pawn-shop revolver. All it did was freak him out, so he started screaming at me and stomping around below the porch, but he knew I had the gun, so he wasn't man enough to get any closer. Anyway, we hollered at each other for a while, and then I went back inside and called somebody about it."

"Tino?" Red asked.

"Yeah, which was dumb, because then he starts talking about coming over to make sure I'm gonna be okay. He's a sweet kid, but he ain't no match for someone like Dub, and Dub wasn't exactly a badass." She looked at her wristwatch. "Okay, long story short, Tino comes over, and by the time he gets there, Dub has already gone off to hunt pigs. I was hoping that would be the end of it, but Tino takes my thirty-eight and goes wandering off in the dark looking for him, so I got no choice but to follow. Eventually he sees Dub's spotlight bouncing around in the trees near the back fence, so that led Tino right to him. Dub saw him coming and he pulled out his hunting knife, trying to be a tough guy or something. Luckily there was enough moonlight for Tino to see what Dub was doing, or—"

"You think Dub would've stabbed him?" Red asked.

"Pretty sure, yeah, because just the idea that Tino would show up at our house would piss Dub off royally."

"I can understand that," Red said.

"But Dub didn't know Tino was carrying my revolver, and as soon as Dub raised the knife, Tino fired a shot."

"Holy—"

"I know," Mandy said. "It was like watching something on TV."

"He shot Dub?"

"No, he shot the ground in front of him. A warning shot."

"And then what happened?"

"Dub got scared and started running for the fence, and Tino ran after him, still carrying the gun, even though I was hollering for him to stop. So then I go after the both of them, and I get there just as Dub climbs over the fence and runs into the road."

Her face got all scrunched up and tears ran down her cheeks. Red didn't know if he should reach over and pat her shoulder or what, so he just sat there, feeling kind of useless.

She said, "It all happened real quick-like. There were headlights coming, and I think Dub was planning to flag 'em down and ask for help. Or maybe he just figured Tino wouldn't be dumb enough to take another shot with witnesses around. Well, it turned out there was two vehicles coming. First one was a four-wheeler, and it swerved, because Dub was standing right in the middle of the road like an idiot. They missed him, but they lost control and ran into the ditch. Right behind the four-wheeler was one of them Hummers, and they didn't have time to stop or even swerve."

A Hummer, Red thought. Just as he'd suspected all along.

"They smashed right into Dub before he knew what was coming. I can still remember the sound of it."

Like hitting a deer, I bet, Red thought, but he didn't say it out loud.

"Me and Tino didn't know what to do," Mandy said. "I was gonna call the cops, but Tino was telling me to hold up, because the cops would say—"

"That Tino chased him out into the road," Red said.

"Zackly. You know how they are."

"Sure do. It's like they got nothing better to do than enforce the law."

"They'd find some reason to blame Tino, and probably me, too, which is bullshit. So we sat there in the dark and just waited to see what would happen next."

"And what *did* happen?" Red asked. He was mesmerized by this point.

Mandy took a long drink from her mug, bracing herself to tell the rest.

Then she said, "The Hummer came to a stop before running over Dub's body in the middle of the road. I could see him in the headlights. Just a big old lump. Not moving. Luckily, we were too far away to see all the gory details, or I probably woulda lost my shit. Then the driver climbed out of the Hummer and walked over to check on him."

Red couldn't stand the suspense any longer.

"Dickie Loftin, right?" he asked. "He was driving the Hummer?"

#

"We'd all been drinking," Creed Loftin said. "I'll admit that right out front. That was kind of the point—at least for Dickie. To get busted for drunk driving. So, being drunk and all, he was hauling ass pretty good on the four-wheeler—like forty miles an hour, and maybe fifty downhill. I was worried he was gonna hit a deer or something, but instead, he slowed down and came to a stop in the middle of the road. Turns out he'd run out of gas."

Creed smiled at the memory.

"He was pretty pissed, too, and he bitched Skeet out real good. He was already in a foul mood anyway because he'd had his eye on a woman at the party, but she turned him down."

Carlotta King, Marlin thought.

"Anyway, Skeet told Dickie to calm his ass down, because we could just run into town and get some gas real quick. But Dickie was being kind of an asshole about it, and finally he says let's just forget the whole damn thing because he wasn't in the mood for it anymore. Skeet says fine, but somebody still has to go get gas. So me and Dickie did that while Bricker and Skeet stayed with the four-wheeler."

"Who drove?" Angelina Vehreg said.

"I did, and by the time we got to town, Dickie was screaming for a cold beer, so I went into the Lowe's Market and got him some, along with a plastic gas can. When I came out, he was standing beside the Hummer, smoking a cigar. See, Lola bitches at him whenever he smokes inside any of their vehicles. So that's how I ended up talking to some guy in the parking lot who'd spotted Dickie and came over to say hello. Dickie obviously wasn't in the mood, so I ran that guy off. Then we stopped at the pumps near the highway to fill the gas can, and a few minutes after that, we ran into that other guy, Danny Ray Watts, who recognized Dickie at a red light."

"Can you describe the conversations you had with those two men?" Angelina Vehreg asked.

"We're not gonna answer that," Boots Baker said. "I'm sure both of those gentlemen have already told you exactly what was said, and we have no reason to dispute it. Creed, please continue."

Creed said, "We drove back to the four-wheeler and put the gas in it, and then we started back to the ranch. Skeet was driving the four-wheeler now and Bricker was driving the Hummer again. He liked driving it. We'd gone less than a mile..."

Creed started shaking his head, like the memory really bothered him.

"We come around this curve, and suddenly, in the middle of nowhere, there's a person in the road. Skeet had to swerve, and that made him lose control of the four-wheeler and end up crashing in the bar ditch, and by the time we saw him, Bricker didn't even have time to hit the brakes. We hit the guy probably going about forty miles an hour. Rest in peace and all that, but what was he doing in the middle of the road at night?"

He paused to sip some coffee from the mug in front of him before resuming his story.

Bobby Garza shifted impatiently in his seat. Angelina Vehreg was frowning. Marlin knew they were frustrated by the inability to ask questions.

Creed Loftin said, "First thing I did was check on Skeet, and luckily he was all right. Meanwhile Dickie and Bricker were checking on the other guy, and, well, it sucks and everything, but the man was dead in the road. No surprise. Ain't nobody to blame but himself."

Marlin and Lauren were both watching the monitor, hanging on every word. Marlin wasn't sure which parts to believe, but he had no doubt Creed Loftin was distorting the truth.

"So then Dickie starts to call 911, but Bricker says hang on a second, because what's the point? Bricker was on parole, I was on parole, we were all drunk, and the man was dead. Calling it in was only gonna cause problems for all of us, especially me and Bricker. Back to prison. Skeet pushes it a little, saying he'll get all of us a good lawyer, and that's when Bricker says, 'Anybody calls the cops, they're gonna find two bodies when they get here. Or more.'"

Creed Loftin looked around with a grave expression to make sure everyone understood the implications.

"Those were his exact words?" Boots Baker asked.

"Yep. I remember it exactly. Hard to forget."

"So he was threatening all of y'all?" Boots Baker said.

"Yep, and as you all know by now, he means what he says." He looked at his notes again. "So Skeet says okay, well, what're we supposed to do then? Just leave him here? And Bricker says no, we gotta move him somewhere that he won't be found right away, or maybe never. He says we gotta put him in the Hummer, and we'd better hurry before anyone else comes along. But Skeet says if they find just one drop of blood inside the Hummer—or even just one hair—then we're all screwed. He said to Bricker, since you're the man who hit him, why don't you load him up on the four-wheeler and haul him away?"

Marlin's frustration was growing. When a man like Creed Loftin tells a story that is ninety percent true, it can be difficult to ascertain which ten percent is false.

"So that's exactly what Bricker did," Creed Loftin said. "Draped the guy over the rear cargo rack and off they went. He had to hurry because it looked like one of the tires was getting flat."

"Where did they take the body?" Angelina Vehreg asked.

Boots Baker looked like he was going to object to the question, but he decided against it and nodded his approval to Creed.

Creed Loftin said, "I got no idea. None of us knew where he was going. None of us wanted to know."

Angelina Vehreg said, "How long was he gone before—"

"No more questions right now," Boots Baker said. He looked at Creed.

"Well, there isn't a whole lot more," Creed said. "Me and Dickie and Skeet went back to the ranch in the Hummer, and that was pretty much it."

"Why didn't you call 911 as soon as Bricker was gone?" Garza asked.

Boots Baker spoke up. "Because, sir, Alan Bricker was an extremely dangerous and unhinged man—the kind of man who would've tried to make good on his threats and kill all three men later. Even if one of your deputies managed to locate and detain Bricker that night, he would eventually be free again, and then he would come after all of them. That's the bottom line. All three men in the Hummer were afraid of Bricker, which was pretty dang smart, considering what Bricker did two days ago, coming after Dickie and Creed the way he did."

"And what happened on the road that night was an accident, so it didn't seem like that big of a deal," Creed Loftin said. "It wasn't like we were failing to report a murder."

"Yeah, it's only manslaughter," Garza said. "No big deal."

Creed started to respond to Garza's sarcasm, but Boots Baker cut him off. "Why don't we take a short break, and then we can move on to the incident with Danny Ray Watts."

41

"THAT PART I'M keeping to myself," Mandy said.

"Oh, come on!" Red said. "No way! You ain't gonna tell me who was driving?"

"I gotta have an ace in the hole in case something happens," she said.

"It was Dickie," Red said. "Had to be."

"Ain't sayin'."

"Well, I'm gonna assume it was him," Red said. "Unless you tell me otherwise."

"Assume whatever the hell you want. What do I care? Don't make it true."

"You sayin' it wasn't Dickie?"

"He was there," Mandy said. "I'll tell you that much. Took me a minute to figure out it was him. I mean, who the hell expects some famous comedian to step out of a vehicle that just ran over your boyfriend?"

"Nobody," Red said.

"Exactly," Mandy said, appreciative of his support. "Nobody expects that. At first, when he stepped in front of the headlights, I thought it was just some guy who looked a lot like him, but then I heard him talk, and I was like, 'Oh, my friggin' God, that's Dickie Loftin.' He's got that voice."

"Must've been weird," Red said.

"Surreal," Mandy said.

"So, so real," Red said. "What'd you do?"

"We just waited and watched, and then I realized one of the other men was Skeet Carrasco, the car dealership guy. I recognized his voice, too. He lives right down the road."

Red knew that, of course, because everybody knew where Skeet Carrasco lived.

"Was Skeet driving?" Red asked, hoping to take her by surprise.

"Ain't sayin'."

"Damn it!"

"And there was a third guy—big guy—but I didn't know who he was until—"

"Dickie's brother," Red said. "Creed Loftin. Looks like a weightlifter?"

"Right, that's what I was saying."

"I bet he was driving," Red said. "Right?"

"Good try," Mandy said.

"But it was one of them, right? Or was there someone else with 'em?"

"Nope," Mandy said. "Just the three of them."

Red was disappointed that she wouldn't tell him who was behind the wheel, but he also knew that the cops might be able to figure out who it was—if and when Red decided to share any of this information with them. He had been persecuted by law enforcement often enough that the idea of helping them out didn't sit right. Let them figure it out for themselves, and in the meantime, he could keep the information in his back pocket, just in case they came around and hassled him some more.

"So what happened next?" he asked. "How did the body disappear?"

9

"I think the bulk of the story is accurate," Bobby Garza said, "except that Bricker wasn't there. That's the one thing he's changing. Making Bricker the fall guy, because he isn't around to defend himself. Blaming everything on him."

"I completely agree," Lauren Gilchrist said.

"Same here," Marlin said.

"If we can find evidence that Bricker was somewhere else on Friday night," Angelina Vehreg said, "Creed Loftin's story will fall apart."

The four of them were in the break room while Boots Baker and his client waited in the conference room down the hall.

"I'll get Ernie started on a warrant for Bricker's cell phone and credit card records," Garza said.

"Can we get someone over to his apartment complex in Austin to see if any of his neighbors recall seeing him Friday night?" Vehreg said.

Lauren Gilchrist was taking notes.

"Good idea," Garza said. "And check for security cameras."

"We should talk to Carlotta King again," Lauren said. "She ran into Creed as she was leaving the party, so it would be good to have her on record saying whether or not she could see anyone else inside the Hummer. It would be great if she could state unequivocally that nobody else was out there."

Marlin said, "Once Skeet acknowledged that Creed was there Friday night, why wouldn't he have mentioned Bricker, too, if he was really there?"

"That's a good question, and I have about a hundred more," Vehreg said. "I'm sure y'all do, too, but I can tell you right now that Baker won't let Loftin answer the majority of them. For now, we'll have to get what we can and try to poke holes in it later."

"Let's go hear what he has to say about Danny Ray Watts," Garza said.

9

"Bricker decided we needed to talk to those two men who saw me and Dickie in Johnson City that night, to try to make them keep their mouths shut." Creed Loftin said. "He came up with this stupid idea that Dickie was working on a show in this area, but it was secret, so we'd pay 'em some money to keep quiet about it. Both of those guys posted on Dickie's Facebook page, so we knew exactly who they were."

"And you deleted those comments on the Facebook page, correct?" Angelina Vehreg asked.

"We're not going to answer that one," Boots Baker said.

The group was in the conference room again.

Creed Loftin said, "Okay, by now, Bricker had told me flat out there wasn't no way he was going back to prison, and if that meant killing a bunch of people, so be it. I don't really care if I look like a pussy now or not, but I was scared of him, and any of you people woulda been, too, if you had any sense. The dude was crazy. Ask anybody."

Creed Loftin paused to emphasize his statement.

Boots Baker said, "I don't think anyone's questioning Bricker's sanity, so let's continue."

Loftin nodded.

"Okay, well, we obviously didn't want anyone to see us talking to Danny Ray Watts, so we parked near his shop and waited until he left, and then we followed him and tried to flag him down. Bricker told me to pull up next to him, and then he hollered over and told Watts he had something wrapped around the axle of his truck. Watts pulled over, but it didn't take him long to recognize me from Friday night, and then the conversation sort of went south. Bricker got short with the man a couple of times, and the next thing I knew, he pulled out a gun—which I did *not* know he had—and shot Watts, totally out of the blue. I was freaking. That's the truth, and I bet it matches up exactly with Watts's version, doesn't it?"

Both Garza and Vehreg remained quiet.

"So then what happened?" Boots Baker asked.

"We thought Watts was dead, so Bricker started saying we needed to decide whether we were gonna haul him off or leave him there. So we left. Went to that little bar in town and drank for a while, and believe me, I needed it. All along I wanted to come forward and tell the police everything I knew, but I was worried that Bricker might kill me and Dickie and Skeet."

"I can only imagine," Boots Baker said, nodding somberly. "Let's move on to the shooting yesterday at your house. Tell us what happened there."

"That won't take long," Creed Loftin said. "I was upstairs and I heard Dickie talking to someone down by the pool. We weren't expecting anyone, so I took a look and saw Bricker down there, holding Dickie at gunpoint. And now you know why we were all so worried, because apparently Bricker had decided to go ahead and kill us all anyway. For all I knew, Skeet was dead already. So I ran to get Dickie's deer rifle, then went back to the window and tried to shoot Bricker before he killed Dickie. Unfortunately, I missed, but what I didn't know was that the cops were already there at the house." He looked at Garza. "If I'd known that, I woulda let y'all handle it. So then y'all killed Bricker—God bless you for that—and then I called 911 to make sure me and Dickie didn't get shot in the process. End of story."

"Must have been pretty scary," Baker said.

"You got that right. I've never been so scared."

9

Mandy said, "After they figured out Dub was dead, they all agreed that none of them was sober enough to say they was driving, so then they started talking about what they should do instead. It was funny the way they sort of eased up on it—the whole idea of hiding the body and pretending they weren't there. Creed said something about how he'd be going back to prison if they called 911, so that wasn't an option, but a lot of the conversation we couldn't hear very good."

Red was mesmerized. What a story. And he believed it! She was telling the truth.

"They was damn lucky it happened on such a quiet road," Red said.

"That's for sure," Mandy said.

"So then what happened?"

"Skeet and Creed Loftin put Dub on the ATV—on that little rack in the back—like they was strapping down a trophy deer. It was sick the way his legs were hanging down and everything. They're gonna burn in hell for that, I'll tell you that much."

"Dirty bastards," Red said.

"Damn right. And then Skeet drove the ATV and Dickie and his brother followed in the Hummer."

"What time was it?" Red asked.

"Maybe ten-fifteen."

That meant it all happened not long after Red had seen the Loftins in town, and it had been just a few minutes later that Red had seen Tino hauling ass on the county road near Dub's place.

"What'd you and Tino do afterward?" Red asked. "After they drove off?"

Mandy went to drink from her mug, but it was empty again. So Red quickly fixed her another one. The woman could really put it away.

Then she said, "What was your question again? I need to leave real soon."

"I said what did you and Tino do after they drove off?"

"Went back home and figured out what the hell we were gonna do. Then I got up the next morning and called the sheriff, and they sent the game warden, figuring it was some kind of hunting accident."

"But did you—"

"Sorry, really, but I got to go," she said as she rose from the couch, grabbing the plastic grocery sack full of cash. "Sorry if I was a bitch at times. Hoping you won't tell anyone what I said—and if you do tell, I'll deny it all anyway."

9

"We might take a few questions now," Boots Baker said. "But I feel that my client has already given a very thorough explanation as to why things happened the way they did, and why he was afraid to come forward before now."

Angelina Vehreg went straight to the core of the matter.

"Let's talk about Alan Bricker and the party on Friday afternoon at Skeet Carrasco's place," she said. "Did he meet you there at Skeet's place or did you and Dickie go to Austin and pick him up?"

"We're not going to answer that one," Boots Baker said immediately.

"Really?" Angelina Vehreg said. "That's surprising."

Baker shrugged.

"Okay, did any of the other guests at Skeet's place interact with, or even see, Alan Bricker?"

"Gonna skip that one, too," Baker said.

"Did Skeet himself see Alan Bricker?"

"Gonna pass," Baker said.

"These are harmless questions," Angelina Vehreg said.

"Maybe so, but even if my client answered them, you wouldn't gain any useful information."

"With all due respect, Mr. Baker, I'd like to be the judge of that."

"What else you got, darlin'?"

Angelina Vehreg maintained her composure.

"Mr. Loftin, can you remember if Alan Bricker was carrying his phone that day?"

"Nope," Baker said. "Not going there."

Vehreg showed only the tiniest sign of exasperation. "You're not giving me much latitude," she said.

"Now don't get your panties in a bunch," Baker said. "I told you the ground rules at the beginning."

Baker was trying to unsettle her, but it didn't work.

Vehreg said, "The truth is, I'm not convinced your client is being entirely forthcoming."

"Does that mean you won't be dropping the charges?" Baker asked.

"Not at this point, no," Vehreg said.

"That's outrageous," Baker said. "A travesty of justice."

"I'm sorry you feel that way."

Baker waited for more, but Vehreg simply stared at him patiently.

"See here, Creed?" Baker said. "This is why I said you shouldn't make a statement."

"Mr. Loftin, did your brother hit Dub Kimble with the Hummer?" Vehreg asked.

"No questions," Baker said, pushing back from the table.

"If he did, you just need to tell us the truth, even if it's painful."

Baker stood. "Come on, Creed. It's time for us to clear out of here."

42

THREE MORE DAYS passed and there was no progress in the Dub Kimble case.

Alan Bricker's cell phone records showed no activity on the evening of Skeet Carrasco's party. No calls coming or going. Location data showed that the phone itself had remained in the area of Bricker's apartment in northeast Austin, but that could mean he'd simply left it at home. Not everyone carried a phone everywhere they went. Or maybe he'd forgotten it. Certainly that's the argument Boots Baker would make, in an effort to defend Creed Loftin's statement.

Bricker's credit and debit cards likewise showed no activity on the date of the party.

Deputies interviewed several of Bricker's neighbors in his apartment complex and nobody remembered whether he was home on that Friday night. There were security cameras in the complex, but none that covered the front door to Bricker's apartment or the area where he normally parked.

Carlotta King tried to be as helpful as possible, but she couldn't say whether there had been another person inside the Hummer when she'd encountered Creed Loftin as she was leaving the party. She could only say she didn't see or hear anyone else, but somebody could've been inside the vehicle, sitting quietly in the dark.

Karl Hines refused to be interviewed. The ATV recovered from his backyard was indeed the one owned by Skeet Carrasco, but Henry Jameson was unable to pull a single fingerprint from it, or any DNA. Apparently it had been scrubbed from top to bottom.

Tino Herrera's car was found parked outside a twenty-four hour fitness center in Topeka, Kansas. Abandoned, obviously. His friends and family members all claimed that they had not heard from him since he'd left town. They were worried about him. Law enforcement officials were confident he'd taken off for parts unknown with Mandy Hammerschmitt.

As for the Danny Ray Watts case, Creed Loftin was still charged for his role in that shooting, but Angelina Vehreg expressed doubts that she would move forward with prosecution, not without new evidence. It was extremely unlikely that a jury would convict him, considering that Alan Bricker had proven himself to be a violent man, and Loftin's fear of retribution appeared to be well-founded.

John Marlin, Bobby Garza, and Lauren Gilchrist were all found to have responded with reasonable force in the shooting of Alan Bricker. They continued to dig into the Dub Kimble case, starting with a renewed search for his remains.

They obtained a search warrant for Dickie Loftin's Hummer, but they learned nothing from it. Henry Jameson processed the vehicle and found no sign of blood, inside or out. No hair that matched Dub Kimble's. No indication that the body had ever been inside the vehicle. Likewise, no sign that Alan Bricker had ever been inside the Hummer, either. Didn't mean he hadn't been. Just meant they couldn't verify whether he *had* been.

The investigation went stagnant.

Marlin went back to his regular duties, which mostly consisted of keeping tabs on dove hunters this time of year.

He was driving north on Miller Creek Loop on Sunday afternoon when he got a call from Lauren.

"Imagine this scenario," she said. "You're taking a bath and suddenly one of your dogs comes inside carrying a human foot in his mouth. Or what's left of one."

"What happened?" Marlin said, taking his foot off the gas.

"And then he drops the foot into the bath with you," she said.

"Who are we talking about?" Marlin said.

"Lester Higgs," Lauren said. "He called me five minutes ago."

9

It was weird waking up in cool weather, with the windows open and a gentle breeze coming into the room. Plus the unmistakable smell of pine trees. A different world. Different people. Different attitudes.

Mandy lay quietly and enjoyed it for a moment. She knew it wouldn't last forever, but that was okay. She stretched, then reached over for Tino and felt an empty bed. So she opened her eyes and saw that the bathroom door was closed. She hadn't heard him get up, but she had been sleeping deeply for the past several nights. The sleep of someone who has no immediate worries.

She could hear a bird singing a song outside, but she didn't know what kind it was. Some species she'd never heard back home.

She was waiting to hear the sound of the shower, and then she'd go in there and join him. Surprise him. Get frisky, standing up, bracing herself against the Formica wall. Tino was so much more fun than Dub had ever been.

She couldn't help but wonder what was happening back home.

She knew there had been some kind of wild shootout at Dickie Loftin's place near Stephenville, because it had made the national news, but the details were sketchy. Sounded like some nutball had been threatening the Loftins and gotten himself shot by cops as a result. Weird thing was, it was the Blanco County cops, and that was because they'd been serving a warrant for Creed Loftin, who had some kind of connection to the shooting of Danny Ray Watts, and so did the man who was killed. She'd only caught the last few seconds of the report, and then, when she'd started to look it up online, she'd decided to let it go. Why should she care? She was starting over.

Tino was taking an awfully long time in there. And he was being so quiet.

"Tino-Weeno?" Mandy called out. Her pet name for him.

No answer.

"Babe?"

Nothing.

She propped herself up on her elbows.

"You in there?"

Silence.

9

Jessie, Ernie Turpin's coonhound, was hyperactive in everyday situations, but when she was called out on a tracking expedition, she absolutely quivered with excitement, tugging on her leash and raring to go.

"Best if you let us go alone," Ernie Turpin said, doing his best to rein the dog in for the moment. "Give me ten or fifteen minutes and let's see what she finds."

"Sounds good to me," Lauren said.

Marlin nodded.

They were standing outside Lester's house on the Hawley Ranch. Earlier, Lauren had asked Lester to load his dogs inside his truck and drive them a mile or two away to prevent any distractions. Meanwhile,

Henry Jameson was inside the house, processing the foot in the tub, all with the permission of Mack Hawley, the ranch owner, and Lester. No warrant needed.

Ernie let Jessie pull him along, past some cedar trees and down a small hill, and it wasn't long before they were out of view.

"Lester says he was in the bathtub alone," Lauren said.

Marlin grinned.

"Does Lester strike you as a guy who takes baths?" Lauren asked.

She had spoken to Lester for a few minutes before Marlin had arrived.

"A cowboy can't take baths?" Marlin asked. "Light a few candles? Maybe pour a glass of chardonnay?"

They were both in a good mood. Receiving an unexpected break in a case always helped boost the spirits. Now, if their luck held, Jessie would find the rest of the body and it would provide further helpful information.

"Thing is, I noticed two wet towels hanging in there," Lauren said. "Weird, huh?"

"If you think that's weird," Marlin said, "I'm pretty sure I passed Kelly Rundell's car on the way over here."

"Imagine that," Lauren said.

Lester's house was 2.6 miles from the spot where Dub Kimble had been hit by Dickie Loftin's Hummer. None of the search parties had looked in this area when Kimble had disappeared. You could expand the scope of a search only so far before it became impractical.

Marlin and Lauren both wondered if the body had been dumped in this area to cast suspicion on Lester. After all, Dub Kimble and Lester had gotten into a heated argument at the café a few weeks earlier, apparently about Kelly Rundell. Good thing Lester had a rock-solid alibi for the night of Dub's disappearance or that ploy might've worked.

"It occurs to me that Alan Bricker would have no way of knowing that he could implicate Lester by leaving the body here," Marlin said.

"But Skeet Carrasco, on the other hand," Lauren said. "He would know. And didn't he try to steer you toward Lester at one point?"

"He did indeed," Marlin said.

"Interesting," Lauren said.

That brought up two possibilities: Carrasco had told someone— possibly one or both of the Loftin brothers—where to dump the body, or he had dumped it himself.

Lauren's phone rang with a call from Ernie and she put it on speaker.

"Just found him, and it's a mess," Ernie said. "Not much left. Lots of scattering."

"Where?"

"Down in a draw about forty yards from the county road. Looks like some brush had been piled over the body at one point."

"How far from the house?" Lauren asked.

"Maybe half a mile."

"But still on the ranch?"

"Right. I didn't cross any fences. I see some shreds of clothing, so we'll be able to compare that to what Lester was wearing that night. Oh, hang on." There was a five-second pause, and then Ernie said, "I just found a tennis shoe. Dub was wearing blue Nikes, right?"

9

Mandy refused to panic just yet.

She glanced at the motel room door and saw that the chain was hanging loose. She remembered sliding the chain into its slot last night. Maybe Tino had left for some reason. To get coffee from the lobby?

She slipped out of bed, still nude, and her nipples hardened in the brisk Oregon morning air. She went to the windows and peeked around the edge of the curtain.

Her truck—*their* truck now—was gone.

Remaining calm was becoming more difficult. Maybe Tino had run an errand, to get some food or something. First things first. She had to pee, so she went to the bathroom door and opened it. He wasn't in there, of course, but there was a note on the vanity beside the sink.

My sweet little Piggie,

I am sorry. Take care of yourself.

Love, Tino.

Oh, jeez. Oh, damn. That little son of a bitch. It was bad enough that he'd left her, but now she realized it might be even worse than that.

She hustled to her suitcase and unzipped it. Oh, God. It *was* worse. Much worse.

The $20,000 in cash was gone. Every damn dollar.

The dirty bastard had left her high and dry.

She began to cry. She began to hyperventilate with panic. She began to wish she'd never laid eyes on Tino Herrera and his impossibly long eyelashes.

What now? What could she possibly do? The fresh start was officially over.

No truck. No money. No friends or family nearby.

As each minute passed, she began to get angrier.

And then she realized she had been overlooking the obvious. She

228 | BEN REHDER

had no reason to protect Tino anymore. No reason to keep quiet.

She took a moment to regain her composure.

Then she called 911 and reported her truck and cash stolen. The dispatcher took her information and said an officer would arrive at her motel room within the hour.

Then she dialed the cell phone number for Sheriff Bobby Garza in Blanco County.

When he answered, she said, "This is Mandy Hammerschmitt. I figure it's time to tell you exactly what happened to Dub."

43

SKEET SAT ON HIS PATIO on Sunday evening with a sprawling fifty-mile view in front of him, yet he saw none of it.

He'd slept for five hours in total in the past three nights. He couldn't focus. Couldn't keep his thoughts straight.

Everything was falling part. His empire was crumbling.

The Loftin brothers were going to turn on him. Skeet Carrasco had no doubt about that. Why wouldn't they? Neither of them had been returning his calls or texts for the past few days.

That was understandable in the first day or two after that crazy shootout at Dickie's place, but why nothing but silence since then? What was going on? Were they talking to the sheriff about Dub Kimble? They could get a sweet deal from the district attorney. Two against one. Their word against his. He could say they were lying—ganging up on him— but would anyone believe him?

And who the hell was this Alan Bricker guy the cops had killed at Dickie's place? One tabloid TV show suggested he was a deranged Jeff Foxworthy fan, but a savvy reporter dug up the fact that Alan Bricker and Creed Loftin had shared a cell together many years back. From that, Skeet had concluded that Creed had asked Bricker to help him deal with the two men who had seen Creed and Dickie in town Friday night. That's how Danny Ray Watts got shot. Skeet was only guessing, but he figured he was probably pretty close to the truth.

And now what?

They were going to turn on him—and that meant the end of everything.

Prison would be just the start of it. Everything Skeet had built in the past three decades was in jeopardy. His chain of dealerships. His ranch. The millions in the bank. All of it. Sure enough, someone representing Dub's estate would crawl out of the woodwork and sue Skeet for everything they could get. And they'd win. Wrongful death or some such BS.

Even if Skeet got a short prison sentence, the dealerships would tank and he would have nothing when he got out.

Come see Skeet and get back on the street!

Yeah, right.

Come see Skeet and get killed on the street!

That's the kind of thing people would say.

All because of one stupid mistake. Not hitting Dub Kimble—that was unavoidable, drunk or sober, like when a deer runs directly in front of your vehicle and you have no time to react. The mistake was trying to get away with it. Hiding the body. Thinking the truth would never come out. Stupid.

Would've been smarter to leave the scene and turn himself in the next day, accompanied by a lawyer. At that point, a blood test would have been of no value. They couldn't have proven he was drunk. He could've said he simply panicked and left the scene.

Dickie and Creed had sworn they would keep silent until the bitter end, but now he wasn't so sure. Betrayal, pure and simple. Skeet had helped turn Dickie into an A-list comedian by featuring him in an ad campaign, and this was the thanks Skeet got?

Or was he letting his imagination run away with him? Was there some other reason the brothers weren't calling him back? Maybe they—

Skeet was startled by his ringing phone.

First time it had rung today. Karl Hines calling. Skeet's ranch foreman wasn't much of a caller. If Karl was calling, it was important.

"Karl?" Skeet said.

"Mr. Carrasco?"

"Yeah?"

"Sorry, I wasn't sure that was you. You sound a little…different."

"What's up, Karl?"

"I'm working on the fence down here by the county road and the game warden pulled into the ranch entrance just now. Are you expecting him? Somebody was with him and I think it was the sheriff."

9

"Before I spill it all, I'm gonna want two things," Mandy Hammerschmitt had said earlier to Bobby Garza on the phone.

"What's that?" Garza had asked.

"First thing is a bus ticket back home."

"From where?"

"Bend, Oregon."

"I'm sure we can arrange that," Garza said.

"And the second thing is, I don't wanna get charged with nothing myself," Mandy said.

"Well, that will depend on what kind of information you have to share with us," Garza said, "but I'm guessing the DA will be willing to work something out, as long as you didn't kill Dub yourself or participate in the killing."

"Hell, no, I didn't. Not really. It was all an accident."

"Why don't you tell me about it?" Garza asked.

"Because if I do, I won't have anything to bargain with."

"You'll have to trust me on this," Garza said. "That's the way it works. We'll work with you. Besides, we might need you to repeat your story later, possibly in court, and that's why you'd still have leverage."

The line was silent for a long moment.

"Okay," Mandy said. "I'll share the high points. How's that?"

"That's a good place to start."

She took a deep breath, then said, "Dub was treating me like shit that night, so Tino came over, but by then Dub was out hunting. Tino went after him, carrying my thirty-eight, but only to scare him. Dub saw Tino coming, so he pulled his knife out, and then Tino fired a warning shot at the ground."

Garza was taking notes as fast as he could write them.

"Dub turned and ran," Mandy said. "He hopped the fence and went out into the middle of the county road...and he just stood there, like a dumbass, with headlights coming his way. A four-wheeler swerved and missed him, but then a Hummer..."

Mandy stopped. Garza could tell she was getting choked up. He waited.

"The Hummer didn't have time to swerve or hit the brakes or nothing," Mandy said. "They hit Dub and that was all she wrote. I figure he was dead right off the bat, which I guess was good, so he didn't suffer none."

She paused again, and Garza resisted the urge to ask questions. Just let her tell the story.

"Me and Tino felt bad, because Dub wouldn't have been out there if Tino hadn't fired that shot. So we didn't call the police or nothing. We just stood there behind some cedars and watched. I regret that now and want to set things right. The guy driving the four-wheeler walked over to the body first, and it freaked me out when I realized it was Dickie Loftin. I could hear his voice and I knew it was him. Then the two guys got out of the Hummer."

She laughed. Then she sniffed.

"You probably want to know who was driving, huh?" she said.

"That would be helpful," Garza said.

"It was Skeet Carrasco," Mandy said.

"You sure?"

"Absolutely. You track Tino down and he'll tell you the same thing. If you can make the little son of a bitch talk."

9

Marlin and Garza had discussed their next move at length.

Try to get an arrest warrant for Skeet Carrasco based on the statement from Mandy Hammerschmitt? Possible, and maybe even likely.

But they opted instead to approach Carrasco again and give him a chance to explain or refute the claims. Get him talking, if possible. He'd never said he wouldn't talk without his attorney, so Marlin and Garza were within their rights to ask for an interview.

And there was no time like the present. Less than one hour after receiving the call from Mandy Hammerschmitt, Marlin left the Hawley Ranch, picked Garza up, and they drove to Carrasco's ranch.

The plan might fail. Carrasco might refuse to answer questions, as he had earlier. At that point, Marlin and Garza would inform Boots Baker that Creed and Dickie Loftin would be wise to make a deal while the dealing was good. Marlin felt confident the Loftins would cave at that point and point their fingers at Carrasco.

Marlin took a right onto the Big Ram Ranch and drove over a cattle guard between two stone pillars. He spotted a silver GMC truck parked sixty or seventy yards to his right, among the cedar trees, near the fence that ran parallel to the county road. Karl Hines's truck. He could see Hines standing near the fence, apparently working, but stopping to watch them enter the ranch.

"There goes the element of surprise," Garza said.

Marlin nodded and kept driving.

They passed a stock tank on the left that was at least three acres in size, with cattle clustered in the shade of nearby oak trees.

Earlier, Mandy had admitted to Garza that Tino had abandoned her, stealing her truck and $20,000 in cash. She had gotten the money in an informal agreement with Red O'Brien in regards to Dub's injury. Marlin had to shake his head at the thought of Mandy and Red sitting around a table, hammering out a deal. What did those two yokels know about negotiating a proper legal settlement?

Marlin and Garza began the long ascent to Carrasco's house atop one of the highest hills in the area. And to think Carrasco also owned a multi-million dollar home in one of the nicest neighborhoods in San Antonio. Hard to imagine having that kind of wealth.

They passed an intersection of sorts—a caliche road ran perpendicular to the paved driveway, and dust hung in the air to their right. But no dust to the left. That meant a vehicle coming from the house had just turned onto the caliche road in the past minute or two.

Marlin eased to a stop. "Think we should check that out?"

"Probably," Garza said.

Marlin backed up, then took a right onto the caliche road. He followed it for two hundred yards through a thick oak grove, then came to a clearing and saw a Cadillac Escalade, maybe seventy yards away, coming slowly toward his truck. He couldn't tell how many people were inside it.

Marlin braked and came to a stop.

"Does Skeet drive an Escalade?" Garza asked.

"Don't know," Marlin said. "Could be a guest."

"Someone looking for a place to hunt dove?"

"Maybe. Let's give them a minute."

g

Skeet saw the game warden's truck waiting for him and his palms began to sweat. It was over. The end of the line. They were coming for him, just as he'd suspected.

What now?

He was having trouble thinking clearly.

He felt trapped.

He reached over and popped open the glove compartment. Inside lay a silver .357. Nothing good could come from that. He'd do something stupid. He pushed the button to lower the passenger-side window, and he tossed the revolver out the window. Now, no matter what might happen, at least that was off the table.

He placed both hands on the steering wheel.

g

"They just threw something," Garza said. "What was that?"

"I couldn't tell," Marlin said.

The Escalade began to roll in their direction. Slowly. Hardly moving.

Then a little faster.

"That's Carrasco," Garza said.

Marlin lowered his window. Time for a quick chat. Let Carrasco know why they were here. Ask him to come to the sheriff's office for an interview. Or they could do it at his house. As long as he talked.

Now Carrasco was ten yards away and Marlin gave a friendly wave through the windshield.

Then Carrasco gunned it, and as the Escalade flew past, Marlin was startled by a loud pop.

"The hell was that?" Garza asked.

"His mirror hit mine," Marlin said, cranking the wheel sharply to make a U-turn. "That's how close it was. See the crack?"

"He just damaged state property," Garza said. "Grounds to pull him over."

Marlin completed the turn and hit the gas hard, but the Escalade was already out of sight, past a curve on the caliche road.

At this much higher speed, Marlin reached the paved driveway in less than thirty seconds, and he saw that the dust in the air ended there. The Escalade—still out of sight—had turned either left or right.

Marlin instinctively turned left, toward the ranch entrance. Stomped the gas, rounded a curve, then another, crested a small hill, and now he saw the Escalade in the distance, just making a hard right onto the county road.

Marlin reached the road, made the same right, and pushed the accelerator to the floor. He was vaguely aware of the silver GMC truck still parked along the fence line. Karl Hines had to be wondering what the hell was going on.

Garza was on the radio, asking for available units to respond to a fleeing subject. That would have to do, because the powerful Escalade was just too fast for Marlin's aging truck. The Cadillac was once again out of sight.

Why was Carrasco running? What could he possibly hope to gain? Where could he go?

Marlin quickly covered another mile and still the Escalade was nowhere to be seen. It had gained ground too rapidly.

Then Marlin topped a small rise and was wholly unprepared for what lay before him.

The Escalade was parked on the shoulder, the driver's door open, and Skeet Carrasco was standing in the middle of the road, just ahead, his eyes closed, bracing for the impact.

Marlin reacted as quickly as he could.

He didn't swerve—at this speed, his truck might've rolled— but he did manage to hit the brake hard and lock the tires up.

Still, though, there was no chance to avoid Carrasco altogether.

Marlin would always remember the impact—the way the grill guard on his truck slammed into Carrasco. The way Carrasco's head slammed downward onto the hood of the truck before his body went airborne for a sickeningly long time.

Then Carrasco hit the pavement and tumbled for ten yards.

Then nothing. The body lay still. No movement whatsoever.

Marlin brought the truck to a full stop five yards shy of the body. He was aware of Garza on the radio again, asking Darrell to roll EMS immediately. Better yet, see if the STAR Flight helicopter in Austin was available.

Then Garza was placing a hand on Marlin's shoulder, saying, "There was nothing you could do. He wanted that to happen."

Marlin was breathing hard, his heart thundering. "I know," he said.

44

SKEET CARRASCO SURPRISED everybody, including the emergency room doctors who treated him, by making it through the night. And the next day. After another 24 hours, it became apparent that he was going to survive, despite two broken legs, a broken arm, a shattered pelvis, a fractured skull, a punctured lung, a ruptured spleen, and a lacerated liver.

Four days after admission, he regained consciousness, had a bowel movement, and they transferred him out of intensive care.

Two days after that, he asked to see the sheriff. He said he wanted to get some things off his conscience.

g

"I'd been drinking," Skeet Carrasco said, in obvious pain. "I was pretty drunk, I guess."

Bobby Garza was seated beside Carrasco's hospital bed with a digital recorder resting on the arm of the chair. Marlin was standing in a corner, simply watching.

Garza had already read Carrasco his rights. Carrasco had indicated that he wished to move forward with the interview, and he stated that he had refused painkillers this morning in order to keep his mind clear.

"Dickie decided he wanted to do some kind of stupid PR stunt—to drive one of my ATVs drunk around Johnson City. Get arrested. He figured his fans would think it was funny. He was probably right."

The story continued from there, much the same way Creed Loftin had told it, except that Alan Bricker wasn't there. He had never been there.

Dickie had been driving the ATV, just as Creed and Mandy had both said.

Creed and Skeet had been in the Hummer, with Skeet driving.

The ATV ran out of gas. Dickie was drunk and short-tempered. Didn't want to do the stupid stunt anymore. Skeet waited with the ATV while Creed and Dickie went to town for gas. They came back, filled the ATV, and were on the way back to the ranch.

Suddenly a man was in the road.

Dickie swerved, but Skeet couldn't avoid him. They hit him hard and he flew through the air. Dead on impact. Skeet approached the body and recognized the man as Dub Kimble. Poor bastard. What the hell was he doing in the road?

And what now?

They were all drunk. That was the problem. Sober, everything would've been okay, but being drunk meant big trouble.

So they decided to move the body. Crazy, yeah, but what else could they do? Skeet had an idea. Dump it on the Hawley Ranch. Skeet knew Lester Higgs and Dub Kimble had had words over Kelly Rundell, so why not take advantage of that? It would lead the cops in the wrong direction if the body were found.

"Downright shameful," Skeet said. "No other word for it."

So he toted the body on the ATV, then he and the Loftins had carried it onto the ranch. All three of them took part. They covered it with brush, and then took off. Went home and vowed to never speak of it again.

Garza asked a lot of questions and Carrasco answered them freely.

The Hummer had no damage at all. The ATV had gotten damaged when Dickie had wrecked it. Lost part of a rear fender. They couldn't very well go wandering around the crime scene, looking for the fragment, so Skeet asked Karl Hines to haul it off. Get rid of it. Sell it. Whatever. Hines didn't know anything about the circumstances. Hines wasn't the kind to ask his boss questions.

Carrasco knew nothing about the events that followed—Creed Loftin coming back to town with Alan Bricker. Knew nothing about the shooting of Danny Ray Watts. Never knew it was connected.

Garza and Marlin believed him.

Marlin didn't know how hard Angelina Vehreg would go after Carrasco. He'd get charged with intoxication manslaughter, no doubt about that, and possibly tampering with evidence, and maybe a few other charges.

The Loftins would get charged with tampering—and that might be it—but since the tampering involved a corpse, that made it a second-degree felony, and that meant Creed Loftin would be serving some time. Dickie, maybe not, if he could swing a plea bargain, but he was suffering in some other ways. All of his gigs had been canceled. He'd lost every last one of his endorsement deals.

Then there was Tino Herrera. He'd been arrested two days earlier in Pocatello, Idaho, still driving Mandy Hammerschmitt's truck. They found a plastic bag on the floorboard containing $17,673 in cash—Mandy's money, which would be returned to her in due time.

When Carrasco was finished making his statement and answering questions, it was time for the sheriff to share a vital piece of information with him.

Garza said, "There's something you should know about Dub Kimble—something the medical examiner found during the autopsy."

"Yeah?"

"He had a bullet lodged in his sternum."

Carrasco raised his eyes to meet Garza's. "What?"

"That shot Tino fired? Apparently it ricocheted and struck Dub in the chest. That might explain why he ran into the road and stopped in the middle. I'm sure he was panicking and wanted help."

Carrasco had been told about the witnesses in the trees—Mandy and Tino—and the events that transpired in the minutes before the accident, including Tino's warning shot at Dub. But Carrasco hadn't known about the autopsy results until now. If the bullet had come to rest in the soft tissues of Kimble's body, it likely would have never been found. The scavengers would have seen to that. But the rib cage, including the sternum, had remained intact, holding the bullet in place.

Carrasco pondered this information for a moment, then said, "Would it have been fatal?"

Sad. He was searching for a way to absolve himself of the guilt he felt for Dub's death. The situation would have been more bearable if Dub was already mortally wounded when Carrasco hit him with the Hummer.

"I'm not going to lie to you," Garza said. "The answer is no. But I thought you'd want to know anyway."

Carrasco nodded slowly, appearing somewhat disappointed.

A silence enveloped the room, and then Carrasco's eyes met Marlin's.

"You were driving the truck that hit me?" he asked.

"Yep."

"I'm sorry to put you through that," he said.

Marlin had a brief flashback to the day it had happened. He remembered tumbling out of his truck and running over to Carrasco's broken body. Seeing the nasty arm fracture, the bone protruding, the blood flowing at a rate that would leave Carrasco dead in minutes.

Applying a compress and holding it tight. The paramedic later telling Marlin he had saved Carrasco's life.

"That's okay," Marlin said.

Carrasco offered his good hand. Marlin stepped forward and shook it.

9

The word reached Red that Mandy Hammerschmitt had returned to town, but he hadn't heard a word from her. Didn't expect to, really, but then she came bouncing up the driveway to his trailer on a Sunday evening, eight days since he'd last seen her, driving a different vehicle this time. Another old truck, but this one was an orange Nissan. She reached the top of the hill, stopped beside Red's Ford, and killed the engine.

When she stepped out, Red was standing on his front porch. "At least the ball joints are good on that one," he said.

She closed the truck door and smiled at him. "You hear about my little adventure?"

"A little bit, yeah."

She stared at him. He stared back.

"Ain't you gonna offer a girl a cold beer?" she asked.

"You want a cold beer?" he asked.

"Thought you'd never ask," she said.

He went inside and got two beers. When he came back out, she was seated on the top step. He sat down beside her and handed her one of the beers. They both popped their tops and took a drink.

"Dang, that's good," she said.

"Sure enough," Red said.

"Where's that big ol' boy that hangs around here?" she asked.

"Billy Don?" Red said. "He's off running around somewhere."

Mandy took another long drink.

Red was wondering why she was here. Wasn't like they were good friends.

"I was thinking about something on the way up to Oregon," she said. "That night when I came over here for the money. And it occurred to me that you probably didn't intend to give me that money when I was done telling you what happened to Dub. You was just gonna tell me to hit the road. Wasn't much I could have done about it. Am I right?"

"Pretty much," Red said.

"But you gave me the money anyway."

"Yep."

"Why?" she asked.

Red laughed. "You know, I'm not sure I know the answer to that."

He could smell a nice scent coming off Mandy, and he noticed that her thigh was rubbing lightly against his. And good Lord, the jugs on her. She was wearing another low-cut blouse, and as Johnny Carson once said to Dolly Parton, he'd give about a year's pay for a peek under there.

"Whatever it was," Mandy said, "I wanted to make sure you knew I appreciated it. That was the nicest thing anybody had done for me in a long time."

"Oh, sure," Red said. "Wasn't no big—"

Mandy leaned over and kissed him. Not a little kiss either. There was suddenly a warm tongue inside Red's mouth, exploring left and right, and he did his best to keep up and act like he knew what he was doing. Made him wish he hadn't eaten that onion dip earlier, but she didn't seem to care.

Then she pulled back and said, "Why don't we go inside?"

"Sounds good," Red said, and it came out in a hoarse croak.

9

It was the best damn Sunday Red had had in a long time. Maybe ever. Better than most Saturdays, too. They went into his bedroom and stayed there for more than two hours. If he'd given a year's pay, it would've been worth it, but free was even better.

At one point, he heard Billy Don pull up in his Ranchero, and then the trailer shook, and then Billy Don called out for him. Mandy giggled in Red's ear, all snuggled up against him, not a stitch on her. The girl had a body that might not stop a train, but it would damn sure slow it down.

Billy Don called out again and Mandy yelled, "He's busy!"

That was followed by total silence, and then he could hear Billy Don say, "Well, god damn. That's my boy."

They stayed in bed until the sunlight in the window began to fade, and then Mandy said, "There's something I need to tell you."

"What's that?" Red said.

"I don't know if you're gonna wanna hear this or not," she said.

"Try me," he said.

"Might get you upset," she said. "And I don't want to ruin the evening."

"Ain't no way you could ruin it at this point," Red said.

"You sure?"

"Dead certain," Red said. "Believe me on that one."

"Okay," Mandy said. "Here goes. You know Dub's back injury?"

"What about it?"

"He was faking it."

Red sat up abruptly. He knew his eyes were wide and his mouth was open.

Mandy started to grin at him.

"That son of a bitch," Red said. And then he could only laugh.

Want to know when Ben Rehder's
next novel will be released?

Subscribe to his email list at
www.benrehder.com.

Have you discovered Ben Rehder's
Roy Ballard Mysteries?

Turn the page for an excerpt from
GONE THE NEXT

GONE THE NEXT

1

The woman he was watching this time was in her early thirties. Thirty-five at the oldest. White. Well dressed. Upper middle class. Reasonably attractive. Probably drove a nice car, like a Lexus or a BMW. She was shopping at Nordstrom in Barton Creek Square mall. Her daughter — Alexis, if he'd overheard the name correctly — appeared to be about seven years old. Brown hair, like her mother's. The same cute nose. They were in the women's clothing department, looking at swimsuits. Alexis was bored. Fidgety. Ready to go to McDonald's, like Mom had promised. Amazing what you can hear if you keep your ears open.

He was across the aisle, in the men's department, looking at Hawaiian shirts. They were all ugly, and he had no intention of buying one. He stood on the far side of the rack and held up a green shirt with palm trees on it. But he was really looking past it, at the woman, who had several one-piece swimsuits draped over her arm. Not bikinis, though she still had the figure for it. Maybe she had stretch marks, or the beginnings of a belly.

He replaced the green shirt and grabbed a blue one covered with coconuts. Just browsing, like a regular shopper might do.

Mom was walking over to a changing room now. Alexis followed, walking stiff-legged, maybe pretending she was a monster. A zombie. Amusing herself.

He moved closer, to a table piled high with neatly folded cargo shorts. He pretended to look for a pair in his size. But he was watching in his peripheral vision.

"Wait right here," Mom said. She didn't look around. She was oblivious to his presence. He might as well have been a mannequin.

Alexis said something in reply, but he couldn't make it out.

"There isn't room, Lexy. I'll just be a minute."

And she shut the door, leaving Alexis all by herself.

~ ~ ~

When he first began his research, he'd been surprised by what he'd found. He had expected the average parent to be watchful. Wary. Downright suspicious. That's how he would be if he had a child. A little girl. He'd guard her like a priceless treasure. Every minute of the day. But his assumptions were wrong. Parents were sloppy. Careless. Just plain stupid.

He knew that now, because he'd watched hundreds of them. And their children. In restaurants. In shopping centers. Supermarkets. Playgrounds and parks. For three months he'd watched. Reconnaissance missions, like this one right now, with Alexis and her mom. Preparing. What he'd observed was encouraging. It wouldn't be as difficult as he'd assumed. When the time came.

But he had to use his head. Plan it out. Use what he'd learned. Doing it in a public place, especially a retail establishment, would be risky, because there were video surveillance systems everywhere nowadays. Some places, like this mall, even had security guards. Daycare centers were often fenced, and the front doors were locked. Schools were always on the lookout for strangers who —

"You need help with anything?"

He jumped, ever so slightly.

A salesgirl had come up behind him. Wanting to be helpful. Calling attention to him. Ruining the moment.

That was a good lesson to remember. Just because he was watching, that didn't mean he wasn't being watched, too.

2

The first time I ever heard the name Tracy Turner — on a hot, cloudless Tuesday in June — I was tailing an obese, pyorrheic degenerate named Wally Crouch. I was fairly certain about the "degenerate" part, because Crouch had visited two adult bookstores and three strip clubs since noon. Not that there's anything wrong with a little mature entertainment, but there's a point when it goes from bawdy boys-will-be-boys recreation to creepy pathological fixation. The pyorrhea was pure conjecture on my part, based solely on the number of Twinkie wrappers Crouch had tossed out the window during his travels.

Crouch was a driver for UPS and, according to my biggest client, he was also a fraud who was riding the workers' comp gravy train. In the course of a routine delivery seven weeks prior, Crouch had allegedly injured his lower back. A ruptured disk, the doctor said. Limited mobility and a twelve- to sixteen-week recovery period. In the meantime, Crouch couldn't lift more than ten pounds without searing pain shooting up his spinal cord. But this particular quack had a checkered past filled with questionable diagnoses and reprimands from the medical board. My job was fairly simple, at least on paper: Follow Crouch discreetly until he proved himself a liar. Catch it on video. Testify, if necessary. Earn a nice paycheck. Continue to finance my sumptuous, razor's-edge lifestyle.

~ ~ ~

You'd think Crouch, having a choice in the matter, would've avoided rush-hour traffic and had a few more beers instead, but he left Sugar's Uptown Cabaret at ten after five and squeezed his way onto the interstate heading south. I followed in my seven-year-old Dodge Caravan. Beige. Try to find a vehicle less likely to catch someone's eye. The windows are deeply tinted and a scanner antenna is mounted on the roof, which are the only clues that the driver isn't a soccer mom toting her brats to practice.

Anyone whose vehicle doubles as a second home recognizes the value of a decent sound system. I'd installed a Blaupunkt, with Bose speakers front and rear. Total system set me back about two grand. Seems like overkill for talk radio, but that's what I was listening to when I heard the familiar alarm signal of the Emergency Alert System. I'd never known the system to be used for anything other than weather warnings, but not this time. It was an Amber Alert. A local girl had gone missing from her affluent West Austin neighborhood. Tracy Turner: six years old, blond hair, green eyes, three feet tall, forty-five pounds, wearing denim shorts and a pink shirt. My palms went sweaty just thinking about it. Then I heard she might be in the company of Howard Turner — her non-custodial father, a resident of Los Angeles — and I breathed a small sigh of relief. Listeners, they said, should keep an eye out for a green Honda with California plates.

Easy to read between the lines. Tracy's parents were divorced, and dad had decided he wanted to spend more time with his daughter, despite how the courts had ruled. Sad, but much better than a random abduction.

The announcer was repeating the message when my cell phone rang. I turned the radio volume down, answered, and my client — a senior claims adjuster at a big insurance company — said, "You nail him yet?"

"Christ, Heidi, it's only the third day."

"I thought you were good."

"That's a vicious rumor."

"Yeah, and I think you started it yourself. I'm starting to think you get by on your looks alone."

"That remark borders on sexual harassment, and you know how I feel about that."

"You're all for it."

"Exactly. Anyway, relax, okay? I'm on him twenty-four seven." Crouch had taken the Manor Road exit, and now he turned into his apartment complex, so I drove past, calling it a day. I didn't like lying to Heidi, but I had a meeting with a man named Harvey Blaylock in thirty minutes.

"Well, you'd better get something soon, because I've got another

246 | BEN REHDER

one waiting," Heidi said.

I didn't say anything, because a jerk in an F-150 was edging over into my lane.

"Roy?" she said.

"Yeah."

"I have another one for you."

"Have scientists come up with that device yet?"

"What device?"

"The one that allows you to be in two places at the same time."

"You really crack you up."

"Let me get this one squared away, then we'll talk, okay?"

"The quicker the better. Where are you? Has Crouch even left the house?"

"Oh, yeah. Been wandering all afternoon."

"Where to?"

"Uh, let's just say he seems to have an inordinate appreciation for the female form."

"Which means?"

"He's been visiting gentlemen's clubs."

A pause. "You mean tittie bars?"

"That's such a crass term. Oh, by the way, the Yellow Rose is looking for dancers. In case you decide to —"

She hung up on me.

~ ~ ~

I had the phone in my hands, so I went ahead and called my best friend Mia Madison, who works at an establishment I used to do business with on occasion. She tends bar at a tavern on North Lamar.

Boiling it down to one sentence, Mia is smart, funny, optimistic, and easy on the eyes. Expanding on the last part, because it's relevant, Mia stands about five ten and has long red hair that she likes to wear in a ponytail. Prominent cheekbones, with dimples beneath. The toned legs of a runner, though she doesn't run, but must walk ten miles a day during an eight-hour shift. When Mia gets dolled up — what she calls "bringing it" — she goes from being an attractive woman you'd certainly notice to a world-class head turner.

On one occasion, she revealed that she has a tattoo. Wouldn't show it to me, but she said — joking, I'm sure — that if I could guess what it was, and where it was, she'd let me have a look. Nearly a year later, I still hadn't given up.

"Is it Muttley?" I asked when she answered.

"Muttley? Who the hell is Muttley?"

"You know, that cartoon dog with the sarcastic laugh."

"You mean Scooby Doo?"

"No, the other one. Hangs with Dick Dastardly."

"I have no idea what you're talking about."

"Before your time, I guess. Are you at work?"

"Not till six. Just got out of the shower. I'm drying off."

"Need any help?"

"I think I can handle it," she said.

"Okay, next question. Want to earn a hundred bucks the easy way?" I said.

"Love to," she said. "When and where?"

3

Harvey Blaylock was maybe sixty, medium height, with neatly trimmed gray hair, black-framed glasses, a white short-sleeved shirt, and tan gabardine slacks. He looked like the kind of man who, if things had taken a slightly different turn, might've wound up as a forklift salesman, or, best case, a high-school principal in a small agrarian town.

In reality, however, Harvey Blaylock was a man who held tremendous sway over my future, near- and long-term. I intended to remain respectful and deferential.

Blaylock's necktie — green, with bucking horses printed on it — rested on his paunch as he leaned back in his chair, scanning the contents of a manila folder. I knew it was my file, because it said ROY W. BALLARD on the outside, typed neatly on a rectangular label. I'm quick to notice things like that.

Five minutes went by. His office smelled like cigarettes and Old Spice. Rays of sun slanted in through horizontal blinds on the windows facing west. As far as I could tell, we were the only people left in the building.

"I really appreciate you staying late for this," I said. "Would've been tough for me to make it earlier."

He grunted and continued reading, one hand drumming slowly on his metal desk. The digital clock on the wall above him read 6:03. On the bookshelf, tucked among a row of wire-bound notebooks, was a framed photo of a young boy holding up a small fish on a line.

"Boy, was I surprised to hear that Joyce retired," I said. "She seemed too young for that. So spry and youthful." Joyce being Blaylock's predecessor. My previous probation officer. A true bitch on wheels. Condescending. Domineering. No sense of humor. "I'll have to send her a card," I said, hoping it didn't sound sarcastic.

Blaylock didn't answer.

I was starting to wonder if he had a reading disability. I'm no angel — I wouldn't have been in this predicament if I were — but my file couldn't have been more than half a dozen pages long. I was surprised that a man in his position, with several hundred probationers in his charge, would spend more than thirty seconds on each.

Finally, Blaylock, still looking at the file, said, "Roy Wilson Ballard. Thirty-six years old. Divorced. Says you used to work as a news cameraman." He had a thick piney-woods accent. Pure east Texas. He peered up at me, without moving his head. Apparently, it was my turn to talk.

"Yes, sir. Until about three years ago."

"When you got fired."

"My boss and I had a personality conflict," I said, wondering how detailed my file was.

"Ernie Crenshaw."

"That's him."

"You broke his nose with a microphone stand."

Fairly detailed, apparently.

"Well, yeah, he, uh —"

"You got an attitude problem, Ballard?"

"No, sir."

"Temper?"

I started to lie, but decided against it. "Occasionally."

"That what happened in this instance? Temper got the best of you?"

"He was rude to one of the reporters. He called her a name."

"What name was that?"

"I'd rather not repeat it."

"I'm asking you to."

"Okay, then. He called her Doris. Her real name is Anne."

His expression remained frozen. Tough crowd.

I said, "Okay. He called her a cunt."

Blaylock's expression still didn't change. "To her face?"

"Behind her back. He was a coward. And she didn't deserve it. This guy was a world-class jerk. Little weasel."

"You heard him say it?"

"I was the one he was talking to. It set me off."

"So you busted his nose."

"I did, sir, yes."

Perhaps it was my imagination, but I thought Harvey Blaylock gave a nearly imperceptible nod of approval. He looked back at the file. "Now you're self-employed. A legal videographer. What is that exactly?"

"Well, uh, that means I record depositions, wills, scenes of accidents. Things like that. But proof of insurance fraud is my specialty. The majority of my business. Turns out I'm really good at it."

"Describe it for me."

"Sir?"

"Give me a typical day."

I recited my standard courtroom answer. "Basically, I keep a subject under surveillance and hope to videotape him engaging in an activity that's beyond his alleged physical limitations." Then I added, "Maybe lifting weights, or dancing. Playing golf. Doing the hokey-pokey."

No smile.

"Not a nine-to-five routine, then."

"No, sir. More like five to nine."

Blaylock mulled that over for a few seconds. "So you're out there, working long hours, sometimes through the night, and you start taking pills to keep up with the pace. That how it went?"

Until you've been there, you have no idea how powerless and naked you feel when someone like Harvey Blaylock is authorized to dig through your personal failings with a salad fork.

"That sums it up pretty well," I said.

"Did it work?"

"What, the pills?"

He nodded.

"Well, yeah. But coffee works pretty well, too."

"You were also drinking. That's why you got pulled over in the first place, and how they ended up finding the pills on you. You got a drinking problem?"

I thought of an old joke. *Yeah, I got a drinking problem. Can't pay my bar tab.* "I hope not," I said, which is about as honest as it gets. "At one point maybe I did, but I don't know for sure. Probably not. But that's what you'd expect someone with a drinking problem to say, right?"

"Had a drink since your court date?"

"No, sir. I'm not allowed to. Even though the Breathalyzer said I was legal."

"Not even one drink?"

"Not a drop. Joyce, gave me a piss te — I mean a urine test, last month, and three in the past year. I passed them all. That should be in the file."

"You miss it?" Blaylock asked. "The booze?"

I honestly thought about it for a moment.

"Sometimes, yeah," I said. "More than I would've guessed, but not enough to freak me out or anything. Sometimes, you know, I just crave a cold beer. Or three. But if I had to quit eating Mexican food, I'd miss that, too. Maybe more than beer."

Blaylock slowly sat forward in his chair and dropped my file, closed, on his desk. "Here's the deal, son. Ninety-five percent of the people I deal with are shitbags who think the world is their personal litter box. I can't do them any good, and they don't want me to. Most of 'em are locked up again within a year, and all I can say is good riddance. Then I see guys like you who make a stupid mistake and get caught up in the system. You probably have a decent life ahead of you, but you don't need me to tell you that, and it really doesn't matter what I think anyway. So I'll just say this: Follow the rules and you can put all this behind you. If you need any help, I'll do what I can. I really will. But if you fuck up just one time, it's like tipping over a row of dominoes. Then it's out of your control, and mine, too. You follow me?"

~ ~ ~

After the meeting, I swung by a Jack-In-The-Box, then sat outside Wally Crouch's place for a few hours, just in case. He stayed put.

I got home just as the ten o'clock news was coming on. Howard Turner had been located in a motel in Yuma City, Arizona, there on business. Police had verified his alibi. He had been nowhere near Texas, and the cops had no reason to believe he was involved.

So Tracy Turner was still missing, and that fact created a void in my chest that I hadn't felt in years.

OTHER NOVELS BY BEN REHDER

Buck Fever
Bone Dry
Flat Crazy
Guilt Trip
Gun Shy
Holy Moly
The Chicken Hanger
The Driving Lesson
Gone The Next
Hog Heaven
Get Busy Dying
Stag Party
Bum Steer
If I Had A Nickel
Point Taken
Now You See Him

Made in the USA
Middletown, DE
06 June 2020